MUTANTS

When the media report that the village of Wentworth Magna has been overrun by a plague of mutant mice—savagely malevolent, frighteningly intelligent, breeding at an appalling rate, and rapidly increasing in size—most people regard the story as a Silly Season scare.

The Government then clamps down on any further reference to the affair—though 'There has been no censorship', declares an easily identifiable Prime Minister. The Army moves in to surround the affected area, and incinerates vast numbers of the creatures. But not enough: many escape, to continue breeding and growing and spreading further and further across the country.

What has been happening? The answer is that at a pharmaceutical complex not far from Wentworth Magna, the brilliant Professor Quarrier and his staff have been developing a drug which could greatly accelerate pregnancy. Clearly, some of Quarrier's mutant mice escaped from his laboratory. Or did they?

While the plague continues to spread, and people are being horribly slaughtered, the investigation of the cause of the outbreak builds up to a very tense and startling dénouement.

BY THE SAME AUTHOR:

THE CRUCIFIED CITY

THE EVENING FOOL

THE MAN WHO HELD THE QUEEN TO RANSOM
AND SENT PARLIAMENT PACKING

JUDAS!

THE MEDUSA TOUCH

TAKE THE WAR TO WASHINGTON

DOPPELGANGER

SUFFER! LITTLE CHILDREN

THE DESTINY MAN

A MAN CALLED SCAVENER

THE DISSIDENT

'CASSANDRA' BELL

EDGAR ALLAN WHO—?

MANRISSA MAN

THE LAZARUS LIE

GRAFFITI

THE IMMORTAL COIL

MUTANTS

A NOVEL

by

PETER VAN GREENAWAY

LONDON
VICTOR GOLLANCZ LTD
1986

First published in Great Britain 1986
by Victor Gollancz Ltd,
14 Henrietta Street, London WC2E 8QJ

© Peter Van Greenaway 1986

British Library Cataloguing in Publication Data
Van Greenaway, Peter
 Mutants.
 I. Title
 823'.914[F]   PR6072.A65

ISBN 0-575-03844-6

Photoset in Great Britain by
Photobooks (Bristol) Ltd.
Printed by WBC Print Ltd., Bristol

'You ask about my opinion on vivisection. I quite agree that it is justifiable for real investigations on physiology; but not for mere damnable and detestable curiosity. It is a subject which makes me sick with horror, so I will not say another word about it, else I shall not sleep to-night.'

> Charles Darwin to
> Professor Roy Lankester,
> 22 March, 1871

MUTANTS

Chapter 1

IT BEGAN WITH the silly season—that vacuum-filler created by Our Dumb Friends' League to bridge the gap between Ascot and the recall of Parliament or thereabouts.

A Sunday paper had mentioned, almost idly and in passing, strange happenings in a normally peaceful Hampshire village. Gerry Hopkins picked out the item on a hunch that it might be worth a brief TV slot in a world currently sheet-anchored in a sea of doldrums.

Early on Monday a video team set off for Wentworth Magna, with little enthusiasm and less expectation. Boredom vanished almost as soon as it arrived.

At first *and* second sight the village seemed deserted, lifeless. All doors and windows were fast closed though it was high summer with morning temperature in the mid-seventies (Fahrenheit and to the devil with Celsius). Minimal traffic; Wentworth enjoyed a rare privilege, being off the track beaten to death by flows and contraflows presently murdering its like.

The three men—two technicians in a transit van and top presenter Hopkins following in his car—very nearly missed an impression that something was wrong. Parked in their patrol car, two policemen appeared to be in animated conversation. They were indistinct, active, but quite unaware, as it seemed, of the newcomers slowing to a puzzled crawl, then to a horrified standstill.

Gazing down and about them the van's occupants had to discard first thoughts that the quiet country road was shimmering in the summer heat.

They stared in perfect disbelief before Tom Ellans, the senior camera operator, his eye nervously roving, saw them clambering over the lowered window on his companion's side. Two of them.

'Shut that window!'

Harry, his trainee assistant, a pale-faced, serious-minded lad, not long out of school, reacted automatically, wound up the window trying to ignore the sudden proximity of whiskers, tails and pointed noses at his elbow.

'I don't believe it,' half-rhetorically, a voice high on emotion, half fear, much wonderment.

'I think two got in through to the rear,' said Ellans, glancing over his shoulder, snatching a mirror view of Hopkins in his company Ford 'Elegante' peering about him with an equally Silly Season sag of the jaw.

'Three,' said Harry, thinking hard. 'I counted three. They went through the grille—better slide it to.'

'That's all right then,' lacking conviction. 'What's up with the law and orderlies I wonder?'

'Hard to tell—that sunglare on the windscreen.' The younger man leaned over and pointed upwards through Ellans' off-side window. An elm tree, well into its prime, was alive with them. Leaves had been stripped from every branch.

More studiedly, they looked and saw winter in the nearest gardens: trees, shrubs and plants raped of flower and foliage . . . August.

A blanched face or two at the window of a nearby house, beyond naked branches and withered hedges, faintly advertised the situation.

'They need the sanitation people—not us.' Devoutly, Harry wished to be elsewhere. Fairly high frequency squeakings were too audible back of the van.

Ellans fought off a cold sweat. He couldn't stand the brutes at any time, but a *carpet* . . . wall to wall and up to the ceiling.

'We can't just sit here!' irritably.

'I'm not getting out,' Adamski frowned. Plainly, he didn't care if it meant his job was forfeit. No way was he launching into the thick of that lot. In those words.

They missed a good background shot of Hopkins, not over bothered by the creatures, putting a foot out of his car and as hastily withdrawing it as they began to pour through the open door. Not the numbers, but a hideous sense of purpose, real or imagined, gave him pause.

He swatted too thoughtfully at the few scuttlers in the car interior as they dodged and scampered with utmost—contempt? So that he shivered as he shouted, pressing the horn as much for something rational to do as to signal the front runners to get on and get out. And why, he wondered, didn't the cops *do* something, instead of sitting there paralyzed. Unpleasant yes, but not the end of the world. He made a mental note to mention 'inexplicable police inaction' during his three-minute spiel.

The hooting hinted at a sense of urgency without exactly providing a solution. For the two TV technicians still sat gazing and listening, enthralled by the novel scene of total devastation in the midst of so much pullulating life.

Adamski reacted first, troubled by a sense of ebbing will-power. He glanced at Ellans, up to his eyes in enchantment, frozen to that moving picture.

'I think the Boss is signalling we move.' Then, more firmly, 'Seems a good idea.'

Ellans wrenched his attention sideways. 'Drive through 'em?' Squeamish. No relish for the idea.

'We can't stay here all day. Let's get some of the perishers. Do our bit for the country.'

Ellans nodded, activated by the red, white and blue touch. 'We can squeeze past the cops—have a chat on the way.'

The idea of action revived them both.

Slipping into first gear Ellans crawled forward, trying not to feel the slight bump, or hear in his wakened imagination the squelch of flesh and blood.

They closed the thirty-yard gap with Hopkins right behind, sickened all the way by the odd motion of their vehicles. Time for Ellans to debate whether to stop for information or go on, get the hell out of an insoluble, intolerable situation and leave Hopkins to work up a 'verbal' if that was what he wanted. No way, he borrowed Adamski's words, would they take the camera to that lot.

Closer now, unhampered by the sunglare, they saw one of the police officers waving frantically, saw the panic expression of a man in the throes of distress. His co-driver appeared to be dozing, head down and unaware of a car covered with—life.

'My God, no wonder they're not moving!' Adamski all but stuttered. 'They've eaten the tyres!'

Ellans stopped close to the driver's window. The man was bawling at his loudest, 'Lower your window a fraction! Lower it!'

They heard easily enough, but couldn't help comparing the contortions of one with the stark immobility of the other.

'Listen—drive just past. Give me room to open up. Tell your friend to open his door as I come round, then give me room to get in—all right?'

'Right. What about your mate?' Ellans bellowed back, infected by the man's urgency.

'Just move!' Agony in the words, not to be ignored.

The van inched forward just clearing the patrol-driver's door. They waited, tense and silent. Adamski gripped the door handle.

Ten seconds later the fugitive in blue flung himself at the door, leapt in, violently shoving Adamski into Ellans' left side. Somehow the newcomer managed to jerk the door to.

Silence would do for the time being. But never for long. Ellans leaned across the badly confined Adamski.

'You all right?'

'Let's go,' said the police officer—a sergeant. Quieter now, but tones inlaid with hysteria somehow. Hopkins was hooting like a barge-master chivvying a tug.

'What about him?' Ellans repeated.

'Dead.' Briefly.

Ellans accelerated more than the gear was worth. A response of some kind.

Adamski jerked his head backwards. 'You sure we only took two or three on board? Sounds like more to me.'

The sergeant shifted—or shuddered, hard to tell which.

'Get a foot on it and drop me on the Winchester turn-off. I've got to get back fast.'

'Why didn't you—?'

'Radio on the blink. You saw the tyres—think I was going to walk?' Truculence, from one who'd seen too much. Involuntarily, and in broken snatches, he sketched the picture of an experience too many.

The station had received a spate of calls from Wentworth Magna late on Saturday. Then nothing much happened until Sunday evening. More calls, more details, nothing serious but an increase of animals of some kind. Mice? Well, not mice exactly—at least, quite resembling mice; and all over the lawn, officer. One could see them in their thousands. By moonlight.

The force was stretched, traffic accidents, break-ins and what not, the duty sergeant had made nice noises, promised to look into it, and put the mysterious prowlers low on the priorities. Then the calls started flooding in—above five. Something had to be done.

'We got the assignment.'

Ellans listened intently. He wanted to hear more, but some of the sergeant's tale seemed to bother him. 'That's funny.'

'What's funny?' the police officer stared straight ahead.

'This was all in a Sunday paper.'

'All?'

'Well, no,' Ellans conceded. 'Enough to load us in the catapult.'

'You the media?'

'Some of it—Britannia TV.'

'Nothing odd. Some character thinks he's over-run and rings his favourite paper. It just got out of hand.' That's how it looked to Adamski.

'Maybe,' the sergeant struggled to loosen his tie, sweat poured down a hefty countenance. 'All I know is, I don't want to go through it again. These perishers bite.' He lifted a bloodied hand.

His companion? Heart attack. Could stomach them in ones or twos. When they flooded in he just keeled over.

Ellans glanced in the mirror. No sign of Hopkins. It was a very minor road, full of twists and turns.

'This is where I get off.'

Ellans nodded, slowed and eyed the traffic streaming in both directions—comforting, the abnormally normal. Still no sign of Hopkins. No sign of those creatures either, or not a lot.

'Take my advice and abandon this—even if it means a walk home.'

Adamski answered for Ellans. 'Why?'

'How many did you say got in?'

'Two—three maybe.'

'Got a torch?'

Ellans' shrug was constricted but he fished a torch from under his seat.

'Shine it back of the van.'

Struggled round as best he could. The others endangered their necks likewise. They heard the sweetest twittering imaginable, the soft susurrus of scampering and scurrying.

The beam told a sombre truth.

'Christ!' Adamski seemed to choke on the blasphemy. 'There's more than—'

Ellans stared, but said nothing. He tried and failed, and simply stared.

A dozen or more, but not just numbers. One of the brutes gnawed at the grille separating it from the three men, only inches away. At first sight, a mouse, no more than that; but gradually, it was borne in on them . . .

The fright that paralyzes, until some half-remembered instinct triggers adrenalin to fuel the motor nerves and, with a concerted impulse, the three unfortunates scramble out of the van as best they can and walk away fast.

There's comedy in it, seen from the gallery. One pays more for tragedy in the front row of the stalls.

They dubbed him 'the funambulist' in the TV world. Thus much about Gerald Hopkins. Five eventful years with a Fleet Street tabloid suggests the rest. Comparing the advantages of press and TV, he'd opted for the flamboyant life-style that goes with being seen as well as heard.

'I'm tired of being a typewriter,' he told his editor. 'Shake hands with a visual display unit.'

Such language to the boss of the printed word presupposes a prior contract, which Hopkins had made sure of with the new, thrusting Britannia PLC. No problem. His record spoke for itself: brilliant reportage from Beirut, his incredible penetration of an IRA cell seven years since. 'You can't kill a guy with the cheek of the devil,' said an off-camera spokesman, and they left it at that.

Then why, if he was so high-powered, nonpareil and maxi-motivated, should thirty-nine-year-old Gerry be tagging along behind his skeleton crew for a three-minute follow-up of a story twenty-four hours terminal in a Sunday quality paper's morgue?

Curiosity is the whole answer.

Written into his contract was the proviso giving first refusal of any story, however banal or bizarre. If it came to naught—fine. If it proved bonanzorial—his word—better still. He collected kudos as others collect stamps.

'The Street' had lost a wizard and still rued the day.

So the duty editor rings Gerry before he can ring the editor.

'Busy, Gerry?'

'Thirsty. Watching the sprinkler on my lawn drives me spare.'

'Done the papers?'

'Three down and one to go.'

'There's a spot for tomorrow's "Out and About" you might—'

'Mice in Hampshire. I'm interested.'

'Wouldn't I know! At least we read the same high-class crap.'

'I'll drive down early Monday. Ellans, if he's available.'

'Sure. And take some Cheddar. They might need a performance incentive.'

'They're not bloody humans. Tell Ellans I'll be at the Centre around four.'

'What d'you think, Gerry?'

'I think a lot of *any*thing is news.'

But when it's too much?

Hopkins, aggravated by his cameraman's behaviour, could accept, in face of the evidence, Ellans' retreat as a fair example of discretion tossing its head at valour. Especially as he manoeuvred his 'Elegante' past the police car.

He'd witnessed the undignified scramble by the police sergeant from one vehicle to another—had even smiled briefly. But why leave his comrade asleep in the middle of a realistic nightmare?

The question answered itself as he came abreast of the abandoned patrol car; Hopkins experienced the miracle of guts turning to water.

Sights too often of a kind that force men to reach for the bottle with conviction, but this—in a quiet English lane . . . scampering and nibbling with the dedication of piranhas—at a dead man's face.

Hopkins stared about him briefly before taking off at the reckless speed of one who, quite suddenly, did not want to be alone.

But, most men are two men. Hopkins' other self reasserted the dominance it was supposed to have. Reputation, 'ink-stained intrepidity' as his Journalist of the Year citation reads, came to his aid, forced him to rethink and so damn the squeamishness corrupting his lesser being—the coward in armour.

In the time needed to explain *volte-face* Hopkins had reversed his car to a trim little mid-Georgian house almost opposing a nestling parish church. He thought of church-mice and half-hoped the house belonged to the vicar; an articulate observer could make his job easier.

Because he'd donned professional harness, because he dimly sensed the story of a lifetime, Hopkins thrust loathing behind him.

Winterset. A box hedge, stripped of foliage, a lime tree despoiled, the lawn, grey as the gravel path, and everywhere an horrendous activity.

In a blaze of fury he dashed his car at the narrow drive, making a joyful massacre of everything in his path, stopped at the steps sideways on to the portico'd door and pressed the horn hoping persistence would pay.

Timely, the appearance of an elderly gentleman in Wellingtons, disreputable trousers, shirt-sleeves rolled, a dog-collar badly awry, a blood-stained poker in one hand.

'No time to lose! Jump out and run!' the booming but modulated tones of one above sounding-boards.

As Hopkins hurtled through the barely opened door it slammed shut behind him.

'Only a dozen or so remaining but that's a dozen too many. Here, lend a hand, dear fellow. There's a knobkerry on the hall-stand—grandfather and the Zulu Wars—grasp it and do mayhem. Introductions later.'

All this as a frail-seeming but agile minister laid about him with prehistoric grunts, in corners, on stairs, even vandalizing a small antique table on to which one of his enemies had clambered.

Hopkins seized the mace-like object and giggled for no apparent reason as he fenced at rather than clubbed whatever crossed his path.

'That's no use! Do it with hatred and you won't miss.'

The guest responded, abandoned his sense of the ridiculous and went for them. Got quite good at it; could even attempt fractured converse.

'Hatred? You?'

'Essence of our faith, dear fellow. Christians are awfully good at it.'

'Historically,' Hopkins amended.

'"Historically" my—foot!' and that was the last of the rodents laid low in the shattered and splattered hall.

'Let's retreat to my study. It's quite free of the little perishers and you can watch from the windows there if you haven't had enough.'

The study: a gem of a quite unspoiled period room. Small but exquisitely appointed, as period people might say and, the walls of course, lined with oaken bookshelves housing tomes such as those very people might have perused without cutting the pages.

Highly civilized—and uninfested.

Inevitably the vicar shed some of his dynamic pose as he closed the door. He looked old, extremely tired and a bit defeated as he leaned his sixty-nine years against the woodwork; his smile barely covered the facts.

'Too old for such capers.'

'Rising to the occasion says otherwise.'

The other man inclined his head to the graceful compliment.

'I could do with a strong drink. I hope you'll join me.'

As one who could always do with a strong drink Hopkins nodded.

The minister prattled as he poured two tumblers half-full of a well-known Highland brand.

'Chalmers—Ned Chalmers, present incumbent of the parish. I won't offer you soda water because I don't believe in it.'

'An atheist, militant churchman.'

'I've never recognized Schweppes as a deity. Your health.'

There's a way of drinking that marks out the hardened bibulant. At any rate, Chalmers grinned knowingly and sat, very nearly collapsed into an old swivel chair at his cluttered desk. He waved Hopkins to a nearby seat facing the window.

'One has heard of the *mus*, but this is ridiculous.'

The reporter warmed to a man who could lighten the darker reality. 'As a matter of fact that's why I'm here.'

'Good heavens! You're not from the sanitary department?'

Hopkins was afraid not, mentioned his name and professional interest.

'"Calamity Hopkins"! Always present when inexplicable disaster strikes. Ominous. I've seen you on the Box. Effective, in a spine-chilling way.'

'I only report. I don't initiate.'

'Sincerely hope it isn't a reason for your existence, dear fellow. That kind of meander can be—addictive.'

Hopkins frowned, being too intelligent not to have pondered that view of things in bathroom privacy. He thought of brass tacks and how best to narrow the scope of discourse.

'But for now, we have a burgeoning situation. My job is to chronicle.'

'No cameras?'

'My team backed off—understandably. Even so, I want to get some of this on tonight's screen.'

'More than that,' barely audible the words, inescapable the note of tragedy ill-defined.

'Has it occurred to you, Mr Hopkins?' he continued in a less ruffled vein, 'We sit here exchanging whisky-flavoured pleasantries, much like two characters in a Morlar novel, playing prologue to some awful, usually irreversible disaster.'

'A fantasist,' thus Hopkins dismissed the man who was thought to be long dead.

'A realist—if I may demur. The visionary is seldom anything else . . . the point is, you must return to London at once—alert the highest authorities—'

'Through TV?' Hopkins' amusement was shortlived.

'And the lowest. That goes without saying.'

'Even a reporter needs a reason for being alarmist.'

'You can see for yourself.'

'I see an inconvenient plague of mice—a local phenomenon.'

Hopkins felt vaguely upstaged, experienced a pang of professional jealousy. His was the right to sound a sensational note, not this backwater country parson, no matter what lurid novels had purpled his thinking. He dissembled carelessly. 'I admit a local plague is distasteful, even destructive, but they had worse in Egypt.'

'I'm not sure.' Chalmers gazed solemnly out at the window. The 'funambulist' thought on Woodforde's pondering the prevalence of wild garlic in mid-winter and, indeed, the faintest hint of an eighteenth-century cleric besotted by local phenomena showed in those classical English features.

'In that case, what am I to tell the viewers?'

'It isn't what but *how* you explain—and exhibit.'

'I said, I have no camera team.'

'You don't need one—'

'I'm sorry to interrupt, but do you know anything about TV?'

'Only what I've seen.'

'"Seen" is the operative word. We flick from newscaster, interviewer, to visual display at every possible opportunity, because the box populi doesn't believe in anything but pictures—every other sense redundant, suspended—at most they'll accept a blow-up, a cut-out or an animated graph.'

'Didymus should be your patron saint.'

'I agree—but that's how it is.'

'It's more serious than you—'

Hopkins misunderstood entirely. Supposed the old man was seeking assurance.

'I'll play it to the hilt.' An unprovoked vision of the dead police officer reminded him . . . 'I didn't know mice were carnivores.'

'Do we know *what* they are?'

A touch of senility? And why the suddenly, imperiously pointing finger? The almost patriarchal command to look?

Mindful of duties owed to one's host, Hopkins complied.

'Now, tell me what you see.'

The journalist obliged after a superficial glance. 'Mice, carpeting your lawn, nibbling the flower-beds, mice everywhere, your summer-house is lousy with them, probably thousands within my visual range—what more?'

Features twisted into the likeness of a sardonic man of God. Very unseemly.

'You are looking, my friend; not *seeing*. One more general curse of the age.'

'I don't understand.' Even journalists have a blindly truthful streak.

'You may be witnessing a projection into the twenty-first century . . . why not?'

Natural enough. Such a perfect little world being eaten alive by myriad imperfections. Thoughts merely, which Hopkins had no intention of translating into offending words.

'Come now, it's not that bad. As I said—'

'It's worse!' insistently.

Whisky—on an agitated stomach. Or too much familiarity with Revelations.

Hopkins got no further with his flip diagnosis. Chalmers was striding to the door, flinging it open and stepping outside. After moments of noisy activity he was back with a celerity that can belie advancing years. In one hand dangled the broken corpse of a perfectly ordinary mouse. Or at least . . .

Forced to look closer, to *see*, Hopkins' instant revulsion went beyond anything experienced thus far. If there are sermons in stones then surely sight of a dog-collared urbanity purposefully swinging a large mouse by its hind leg might suggest the kind of gruesome parable favoured by long ago fans of Gothic horror stories?

What next? he wondered as he withdrew an inch or two from the thing thrust quite abruptly under his nose.

'Show *this* to your doubting Thomases, Mr Hopkins. This and no more if you prefer. Point out, in abicidial language, the uncanny likeness to *hands*, of the forepaws—zoom in on the opposable thumb, compare with a lantern-slide picture the eyes, note that they not only resemble those of man, but that they're also pale, china blue. Note the ears, the total configuration of the face . . .'

Things unnoticed, salient features unremarked. Fresh cause for repugnance; yet Hopkins could still detect ambivalence in the minister's excited harangue; a biology lecturer, expatiating on a newfound species.

'It's sickening.' Well, being human he had to make a conditioned response of a kind. We seldom shudder nowadays. Words cover our fears and our ignorance more—intelligently.

'You see why you have to go back?'

Hopkins regarded the man with the mouse in dazed fashion. Truly, to *see*, and then go out into one bit of this world where they lived, savagely, a satirical echo of his own breed. It all looked different now.

The vicar had opened the casement, tossing the corpse among its seething fellows before closing it firmly and quickly.

'I'm not concerned with your brand of sensationalism—or anyone else's. I'm only convinced of the need to broadcast what you've seen, what's happening in Wentworth Magna.'

'A few sports of nature,' feebly.

'You've seen them—close and in detail.'

'Even so—'

'And observed their tremendous rate of reproduction—'

'Phenomenal I agree, even terrifying, but mice after all.'

'Dear fellow, haven't you understood? Mutations! Mice endowed with markedly human characteristics . . . what does that suggest to you in a meddlesome age that can leave nothing alone?'

Chapter 2

SHE LOVED, BUT had long since given up trying to understand him. Married to Quentin Quarrier—a figure of speech and little more.

Helen moved with a stately restlessness from room to room of a substantial house so fashionable in the early thirties. An architectural pastiche with a large dash of the 'noov' nineties and a touch of Tudor. 'Jesus Quist but it's quaint,' was Quentin's first irreverent reaction.

The gardens surrounding and pre-dating the house were laid out faintly to resemble those of Hampton Court, even to the once neglected maze now trimmed to perfection.

It was the maze that had attracted Quentin on their first viewing of the property.

'Quaint or not, I like the house. It has a shamefaced air—apologetic for failing to live up to its pretentiousness. I hope that's it, Q.'

'The maze does it, I think.'

'The maze?' They were driving back to the estate agent to talk terms.

'Well, it's a feature—a problem in green to be solved.'

She'd smiled, privately baffled how a decision to involve every penny of their capital could hinge on an overgrown tangle of box worth fifty pounds at most.

T'was ever thus, she could muse ten or more years on. Whimsy at thirty-eight was amusing, even endearing, but at the end of the forties trail?

Pausing at the morning-room window with its favoured view she ran a finger along the Duluxed frame—Hyaline white—not searching for dust so much as for flaws in her current concern.

After all, he was old enough to know his own mind. Or was that to confuse with the brilliance he exuded, now as always? The gifted research Fellow snapped up by HMG's department of experimental and scientific development, snatched away by Price-Pearson and all devoured by a merger creating one of Europe's mammothest drug concerns. It meant Quentin could choose his own terms and he chose comparative anonymity.

She'd welcomed that loss of small-is-suitable identity; preferred to watch at a distance the ulcerated rat-race degenerating into an alcoholic smart-circuit demanding endless demonstrations of wife-loyalty to those never-ending social jamborees inseparable from big business fix-ups.

'A problem in green—to be solved,' she echoed the rusting phrase at sight of the maze beyond the sunken patch which doubled as a Dutch garden in May and held Jonas's surplus annuals for the rest of the season.

The children, she decided, were late home from school. They'd be all right. Three together. Safety in numbers.

They all adored the maze, now trimmed to perfection by the day-a-week gardener who stayed in love with it long after Quentin had outgrown its novelty.

Just visible as it was from the Avenue, she'd once been mildly amused at sight of Jonas coming along the drive with secateurs and a purposeful air.

'Surely it isn't your day?'

'Nor is it, Mrs Quarrier, but my eye snagged on a sprig out o' kilter on the roadside of her. Couldn't have slept for thinking of it till Tuesday come.'

Her. Whatever men love, ships, mazes, cars—even women.

She recalled Quentin's reaction to the bit of trivia such as wives reserve for their husbands after hours.

'Possessiveness—the paternal instinct—inherent in the generality—Jonas no exception. I bet his kids never have a hair out of place.'

Half-aware that she'd set herself to remember those undercurrents of bitterness at mention of children, a light touch, more apparent than real, imperfectly concealing his disappointment at their childlessness, she could also regret his cynical attitude to the world at large, his inability to grasp the most commonplace facts. Jonas, after all, was a pensioner and a widower, with not a 'kid' in sight.

Everything about Quentin seemed to have a scientific basis, even his jerky phraseology came of interminable jottings on a pad alongside microscopes, long carried over to the cassette-recorder memorializing his every ineffable utterance—as he'd explained with an archbishopy grimace.

So much to remember at this undoubted watershed in his career and so, of their lives 'to-get-her' as a one-time feminist friend would pun with a curling lip.

Were their problems ending, or just beginning? Probably a new brand belonging to changed circumstances.

'I'm quitting Price-Pearson,' baldly, not half an hour since.

She saw no reason to exclaim, or even look surprised. He'd hinted at the possibility for months. Too much internecine stuff. Too much bare-backed jockeying for a boardroom place. Quentin was only a promotion away—but he no longer relished the role of a minor tycoon in the new, slick and sham world of businessman in a white lab coat over a carefully tailored grey suit.

Not exactly on a wave of enthusiasm she returned to the kitchen—a small matter of fixing supper. Culinary she did not feel. Would have preferred to talk but he was in his den writing up a report. She hummed a minor fugue on sacrosanctuaries and watersheds.

He never failed to surprise. Easily succeeded an hour or so later when she was red with heat and vexation over those blistering onions. Came on her unexpectedly as she rinsed odd dishes under hot and cold running water.

'You didn't ask why?'

Starting at the sudden voice so close behind her, Helen turned, instantly confused by his strange and quite unfamiliar expression. It verged perilously on the unpleasant.

'I imagined you'd tell me after a meal,' she smiled and reached for a drying cloth. 'Bomb-shells before the soup—fall-out after Brie and biscuits, remember?'

His expression changed to something more familiar and re-assuring. A boyish grin is little the worse for being out-of-date.

'Right. It's always been like that. But it didn't seem fair—breaking the momentous and leaving it crying in your lap.'

'Have some coffee—it's an hour till supper.'

'No—I'll just sit.' Which he did, looking about him like any inquisitive visitor.

She poured a cup for herself from the Cona machine, preparing to wait while he went walk-about in his mind before explanations came.

'The colour-scheme's appalling.'

She glanced at the pale-blue walls and thought, there we go. What *has* décor got to do with watersheds?

'Kitchens,' he confided, 'should have a *ruddy* look. Like half-cooked steaks.'

'You're confusing kitchens with housewives.'

'Right again. I'm probably harking back to the good old days.'

I have been right twice in as many minutes—there are tenter-hooks in it somewhere—covered her spoken platitude. 'They weren't always that easy.'

'Oh—much further back. Before our time . . . I was thinking of alchemists, beavering away over a hot stove in the basement. Cooking for dear life every ingredient they could lay hands on—just to bring an underdone philosopher's stone out of the oven. Garnished with juniper berries. Sheer Sunday Supplement.'

She smiled at his interpretation of things but looked for the tenuous link. 'What couldn't they have done with micro-ovens?'

'Useful in the labs,' he admitted, before describing what could be done with a mere kitchen blender. 'The French taught us that one.'

Helen waited, half-persuaded he'd made a neat introduction to those explanations. And, in an attenuated fashion, he had.

'Everything's so different now—especially this last yearabouts. One big happy family in the old days—Mathieson, as he used to be—and Galvin, remember? And poor old Jones Miner, brilliant chemist out of a pit village—most of us middle-young enthusiasts. What a fry-for-all we planned to cook in Price-Pearson's crucibles. Price-Pearson's Patent Potent Panaceas. We had it stitched—actually did alleviate some of the world's ills. Then we "re-located" what—ten years ago—eight? Galvin dead, Jones kidnapped by the fairies and Nick Alladyce not far behind. Mergers, new ideas, cost analyses, quota postulants—whatever the hell *they* mean other than an extra flick of the whip—then, to cap it all, I'm told Buckfast is needed in the Zurich division and they *lend* me Mrs Chandrasakar.'

'But she's been with you for at least a year.'

'As a distant adjunct—not as a Number Three—or a number anything. No—it's the last straw.'

She wanted to know about other straws. And wasn't the Mrs Chandra thing a simple red herring, symptom of a deeper disquiet? He'd often talked of 'that Hindu woman' with nothing worse than amused tolerance.

Alarm bells rang faintly though Helen could have sworn she hadn't touched them. For the moment she played the red herring.

'You say she's competent?'

'Genetically? She has much the same qualifications as Buckfast —and it ends there.'

For some reason this simply would not do; not for Helen. 'Research,' tentatively, 'you've said so often—'

'And I'll go on saying it!' flaring and staring her out of countenance. 'Not only does that strawberry soufflé look delicious, but you can't quantify or specify—aptitude.'

'Then how does she offend?'

'Offend?' he seemed genuinely surprised. 'Good grief, you think I'm being racist? Look—after twelve years I know Buckfast's brilliance. He *fits*. And chemo-geneticists aren't thick on the ground . . . she—just doesn't fit.'

Believing in his earnest manner, Helen simply could not believe in the matter, so she saw no point in asking bluntly 'Why not?' Pettiness, speciousness, so much salad-dressing to cover a leaf of damp lettuce. Truly not racial or sexual prejudice: she knew him better than that.

Something more fundamental was wrong, had been, she now realized, for days, if not weeks—since—since when? Looking at him, at the new lines straining at his mouth's corners, she thought of a man waiting for a train that had already crashed a mile from the station.

'So you resigned?' inconsequentially.

'My contract is up for renewal in a month—that seems a good time . . .' then, as if more were needed, 'On a question of pique, or a suspect principle, you could fault me . . . but it's more than that.'

'Quentin—'

'The oven smells eloquent—what is it?'

'Mrs Beeton's pot roast—second class.' Words bandied while she worked on the solution to an unspoken riddle. A link was missing in his chain of non-sequiturs and, not for the first time, Helen would follow into the maze in search of a stranger called Quentin Quarrier, and hope to find her husband somewhere in the middle. Meantime, there was supper to think of. The children had already eaten and gone their impetuous ways . . .

Later they ate in customary silence except once, when she suddenly found the thread; and it led to such a startling conclusion that she had to cover with a totally unrelated question.

'You said not long ago, you were on the verge of a breakthrough.'

'Did I? Probably on the wrong "verge". Must've meant "of a breakdown".'

But she was thinking as she nodded, not once, in all his meandering, had he mentioned Remington. Strange, considering he hadn't been the same man since Rem's death. Since then . . .

The evenings at home followed a pattern. Reading mostly. Novels for her, technical horrors for him; intervals of coffee laced with small talk occasionally, a last drink of something stronger and, if they remembered, a glimpse of *the* news programme on TV.

Later, she would recall that he'd made a point of switching on in good time. Most unusual.

The news headline rang the same cracked bell—a tocsin summoning nobody to a funeral. Helen could never quite fall with the pound or rise with hopes of yet another strike settlement. Almost any event catastrophizing the great wide world left her unmoved, as being practical enough to know she could do nothing alone to alleviate the daily quota of misery. More and more she set herself not to watch, felt unclean, as if bystanding one kind of accident or another—like ghouls who turn up for a disaster and not a pin paid to enjoy the gory peepshow.

Tonight's offering would challenge such fastidiousness.

'Strange rustlings are to be heard in Hampshire's Wentworth Magna,' the newscaster began, winsomely 'Gerald Hopkins reports with an eye-witness account of a sudden plague of mice infecting this remote and picturesque village.'

'That's not twenty miles from here—nearer.' Helen seemed to be sharing her information with the female simpering sweetly from the screen.

'Gerald looks more than his usual haggard self,' Quarrier said.

Very likely, Hopkins still bore the marks of those moments when he'd struggled six feet or so to his car as Chalmers closed the door against mice and men. No need to exaggerate the effect on lineaments; the squarest eyes of the dullest viewer could sense that something was amiss.

He'd demanded, and got, five minutes clear . . .

'Someone phones a reputable Sunday paper at seven o'clock on Saturday evening last.

'The unknown warned that an invasion of mice might be imminent in the village of Wentworth Magna quote, or its vicinity, unquote. He thought the editor might be interested. Some of you may have read the item.

'According to the vicar, no mice were seen at seven o'clock or for some time after in the village that Saturday evening.'

Now that, Helen thought, was significantly interesting. She glanced at Quentin, indolent in his favourite chair, half-turned to watch the sudden image of Hopkins. He caught her eye.

'The old master still. Knows how to grab one's attention.'

She nodded, listening the while for nuances.

'We took a camera team to this once attractive village . . . so much time wasted . . . I'm not exaggerating when I tell you we were all lucky to escape alive. By now, of course, the rescue services will be doing whatever has to be done, but already one police officer has died. There may be other victims—the authorities are not saying very much, and all phones appear to be cut off in the area.

'Wentworth Magna is being eaten alive.'

Again Helen's gaze veered in search of Quarrier's reaction to Hopkins' stylish sensationalism, but he seemed preoccupied, frowning at some quite unrelated thought.

'Behind me,' the 'funambulist' continued, 'a blown-up still of a mouse we can all recognize, the kind of animal made human by Disney and Bea Potter. Keep it in view as I tell how I fared in this doomed village—not too strong a word for what's currently happening.

'To fight one's way through hordes of these things to reach safety is to say goodbye to Mickey and all that.

'Somehow, I got to the only house showing signs of life. The vicarage. It was the Reverend C. M. Chalmers who not only sheltered me but provided my first real insight into the nature of the problem. What you now see is credible enough because it's familiar. No need for a second glance.

'But take a look at the next enlargement of a being as unlike its original as hamburgers to roast beef.'

'Good God!' That time-worn and universal reaction shared by Helen with millions forced to make an odious comparison. She could easily forget to note Quentin's response—which must have intrigued.

The eyes and ears were too familiar.

'Some of these things,' Hopkins continued, 'got into our transport. I abandoned my car a mile or so beyond the village.

'It was too crowded.

'I had the car towed back to Town. We managed to collect a few in a metal box. The rest were incinerated. They ate their progeny, mated, gnawed at everything as they grew. . . .'

The camera panned to a cage the size of a packing crate, strongly meshed on all sides.

'What you see is what's happening in a village grown quiet as the grave, trees leafless, phones dead and houses barricaded, a target too late for rescue parties most like.'

He made a flourish towards the cage, like a magician conjuring the highest point of horror from his Grand Guignol routine.

Helen leaned forward, not entirely oblivious of Quentin; soul mates on the distaff side seldom are; and he surely had a professional interest beyond his present negligent attitude, the half-contemptuous smile that seemed to slide down his nose, as she would tease in his superior moments.

An unforgettable image compelled attention.

The cage shook to the movement of an animate mass, was filled with pulsating life, a biological time-bomb not clearly understood until the camera zoomed close enough to define just one of the growths clinging to the mesh with hands, clearly recognizable hands, hands small but active, now holding on with one while the other pushed away a jostling neighbour. As if, mob-like, it was camera-conscious, it stared sentiently at you, the viewer, at everyone installed before a screen, at Helen forced to close her eyes against an impression of malevolence once belonging to none but the human race.

'Don't let them escape,' murmured in confidence to no one in particular. Caged, they were sickening. At large. . . .

The camera returned to Hopkins as the studio hands wheeled their obscene cargo out of view.

'They'll be incinerated immediately,' he assured, adding, as if in afterthought, 'there were six in that crate three hours ago . . .' left time for that to sink in.

Again Helen glanced at her husband. Searching for signs of shock and concern she was bound to miss the less obvious, a deepening of his temperamentally inner tension. Mildly annoyed, she said nothing but thought how futile it was to be violently agog when the feeling can't be shared.

'Hundreds, yes, thousands certainly, millions maybe; whichever, I tried and failed to alert the highest authorities. If "they" are watching this programme the message is the same. At the moment this is a minor ecological disaster—should it spread beyond that miserable village's confines, someone will have to answer a clear-cut charge of criminal negligence.' He ended on a sting-in-the-tail note which made him unique in his line.

'After all . . . these monstrosities eat people.'

Uncompromising stuff, yet, out of sight of 'these monstrosities' it seemed a trifle melodramatic because the amorphous mass was already shifting by more or less degrees into another gear, preparing to absorb the next item, and the next . . . and the next.

While a well-known author is being persuaded to explain how he absent-mindedly left his latest best-seller in his mother's work-box forty years back, Helen watches, listens, and hears precisely nothing.

'What?' she jerked out of arm-hugging abstraction.

'I said "must we suffer alarmists *and* charlatans?"'

Compliant, Helen switched off the insufferable scribbler but wondered aloud if it didn't all rather call for something stronger than bedtime cocoa.

'Whatever you're having.'

'I thought,' she reverted, 'you liked Hopkins.'

He tossed a sheaf of papers on to a sofa table and reclined, hands behind head to stare at the ceiling—odd, his expression, uneasy, belying an appearance of ease. He couldn't possibly be wondering how the ceiling came to be there.

Nothing said till drinks are prepared and sipped. They had outrageous tastes in the jug and bottle line. Within their restricted circle tomato juice and claret held the record.

'He only does it to annoy,' one pomposity who prided himself on his cleft of centre palate had lisped.

'You were on about Hopkins. Yes, I do like him, his style, which is as much as one *can* care for in journalists. He's few people's stooge as far as I can tell.'

'Oh?' and how would he know? her inflection suggested.

'Obviously not a simpery sycophant—no kow-towing to the latest Almighty. Remember how he stood up to "her" on the last "Eye-to-Eye"?'

'Then why not respect his judgment on this?'

He stared stolidly at the ceiling. 'Hopkins has to make a living; once in a while that demands over-reaction, bargaining with his sense of proportion if you prefer.'

'But you saw for yourself,' she objected. Petulance had no place in her nature, but bewilderment at the drift of their dialogue clearly showed. Chats about journalism and its practitioners simply didn't count.

'I saw what you saw,' non-commitally.

She frowned, sensing evasion, at which Quentin was an acknowledged master. Not for the first time she regretted a superficial interest in his work and so, consciously, implied a connection of some kind between A and B.

Certainly, he'd never encouraged her to look too far below the surface, to 'share his microscope'. 'Beautiful women should have no truck with mysteries, with miracles, with the abstruse, for they are, *sui generis*, of all these things', Helen could recall how he'd declaimed thus, long ago, one eye on her and a hand tucked into the waistcoat of a three-piece, like an Ebury Street Napoleon surrounded by cocktail courtiers.

With an effort she found the pertaining word. 'Mutants?' but query-quavery, much as a fourth-grade schoolgirl might be overwhelmed by the good looks of a sardonic biology master.

Faintly contemptuous the slow turn of his head, eyebrows poised high above a blank stare. When *that* trait appeared, Helen knew she could thump him without compunction.

He might have responded from those supercilious heights but luckily the phone rang leaving her to worry whether it would wake Martin and set him coughing again. Martin was her youngest.

The Superintendent easily visualized a picture post-card village noted for its wealth of thatched cottages; he also narrowed his gaze against a show of argument that came damned near insubordination.

'What are you aiming at?'

'This is an emergency situation. Even the TV people picked it up somehow, sent a camera crew down for a story.'

'How do you know?' the duty Inspector barked.

'They came to my assistance or I wouldn't be here now. As it was, they're not sure what happened to Hopkins. He was following in his car but—'

'Gerald Hopkins—the newshound?'

'That's right, sir.'

Long time Baker stared hard and all but through the officer. Disconcerting to those netherward of the law, but Tiller had suffered too much to fear a basilisk eye.

Hopkins . . . not one to go chasing wild geese. Two and two suggested a decision had better be made.

'D'you know the people in Wentworth Magna?'

'I should do, sir. My uncle was born and lived there—'

'Does he still—?'

'He died five years back. My aunt moved.'

'Who *do* you know?' impatiently.

'There's Edmund Percy and—'

'Think of someone who'd likely be home now—'

'Well, I reckon Mr and Mrs Chilham—'

'Ring 'em.' Baker indicated the phone.

Tiller found the number and dialled.

They waited. . . .

Tiller replaced the receiver. He looked pale and utterly wretched.

'I know the vicar slightly—I'll try him,' said Baker in milder tones. He dialled the number.

The line was dead and so, no doubt, was Chalmers.

Ten-forty. Long past time for meaningful action, but what could be done was done.

Baker called out every available man, rang the local authority people.

'We've heard, but there's nothing we can do.'

'I want flame-throwing equipment—you've got it?'

Peering out of the lowered car window brought Barker to the farmer's level, uncertain, unwilling to credit his senses.

'Never saw aught like that in my fifty-odd years. Never.' Breath-taken tones, a token of wonderment.

The Superintendent heard those words as from a great distance ... further surely than the few hundred yards separating them from that heaving mass, ebbing and flowing like a furry tide. Uncanny silence belied by a mad chorus of squeaking.

'They're spreading slow,' the farmer gestured at the ground only yards away. A few of the creatures were scuttering and scurrying back and forth; and always nearer, like a reconnaissance party. They could be seen in some detail.

'Them's not mice—not my sort anyway.' He spat to relieve some indefinable feeling, apprehension perhaps, then stumped back to his tractor drawn up in the lay-by behind them.

Baker glanced at his driver who gazed at the scene as one mesmerized, almost regretted ordering Tiller to bring him. The man was far gone in fear.

'You'd better sit tight, Tiller. We'll see what can be done.'

'Don't go, sir. I mean—'

That would have provoked strong language elsetimes, but Baker ignored it and left the car to tumble his men out of the van. Was suddenly struck by the idea of vulnerability—for them all—against such multitudes.

A fire-tender came to a screeching halt. A section officer, clumsy in his gear, climbed out and recognized Baker at once.

'Where's the fire then?'

The Super explained tersely.

'Mice! Jesus, we can't deal with mice—not our job.'

'You've got equipment—?'

'What kind—mousetraps?'

'Foam—'

'Some, but—'

'Try it. Try anything. We've got to reach those people.'

'What people?'

The age-old problem of communication, not least when things are bizarre. Nobody's fault. Not Baker's.

He explained once more the need to clear a way to where eighty-odd people were trapped.

'You mean they're all over?'

'Thousands.'

'. . . mice?' unthinkingly the fire-fighter scratched his helmet.

'For Christ's sake don't stare at *me*! Look along the road there.'

The man did so. His colleagues, drifting along from natural curiosity, also looked. A few more pale faces, glances exchanged—eight police officers, six firemen. Qualms were clearly prevalent.

The youthful-looking section-leader cleared his throat. 'We'll try foam—there's no water till we're in the village—that'll be a mile along.'

After a murmur of assent, he felt a bit more confident in his new promotion.

'My men'll give you any help you need,' Baker promised.

The fireman glanced at them briefly. 'Don't reckon a baton charge'll get us far.' The little group grinned at its scowling rivals and moved off, buoyed up by the show of oneupmanship.

Short-lived their buoyancy.

The tender eased past the police vehicles and made progress for a hundred yards or so. A strange covey of masked men, well-covered, while a man on top directed a stream of foam at the unholy mass ahead.

Difficult for the onlookers to judge the effect but it hardly mattered. Quite abruptly the scene changed as the hordes fell away from the wheels or the foam; whatever the cause they seemed to regroup, to coalesce, to become one enormous monster congealed for a purpose.

Intense watchfulness turned to speechless amazement as the bright red tender seemed to merge, chameleon-like, with a great surging tide of mouse-coloured life, swarming and skittering over men suddenly fighting hysterically to rid themselves of unspeakable four-legged filth . . . the thickest mind could recognize malignancy in that onslaught.

The tender began to back crazily, short of a rational touch on the steering, panic written all over its progress. By a miracle it cleared Baker's car and the van behind, giving a momentary glimpse of ashen faces under the blackness of helmets. It careered into a ditch ten yards behind them and keeled over.

Baker and his men ran back to help then slowed to a standstill. Sprawled on the ground was the young section-leader who'd plied the jet of foam. He'd toppled off as the vehicle lumbered on to its side.

A cluster of mice gnawed at his clothing, sniffed at his face which he was trying to cover with one hand, the other beating feebly to shake off others clinging to his sleeve. More and more of them were closing in to crawl over him till he seemed, all suddenly, garbed in a living shroud.

Wits were recovered and men, in a paradoxical frenzy of fear and loathing, rushed to his rescue. More of the brutes were appearing as from nowhere, as if sprung from the very ground beneath them but, above all, memories would be vivid of the manner in which they clung with ease, with tenacity to any and everything. They would cling, even as they were battered to a pulp.

And that eerie way they stared at you . . . almost human.

'Where the hell are they coming from!' a breathless futility from Baker to—anyone.

'Jesus, look at his face!'

They formed a ring to protect a man rigid with terror, too stricken to make a bid for survival.

Somehow they dragged and carried him to the police 'transit', fighting maniacally with a phenomenon beyond their understanding, fear spurring their fury, until he was hurled to safety, face streaming with blood, left arm broken and hanging uselessly.

Useless.

A brutal transformation; not even Baker was the same man as had driven sceptically to the scene. Wild-eyed they gazed on the chaos and the carnage, darted fearful glances in every direction, searching out the reason for it all.

'Everybody back into the van, you chaps too!' he shouted to the fire-fighters.

Baker slammed the doors on the last of them, ordered the driver to back into the lay-by and wait.

'What about you, sir?'

'Just do as I say!'

A born leader is even more formidable on his own. Every inch an antagonist Baker was concerned to the point of despair for the public he served, for those under him; now he'd only himself to think about.

He ran back to the approaching Council van still beating at a dozen animals clinging to his legs. The driver's face looked mighty comical as it leaned cautiously out of the lowered window. Baker giggled hopelessly at the sight of those weasely features above him, watching with open-mouthed astonishment a police officer apparently flagellating himself to death.

'What's all this then?'

Stern-faced but inwardly hysterical, Baker bellowed a warning to keep his mouth shut or some of those perishers would be down his gullet and dining on his guts before he could say tea-break.

The driver shut his mouth, but opened it again, just wide enough to ask: 'Where they all come from?'

'Don't ask stupid questions. You've got flame-throwers?'

'Only one. We're not arsonists.'

'Portable?'

'Yes—a backpack.'

While another man fixed it on, the driver explained: 'Press that trigger there—it's a pizo-job—instant ignition. Keep the nozzle pointing away whatever else.'

'How long on capacity?'

'Depends. Short bursts'll take you further. Half an hour say.'

Once they'd finished, the driver with his mate and alacrity regained the cab still fighting off the first of their attackers. The driver looked badly shaken.

'You're not going into the—?'

Baker ignored the doctrine of negative despair, had turned already to jog as fast as the bulky equipment allowed, straight into the maw of a biological glut.

They watched, fascinated, not wholly believing in the figure of a man struggling into the teeming distance behind sudden bursts of flame. Only Tiller, remembering his dead comrade, sat with closed eyes, repeating over and over again 'The fool. . . .'

The way was strait enough. Shrugging off his years the Superintendent went steadily forward, slipping sometimes as his boots ground to pulp whatever came underfoot. Disappeared from their view as he followed a sharp curve— and very nearly faltered.

A carpet of them. Not just the road but the verge, the hedges, trees, everything pulsated with life. A horrible slow motion vista perceptibly quickening until the turbulence at his feet had a nightmarish speed signifying Nature out of control.

He prayed blasphemously and triggered the ignition once more, unleashing a stream of fire three yards ahead of his course. Almost forgot to stop, still fascinated as he was by the novelty.

Again it cleared a suddenly charred and smoking path, sent the survivors scurrying away to either side.

He smiled grimly. If Emmy could see him now. Emmy was his wife. And now, a thief-taker, close to retirement, reduced to this.

None saw his pathetic heroism that day. Warding off the importunate hordes as he broke into houses, the village shop, the sub post-office, the vicarage, to find no more than remains.

Not one living soul.

First witness to a massacre, Baker, sickened and exhausted, turned away from the unendurable, took the scorched path back to sanity. Once more they were crowding him like beggars at alms; after a few yards he was forced to use the flame-thrower, pressed the ignition viciously. A pathetic flame, barely enough to light a cigarette, flared and died, and that was all.

He began to run, flailing his arms wildly as the mice swarmed, uncannily sensing defencelessness. New-found fear set him cursing and beating at the things climbing his body. He stumbled as he fought to rid himself of a weapon become an encumbrance. After prodigious efforts he struggled out of the harness and flung the whole thing ahead of him. It made the going easier, but there was no shaking off the gnawing, the nibbling, the faeces in his hair, the clambering and clinging.

Momentarily he *saw* in detail, a grinning miniscule on his sleeve as he brushed others from his face, a split-second image of a gargoylish countenance, clinging to him with . . . hands . . . tiny, perfectly formed hands. . . .

Baker degenerated into a distracted version of his former self, blundered on, screaming obscenities, blasphemies while the victors celebrated imminent victory.

He very nearly came out of those jaws, showed up once more, shouting, stumbling and scream-laughing, a thing of rags, bloodied but defiant, though beyond articulating what he was defiant about, till he fell, too far from rescue, totally overwhelmed by a soft grey enemy.

The episode illustrates a point. For all Hopkins' stage managed demonstrating, the really sensational news about the events at Wentworth Magna had happened hours ago and it went unrecorded. Not that those who'd experienced the horrors were in a condition to tell the nation exactly how serious the situation had become.

Chapter 4

'Who was it?'

Quentin, in his ambiguous mood gracefully ignored the familiar query. True to his oblique cast of temperament he inwardly played back the cryptic conversation with Alladyce, a close colleague and friend from the Price-Pearson complex.

'Quentin!'

'At your service.'

'Did you see "Eye-to-Eye" just now?'

'With whom?'

'No joking!'

'. . . Yes, I did see it.'

'You realize what's happened?'

'No.'

'Quentin, there's bound to be an inquiry—hadn't we better be consistent?'

'About what?'

'Man, they have to be ours.'

'Man, I don't agree.'

'The growth and reproduction rate!'

'Well?'

'That last batch, Rem said you used HFH.'

'He didn't need to say, I told you.'

'Well?'

'. . . I'm uncertain whether you're driving at something or just trying to run me down. You were in on the series.'

'Only at the end. You know damn well I was away for six weeks.'

'Very well, Nicholas. You were away for six weeks nervously breaking down all over the place—'

'When I came back the X700 series was in bloody chaos.'

'Excess irradiation.'

'Look, Quentin—'

'What are you getting at? You want me to admit to God knows what while I'm spending a perfectly docile evening at home with Helen—'

'It happened not twenty miles from Price-Pearson's.'

'Understood. I just refuse to meet repercussions till they percuss.'

'It's too much of a coincidence!'

'The X700s had a top rating—we simply don't know what happened to some of them, that's all.'

'Are you going to admit that?'

'I don't have to admit anything! We're not responsible for what we don't know about.'

'That's being simplistic.'

'. . . Very good, old son. Now you go and dip your head in black coffee and let me know tomorrow how you reached a conclusion suitable to your present state of willies.'

He erased the play-back, gave a melodramatic sigh and slumped heavily on to the sofa.

'Long hot summers are much overrated.'

'Was that Nick?'

He glanced warily. 'How did you guess?'

'I didn't. You have different voices for different people. With Nicholas it's peremptory—even hectoring at times.'

He picked up *New Science*, flipping its pages to no great purpose. To Helen's watchful eye it read like an Indian smoke signal. Determined evasiveness.

Conscious of, and cornered by her uncompromising eye, he tossed the journal aside and grinned for a token of mock surrender.

'Nicholas is a much respected fellow-toiler and squash partner but he's scared of his own shadow. He earned his breakdown trying to reconcile science and ethics.'

'Can't they be?' she felt vaguely troubled, as if watching a loved one relapse after a successful operation.

'Not particularly. One *can* rise out of the other—but it's *ab initio* stuff against the superficial expedience of *ad hoc* hang-ups.'

Helen nodded, unconvinced by Latinisms he tended to trot out to obscure the plain English of a difficult situation. Nick's recovery and Remington's death had almost coincided. She set herself to think it out carefully and logically, in best male tradition.

'But was it ethics or something that happened at the labs that put him off-course?'

His reaction startled her. A matter of sitting bolt upright, abruptly, as if she'd made an insulting remark. Some notion, triggered by her penetrant questioning, seemed badly to have got to him.

'Nothing escaped from Price-Pearson.'

She stared at the scowl and the strange assertion; at a man studying some image in a fourth dimension far beyond her understanding.

Strangely enough, she'd forgotten the news item which all this was about.

'Nothing, Q?' tentatively, as not to disintegrate a fragility, whatever it might be.

He refocused, bestowed some of his attention, but with a constant shift of vision.

'It's a bloody peculiar world, eh? The crapsters work overtime to reproduce video mutants, guaranteed to climb the collective spinal cord, and all the time *we*—'

He broke off. As if a sentence could end in a booby-trap. 'Let's go to bed.' Decisively.

'Let's not go to bed while you've something unresolved on your mind.'

'Did I say I had?' flaring like a small, spoilt brat, badly caught out.

'Nothing said, everything implied,' handling with care, like a psychiatrist leading the way to abreaction. 'Perhaps the Hopkins item climbed Nick's spinal cord.'

'A professional interest that's all.'

'Then why shout at him?'

'I don't recall shouting.' Pompously.

'Raise your voice then. Or how could I hear "I don't have to admit anything"?'

'Everybody seems to be driving at something tonight. Hope your licence isn't overdue for renewal.'

'Q, come down to earth and let's talk it out.'

'"On what non-existent basis?" said he, cutting the ground from under her feet.'

'I'll try to give you one. Not fifteen miles from here a village is overrun by what we'll charitably call "mice". Eight miles in the other direction is a drugs concern prestigious enough to warrant a security system Fort Knox could envy. I know, because my husband is highly employed there as a geneticist with a bit of biochemistry thrown in as make-weight. You follow me thus far?'

'I'm treading on your heels and I hope it hurts.'

'He doesn't discuss his work much—outside in-house politics—but I do gather he's into the fast fertility and pregnancy business and that requires—apparently—inflicting the usual unspeakable procedures on small creatures incapable—until now—of defending themselves.'

'You're flogging an open secret! It's been with us a long time. With me.'

'Accelerated pregnancy . . . six months . . . I still think it's a—questionable theory.'

'It's more than a theory!' reaction of a badly riled man.

'Oh?' with an advocate's speed. 'So Nicholas and Rem and the rest *were* working on this thing till Rem died and Nick cracked up?'

'It isn't as simple as that!'

She recognized the cut-off point severed by an exclamation-mark and damned her enthusiasm as an amateur prosecuting counsel. Knew he would clam up to avoid a row when both were too intelligent to indulge in slanging matches.

The solitaire board, her constant companion and occasional solace since childhood was always at hand. She took it up now, an instant palliative, equivalent of an executive's comforter and problem-smasher. But she went through the leap-frog motions in desultory fashion and, as the silence grew lengthy, so the atmosphere cleared and visibility returned to about what it was before a vigorous depression called Hopkins appeared on the screen.

'Not that one, you'll end on four,' he'd been watching her and the board, thinking of other things, but fascinated, as always, by a problem however banal. She smiled and replaced the peg. Sure enough it came out to a triangular three.

'It's not fair—I've been playing this for years and I still get it wrong.'

'It's a matter of progression—no side-tracking—shifting things around, molecules, haemoglobin, two kinds of protein change, which is right? And think of the build-up—no, don't.'

Very nearly flippancy, imperfectly masking a downturn of spirits, a negative mood. To gain time she put away the worn solitaire board and stayed by the window to admire the evening blue.

'It's not that simple,' he repeated, but with an apologist's mildness.

She crossed to sit at his side, took an unresisting, half-responsive hand. 'You mean you can't talk about it?'

He nodded, reluctantly. She noted more grey than usual in his very dark brown hair.

'Then don't.'

'Logically, I can't find much to talk about.' He tried, and failed to look her in the eye; she needed nothing more to convince her that Wentworth Magna's tragedy was his, wholly or in part. A visual image, too subliminal to make her flesh creep, reminded her of the strange company he was forced to keep in his working life.

'It doesn't matter,' she promised. 'You're leaving anyway.'

An anguished glance, as if she'd mocked his dearest remembrance. 'That's the nub in a nub-shell. I'm not sure I can now this has blown up.'

'Why not?'

'They won't let me.'

Four words. More horrifying than any furtive image. Incredulous the stare! Unbelieving the echoed 'Won't *let* you?'

The Chairman of the Price-Pearson board of directors, no less, wouldn't let him . . . banal to say it seemed like yesterday, but two years *is* a short time in biotechnics, and to Quentin, now wading in the shallows of a dilemma threatening, among other things, his freedom of choice, that fateful meeting, 'the day of the green light', did indeed seem too recent.

The *dernier cri* office in their London HQ reflected Price-Pearson's standing in the drugs and pharmaceutical world. Exotic woods from Brazilian rain forests were reconciled with huge plaques in gleaming bronze bas-reliefs depicting nothing very much. The T-shaped desk was breathtaking in craftsmanship and managerial insolence. Three chairs faced Sir Rufus seated at the top of the T's cross-bar. Two were set on either side of the angle thus formed. Another was placed at the very bottom of the vertical. At this distance sat the humbler employee. Executive directors used either of the two just mentioned. If the news was favourable one sat on Sir Rufus's right hand. The inferior chair was seldom needed. The Chairman practised the art of delegation to perfection.

'Take the right hand pew, Quentin.' He activated the recorder—nothing was left to chance in the dangerously competitive world of this industry.

At every day's end his secretary, escorted by security men, would take the tapes for storage in a special strong-room beneath those elegant Curzon Street offices. Every word uttered in working hours was captured and confined for the duration or forever (whichever proves to be the longer). Thus, no slip-ups, no betrayals, no denials or recriminations.

Time wasted to describe physically this true-to-form tycoon. More interesting to consider the gadget in his hand, much like a pair of nail-scissors with a steel band attached and acting as a spring. The trick was to bring the blades to a vertical position, point upwards as far as possible, by flicking one blade to match the other, a tactile exercise which appeared endlessly to fascinate Sir Rufus. Unfortunately it fascinated his captive audience too, high and low alike. Which was what it was all about.

In the thick of discussion the viewer's concentration went distracted to less than one hundred per cent and Sir Rufus who could play his game—selectively—very nearly blindfold would draw certain conclusions.

Strong-minded individuals ignored the ploy. Quentin, 'a highly-placed hireling', was one of them.

'Shouldn't be surprised if you're in my place one of these days, Q.'

'Over your dead body.'

'Vulgar but correct. Meantime, your rare gift as a practising boffin *and* administrator doesn't go unnoticed. I've authority from our European masters to nominate you for a board directorship as and when I think fit.'

'Why?'

'Partly because you're not slow to ask questions without preamble. I suppose that's the merit of scientific objectivity.'

'I like to think I'd have that whatever I was doing.'

'Wouldn't get you far—not in the non-scientific sectors.'

'Again, why?'

'The tolerance? Because your breed knows things we don't—that spells dependency—ours—up to a point.'

Q nodded, wondering had he donned his one and only tailored executive duds just to be told the indisputable facts of life? He waited for more.

'Coffee? I don't encourage alcoholics as you know.'

Q said yes to both parts, aware that Sir Rufus was secretary and treasurer of his local AA.

Coffee materialized seemingly unbidden, was poured, *petits-fours* offered and accepted. Time passed in a sipping, nibbling silence.

'Obviously you're here for more than a cosy chat.' Sir Rufus returned briefly to his scissors. 'It comes,' one eye remained on Quentin, 'to guarded congratulations and a bit of exploratory surgery—so to speak.'

'On me?'

'On you. I read your paper and lab reports, the feasibility stuff on Accelerated Pregnancy. Frankly I wasn't over the moon because the moon is over my head. Technical jargon of that order doesn't mean much to a layman—naturally I passed it to Mathieson, our scientific guru, for his considered opinion. His response would have warmed your staphylococci.'

Quentin smiled. '"Cockles" is the usual term.'

'I know, but I have to show I'm not a complete scientific idiot sometimes.' Interesting, from a former head of a minor nationalized industry and still active in Lombard Street. 'Anyway,' he continued, 'Mathie convinced me you were on to a winner. Not that I needed much convincing—technicalities may escape me, but in simple terms the idea speaks for itself—if it works.'

'It works.'

Sir Rufus ceased to fiddle with those infernal scissors. Q realized he was supposed to expand his brevity.

'It works so well I had to discontinue the experiments.'

'Why?'

'Technical reasons.'

'Was it scheduled?'

'Well no, it couldn't be. Everything's cleared with this end officially.'

'Then how—?'

'Weekend stuff. Unpaid. We use the lab facilities to follow up pet projects.'

'We? D'you mean everybody?'

'Just a few of us, addicts I suppose, but it's less harmful than drugs.'

Sir Rufus pondered this for longer than seemed decent.

'Who else was in on this?'

'Remington, Alladyce, Sanders sometimes.'

'All genetic wallahs?'

'Only myself and Nick—Alladyce, that is.'

'Your deputy H of D?'

'No—that's Rem—Remington.'

'Quentin, apart from its Nobel Prize possibilities, do you quite appreciate the wider implications of—?'

'I stated them in the opening paragraphs.'

'Some perhaps—but it *was* a rhetorical question . . . you've taken our European brass by storm. Doctor Schweiker thinks it's the greatest genetic advance since Adam's rib.'

Quentin nodded gloomily, could think of nothing modest enough for a response. A sequel must be hidden somewhere in the flannery. He studied the undissolved sugar crystals in his cup wishing he could spoon them out.

'Upshotwise, your inspired bit of tinkering is taken on board, lock, stock and crucible. No financial holds barred.'

It's conceivable, judging from Quarrier's expression, that he wanted to say: I didn't mean to do it. The benefit of that doubt can never be resolved. On the other hand, Sir Rufus had none.

'You're to drop everything else and concentrate a hundred per cent on your brainchild.'

Quarrier liked nothing of this. R and D didn't work like that—or shouldn't. Research was an evolutionary concept, not an old-fashioned army exercise in tactical manoeuvring.

'I stated the inherent dangers,' he repeated carefully. 'Genetic change—even in animals—can destabilize—in a settled society it could mean potential disaster.'

'Of course, that's the cautionary side of the coin. Like any great idea it's bound to have a double edge—but that's the sociologists' problem.'

Sir Rufus concentrated on his scissors to mask irritation. The wild one was supposed to be tamed enough to jump through the hoop and here he was denying the Lord. Ah! of course! He'd forgotten the sugar.

'Incidentally, I'm authorized to double your salary, unlimit your expenses—and ditto your team *pro rata.*'

Quarrier stared blankly to the point of insolence. Sir Rufus beamed, assuming his employee had been struck dumb by munificence. The beam faded as Quarrier continued to stare. Puzzled, he leaned forward, flipping the scissors without playing the game.

'Not enough, your highness—or what?'

'The procedure has a limited application.'

'State the limitations,' coldly.

But why? They were in the preamble. Obviously ignored, as Sir Rufus chose to ignore them now.

'It's a risk reduction in certain cases—the danger of prolonged pregnancy. It doesn't go further—I mean, it shouldn't.'

Top dog smiled and relaxed. All was now clear. Mere scruples were involved, and those could be tidied away, swept under the carpet. What else was top dog there for?

'Quentin,' confidingly, 'the name of the game has changed. To quote Mathieson, your discovery could transform procreation as Darwin revised ideas of our origins—no, let me finish. This *is* social, political and economical dynamite—it's known to very few and it has to stay that way. Everything about your scheme on record is now in one of Zurich's deepest bomb-proof vaults. If that little sewer full of other people's projections got breached, Pandora's box of tricks wouldn't compare.'

'If it's all so secret—' Quarrier was awed, and a bit scared in spite of himself.

'*Nothing* is that secret; things are simply left—not to be known—left on ice—there's a rumour of a process that could wipe out our present hi-tech infrastructure at a blow—it depends basically on a single crystal—the inventor committed suicide—I'm told. Otherwise, formulae that don't bear thinking of even in a sci-fi horror film.'

'. . . and you put my theory in the same bracket?'

Sir Rufus nodded. 'In all but one respect—that it should go forward under the strictest controls. Now, when something's that secret we have no choice but to inform the government of the day.'

'The—?' too stunned to finish the echo Quarrier, out of all character, felt himself to be a very small fish floundering in a sudden sea of Sargasso.

'Everything scientific is more or less under surveillance, but this—we need more sophisticated protection than we can afford. You can imagine how our friends would mug us for a sight of that paper—as for our enemies—'

Floundering. 'I simply—don't understand. This is supposed to be a boon and a blessing to mankind.'

'That Waverley pen nonsense! You could as well use one to sign a death warrant as write a sonnet. Nowhere is a sacrosanct, Quentin—least of all the laboratory. Now, I have another appointment. See Mathieson—he's expecting you. And be prepared for a visitor down there in a day or two.'

'What enemies!'

Sir Rufus stood firmly on his dignity. Quarrier stayed sitting.

'The buck stops elsewhere on that one. But remember, you committed us to the programme, now you're committed. If there's a cat in the bag and you prefer the quiet life—drown it. Before it's too late.'

He shot out a dismissive hand. 'You've got a world beater, don't spoil it.'

He'd reached the door before Sir Rufus enquired, quite mildly, 'You didn't mention your reasons for discontinuing experiments.'

'I thought I'd mentioned—I had to.'

'Yes, but why?'

If I talked of lag and log, of exponential growth expressed as log $\frac{N}{NO}$ = K4 when K is a constant the bloody oaf would think I was trying to pull his rank. Instead:

'It—got out of control. I had to abort the whole batch.'

He left the building immediately. Mathieson could wait.

Chapter 5

GIVE OR TAKE a comma here, a phrase there, one has a reasonably authentic gist of a two-year-old duologue, and though the Zurich parent company still refuses to release the relevant tapes requested by the Committee of Inquiry, enough has leaked out to fill in some of the blank areas.

A sleepless night gave Quarrier time to regret that day. So many significances in a single conversation; warning signs he should have heeded and acted on more instantly, washing his hands of the whole affair, emigration to begin a new life, unfraught . . . unfettered.

'Who else was in on this?' he recollected the blare of trumpets almost drowning a note of anxiety in the Chairman's question.

Too late. Two years too late. Rem, car-crashed and kaput. Alladyce, a broken reed.

He'd arrived at the complex next day long after his usual time.

The Price-Pearson laboratories were set deep in more or less sylvan tranquillity, but idyll stopped at a steel-mesh fence surrounding a swarm of production units and the main R and D building, a radial affair aggressively futuristic, but dangerous. Much of the cladding was fallen from the walls. A storeman had been struck and killed by a detaching fragment: victimized by kitsch architecture.

No obvious security at the main gate. From a small block-house the guard could communicate by a sophisticated Tannoy system with suppliers and other outsiders, giving them access if they matched with the 'authorized entry' schedule. Every employee carried a mini-computer/trans/receiver. A sealed-in code, known only to the central computer and changed weekly, automatically transmitted this cypher to the personal computer and block-house alike. As the unit holder approached the gate it was activated to open by compatible electronic signals.

A preoccupied Quarrier slowed and drove through at walking pace, watching, via his rear-view mirror, the gate slide to—cutting off retreat like a trap set and sprung by invisible forces. The computer on the seat beside him had made it possible; an accomplice, cold, detached and totally indifferent.

Unusually he'd sat awhile in the crowded parking lot, portrait of a poor chess-player, short of next moves. He felt fragmented, less than the sum total of parts, one of which was with Helen, another still festered with remembrance of yesterday's revelations. The dejected remainder simply languished in a steel-blue Rover that went with the job.

The job. He smiled grimly, jabbing at the button giving 'in-house' access, category 1. Which meant he could pass through every door in the building including the ladies' toilets. He pocketed the hateful computer and allowed his reluctant self to be absorbed, to become more—compatible.

From the foyer he passed the convention hall and turned into a corridor creating the distant eighth spoke of the radial. His territory, on two floors, a dozen laboratories defining his immediate suzerainty where he could add or take away, advise, hire or fire, initiate tangential experiments simply by drawing on a specialists' pool—and claim first dance with the prettiest girls at the Christmas Stomp.

He'd insisted on a 'working' secretary, one with a science diploma good enough to allow her at the least a rough understanding of his dictated material filled with highly technical jargon.

Unusually she stood at the door leading to his office at the far end of the corridor. Young and attractive, her brightness was marred just then by a vaguely worried air, a rehearsal of the harassed middle-aged housewife yet-to-be, taking hurried steps to meet hubby with unwelcome news.

'You can't be missing me that much!' Nothing personal, no evidence of a 'situation', merely Quarrier's off-beat line of humour from which all suffered.

'Doctor Quarrier, there's an unscheduled visitor waiting to see you.'

Her anxiety amused. In the perfect secretary's book such animals don't exist.

'It does happen, Laura. It does happen.'

'But he looks—' she paused long enough to put him on the alert. For all her twenty-three years he'd discovered in Laura a shrewd judge of character, not pedantically so, but much implied.

'What does he look?'

'A little man with a lot of authority.'

Interesting. The sort of assessment only a female would dare to flick off her cuff in an intuitive moment.

He smiled and asked were yesterday's lab reports on the stove.

'On your desk.'

'Same thing. It's where I really cook the books. Let's hope they've boiled all over our visitor.'

Vanity, vanity, all is molecular, he repeated *sotto voce* the old student adage, followed Laura into her sanctum and continued on to his, conscious of Sir Rufus's warning words—a visitor—be prepared—a day or two.

And the future was here, now all suddenly. A fleet image of Scrooge cringing before Marley's run-down of visitations set him grinning enough to double as a welcoming grimace to the— unwanted.

'Jeremy Dysart. Special Operations. But I imagine you'd like to verify. It's all on this bit of plastic.'

Which the fellow offered through a cloud of cigarette smoke; had obviously made himself at home.

'You'd better sit down—again.'

But he was thinking, oh my God, we're into the world of trashy fiction; studied the photograph with insolent care. The slightest discrepancy and he'd alert the security staff and enjoy watching the impostor being thrown out.

Malheureusely, he decided, the steel-blue eyes, blondish beard, nose made to snub, dark complexion at odds with straw-coloured hair, the thirty-two years of it all proclaimed parity with the living presence; Quarrier returned the ID signed by the Home Secretary no less.

'I understand we were at the same university. Not the same time of course.'

'Some of my worst enemies attended the very same lectures.' Dry as air-conditioned dust.

Dysart chuckled, an adept at converting rebuffs into pleasantries, crossed one casual leg over the other. Laura was right. His mere five feet eight took nothing away from an outsize assumption of being— necessary.

'Your witticisms were still being quoted in the quads years later.'

Quarrier said nothing, pushed his briefcase into a small locker and sat at his desk squarely facing the ex-undergrad.

'You were cleared through head office?'

'That's correct. Why?'

'I'd wonder how you got in otherwise.'

'The computer code? Believe me, we'd crack that very small nut if we had to.'

'How can I help you?'

'I hope that'll be mutual. D'you mind if I smoke?'

'Please continue.'

American-style, Dysart shook out a cigarette, lit it with a Dupont. Quarrier thought of little Jimmy Bond and the gadgets he employed to conceal his sweaty socks. He looked elsewhere to hide growing distaste, apprehensive and conscious of having set something in motion with not a handbrake in sight.

'Don't feel inhibited by your very natural hostility. I promise it doesn't bother a jot. Occupational hazard. Uncouth ones'll even swing a punch.'

Was the fellow a mind-reader? Quarrier damned his adrenalin overflow to hell and felt uncouth.

'I suspect,' Dysart continued in a maddeningly conversational style, 'you won't like much of what I have to say, but bear with me—only doing my job.'

Determined to say the minimum, Quarrier silently wondered was he mistaken about the ghost of a foreign inflection?

'And I'd better remind you—your outfit came to us—we didn't approach first . . . Price-Pearson owes a large slice of its lucre to fat HMG contracts—12 million quidsworth last year—'

'Not my department. You want our commercial director.'

Dysart leaned forward in a thrusting, aggressive manner. 'Sorry! Perhaps I'm long-windedly making a point, to wit: your firm has extensive and profitable tie-ups with my firm. And if something touching the national interest turns up, we're required to know about it.'

'I think you've been misinformed. A, my paper is exploratory—

even speculative. B, far from being in the national interest, it has only a very limited application.'

'. . . I wouldn't describe you as naïve, Doctor—not on the basis of your parley with Sir Rufus—or what did you mean by "inherent dangers"?'

They eyed each other on the I-know-that-you-know-that-I-know principle. For sure, one of them found himself at a disadvantage. He could only respond with irrelevance dressed as bluster.

'I totally resent the notion of a private conversation providing third-party entertainment!'

'I don't blame you one bit. *I* found it utterly boring.' Amiably. 'But, the world we live in. Where would we be without it? Dead, I suppose . . . let's be specific, Doctor. Your idea *is* dynamite, not least because you've gone beyond imminence, or why abort it?'

'Apprehension!'

That, oddly enough, was the first time Quarrier had admitted as much to any but his shaving-mirror image.

Dysart nodded like a sympathetic psychiatrist. 'Dynamite . . . can you be surprised if the powers-that-are show a lively interest?'

'A very limited application,' Quarrier repeated, dwelling on each word.

'But you're the first to stress those "inherent dangers".'

'Of course! I'd be failing my own code if I didn't glance over my shoulder at consequences.'

'You worked with rodents.'

'Mice.'

'Accelerated the breeding process.'

'Yes.'

'Ending up with more of them than you'd bargained for?'

'. . . That's—a simplistic reading of my work.'

'Simplistically a scalpel is lethal enough to kill or cure.'

'I see a useful solution to the problems some women have in later stages of pregnancy. Nothing more.'

'The road to hell is paved with self-deceptions. . . I'll tell you what I see.' Dysart leaned forward, mettled with the familiar eye-glitter of a dangerous visionary. 'A biological weapon with a finesse that makes an H-bomb blood brother to a stone-age cudgel. What price the Caucasian granaries, the wheat-fields of the Eastern bloc against an endless outpouring of *mus myriapara*?'

'There is no such species,' evenly.

'Call it what you will, you can't deny your own creation . . . strange, to think the ancients prophesied according with the scurryings of mice—myomancy wasn't it? Maybe they divined what you were getting at.'

'You're into fantasy, Mr Dysart.'

'War *is* a fantasy, Doctor. Preparation for it is the only reality. This time it could make your inspiration crucial. We know such a conflict would be prodigal of life. Time itself would have new meaning. And how outstrip the battalions of dead except with begetting regiments? Very well then, advantage is to the side having means to regenerate and repopulate at a rate faster than enemies still burdened with an outmoded nine months' cycle.'

The man's audacity was breath-taking, imposed a heavy discount on Quarrier's colourless reaction: 'That wasn't what I had in mind.'

'A biological short cut, naturally. But the rest—'

'I told you! dangers, potential, economically, possibly social—nothing more.'

'Nothing?' Dysart chuckled, drew on his cigarette, formed a perfect smoke ring and watched it undulate almost to the vanishing point.

'Clinical or cynical, *every*thing is a potential hazard, Doctor. This cigarette, a banana skin, drains, an air-conditioning system, cholesterol, thin ice, you name it. Intelligent use of so many means at our disposal is a sure defence in these dangerous times.'

'Make your point. I've a lot to do.'

'The whole programme is under government seal. Sir Rufus has signed the declaratory instrument committing him and all concerned to the restraints imposed by the Official Secrets Act. That means, no communication even with your nearest and dearest.'

'Now just a moment—'

'I shall require to know who besides yourself has a copy of the report which is, as of now, classified at the very top end of the register.'

Odd associative images! Manet's 'Execution of Mexico's Emperor Maximilian' flashed on to Quarrier's personal display unit—the crowding rifles . . . he felt he must choke at this onslaught, this—he fastened on the neglected 'effrontery' knowing the term could mean nothing to a late twentieth-century go-go man.

'You've—made so many bloody assumptions,' a voice hoarse with anger, 'all of the first order of magnitude. I'll choose only one before you go. If you'd eavesdropped carefully you'd know I can't be pushed—not into researching beyond a limited black-on-white objective. And who the hell is Sir Rufus or anybody else to put me in an OSA straitjacket!'

'Gags, ear-plugs, blinkers, straitjackets—we're all in uniform nowadays. You simply research your theory in qualified silence—why should it concern you what happens after?'

'That's insane! How can I not be concerned!'

Thus Quarrier, cleverly spitted and roasted in one.

'. . . Concern may be selective?' shaped like a query on a trump card.

No one but Quarrier heard the discordant blare of trumpets—a familiar warning fanfare blasting the inner ear. He waited, not trusting himself to speak.

'You headed research into a marketed drug, Bromouracil, which is basically compatible with thymine I believe. What the brochure described as "a new wonder pan-allergy drug" . . . was it six or seven people who died before it was withdrawn? Price-Pearson paid compensation, of course but, d'you know, I searched in vain for a single account of how you and your team beat their breasts or agonized over seven graves.'

'It wasn't my team!'

But Dysart was uncoiling, ready to go. On his reckoning he'd won. No reason to stay.

'Although I'm accredited to your department, that doesn't mean I'm your shadow—they issued me one of those ducky gadgets so no problem about access. The deal works both ways—if you have problems with ugly or unauthorized customers this number,' he tossed a scrap of pasteboard on to Quarrier's desk, 'will always find me.'

The diminutive, exuding a great deal of something not very nice, took his leave; whether Quarrier was quite in charge of the fact is doubtful.

He'd sat on, deep, as they say, in thought. Indeed, for some days after Dysart's visitation, Quarrier appeared, even in motion, to sit on and on.

His staff called it preoccupation. It was more than that: a partial paralysis of will wherewith he simply walked the business of living and working, immune to Helen and the daily motley, societally unhinged because someone had conjured Pepper's ghost to point at him and his share in an indisputable failure—which had killed seven . . . Which he'd learned somehow to live with till a stunted minion of Nemesis had to trip him with his own specious objection very nearly bordering on hypocrisy.

Given his thoroughly confused conscience, none could be permitted to share a newfound dilemma. Quarrier was a man to wrestle with his problems—but not the first to wrestle wrongly.

Granted, he was, at the time, a junior member of the team—a geneticist consultant—allowed, he had reservations about the product. True, the fatal drug had been developed in excellent faith and with a genuine desire to alleviate suffering. What he was being asked to do now rested on a different plane but as with most men of high intelligence, Quarrier's was circumscribed, so that he simply could not think through the fallacy of comparing like with what appeared only to be like.

His passion for the next two years was to be based on a false assumption, on a grey acquiescence enlivened by bouts of technicoloured enthusiasm and, beneath all, a terrible ache born of a new, special kind of loneliness.

Chapter 6

QUARRIER DELUDED HIMSELF that he'd convinced Helen there was nothing to worry about. Now, deep into the night, while she slept uneasily on his reassurance, he turned to the first refuge of the spiritually isolated, memories of past events, the few arcane triumphs, the many inexplicable failures inseparable from the twists and turns of endless experiments, all the thrills of the chase for its own sake, never for the kudos they might bring.

Futile salve to a troubled conscience. He tried and failed, at last, to sleep all from his mind; went stealthily from the bedroom and down to the kitchen. Resurrection by coffee hardly appealed; he mixed a milk shake and went to the den. Opened wide the garden window and drifted into contemplation of the trees still stamped with the colour of night. He'd placed the glass on his desk—and forgot about it. Bored by the negative view, he let his mind take him on the ebb-tide back to the two-year-old times.

And the fraught days; one in particular.

Remington, Alladyce and a satellite group of graduate researchers, had made an incomparable team, working well together, no clash of personalities. He smiled, recalling how he'd once told Alladyce he had none—the moustache had drooped a little more than usual.

'I know,' he'd said gloomily. 'Brown eyes from my mother, blue genes from Dad.'

Remington, older than Quarrier, hewed to a line, was an insensate worker, damned clocks, meals and company rules to hell, and that, thought the extant one, partly explained why the poor old chap was late and lamented. He'd bullied his experiments into success, nagged at chromosomes through prophase, mataphase, anaphase and telophase. 'You can't fool me, you bloody hypocrites!' he'd bawl at mitochondria cowering under his microscope, 'Janus green never lies!'

He'd sworn he was a failed bachelor; couldn't stand women—he said—at any price. Never found one—he insisted—small enough to fit on a slide. When he did—he promised—he'd stain it with phototungstic acid and if it squirmed, he'd marry it. Never did a woman listen with such fond complacency as dear old Linda who'd gone before leaving him heartbroken.

As it's written, as Quarrier recalled it so Rem spoke, a jerky, peremptory style, tattered speech barely covering a fund of good nature and intellectual honesty. Not much of that about in these affluent, troubled times.

The fraught days; one in particular.

After Dysart, he'd gone straight home and stayed there for two days. The rest of the triumvirate had to wait while he went through a course of occidental meditation which roughly translated meant mooning about the house in a melancholy state of utter indecision. Helen had assumed a fit of absent-mindedness when he'd offered to help with the washing-up.

'Wouldn't you care for a dish-washing thing?'

'A, you make it sound vaguely suggestive; B, I *am* a dish-washing thing.'

His colleagues, anxious in their way at his unaccustomed absence, were already in his office when he got back to the Complex . . .

'You've been gone four days!' Rem bellowed.

'I'm entitled to my week-ends—even as the lowliest prime minister.' Very dignified was Q's reply.

'Don't say you've been to Chequers,' Alladyce started to look impressed.

'Not far off, Nick. Nearer than I knew till you mentioned it.'

'It's all right for some,' Rem nursed his grievance still. He was terribly fond of the young. 'Here am I slaving my guts out like an ergotoid twit to demonstrate that erythropoetin is *not* the factor you're looking for, and even Nick's done a bit here and there—'

'Good of you to remember me,' murmured the after-thought with sad brown eyes and overdone moustache.

'Not at all, Nick. Even if you don't contribute much, at least you turn up to earn your daily crust.'

'I had a lot to think about, Rem. I still have.'

Remington called his bluff manner to heel, sensing real gravity in

Quarrier's demeanour. The two white-coated men sat, one primly, the other casually, and waited.

Quarrier found it hard to look them in the eyes, even less easy to discharge the burden of a naturally evasive mind. He fiddled with one of those electronic gadgets used to correct computer errors.

'I want you both to hear me out to the full stop.'

He then gave the gist, a hesitant, fairly condensed version of his exchanges with Sir Rufus and Dysart. Omitted nothing of substance, was heard in total silence.

Oddly enough, Alladyce made the first, very nearly impassioned comment, striking from one so mild-mannered and tediously undemonstrative.

'So you've committed us to finding yet another weapon for biological warfare!'

A blunt, inescapable accusation—between the eyes.

'I've committed no one! Not even myself.' Quarrier leaned forward, arms tight folded, portrait of a man pitting inner against outer tension. 'I'm simply looking for advice and consensus, that's all. We have to make a yea or nay decision . . . Bob?'

The thick, black, bushy eyebrows and the lower lip thrusting aggressively had been known to reduce bloody-minded guinea-pigs to screaming hysterics.

'Is this Dysart the unknown I told Nick I'd seen snooping around on Friday—a fair-haired phenotype displaying incomplete dominance?'

Quarrier wryly confirmed the probability.

'He asked me some bloody stupid question—I told him to shove off.'

'But why let him put you over a barrel over the pan-allergy business?' Alladyce wondered.

Quarrier shrugged. 'I threw a bucketful of ethics into the wind. It's always a mistake.'

'For God's sake! couldn't you tell him you were subordinate to Mathieson at that time? *You* warned Mathie Bromouracil could have a risky feed-back.'

'You're being loyal but rhetorical, Rem. I didn't have the clout in his subject—he headed the project—we had collective responsibility.'

'That isn't the point—Mathieson was far gone but he made the decision.'

'Also not to the point. I conceded—reluctantly—but I conceded.'

'And look where he is now,' Alladyce muttered.

Quarrier showed some irritation. 'The fall and rise of Geoffrey Mathieson does not pertain. I want cast-iron reasons from you and Rem as to whether we should do or die.'

Remington thought that was pitching it high.

'Not much higher than low. Suppose we resign on a Pugwash principle—there are those who'd make it sure-fire we'd never work again—'

'Oh, come—!' Alladyce started to object.

'*They* consider it that important.'

'Do you?' Rem challenged.

'In terms of our original objective—restricted pregnancy? Of *course* I do.'

'Then let's deal with the actual and leave ifs and buts to tinkers.' Decisively.

His two colleagues regarded Remington warily. Even in a mellow mood he was capable of suggesting they strangle Dysart and scatter the remains in the nearest safari park. He filled in their silence.

'I never went along with your decision to abort the project. You were on to a winner and still are. The imprint formula is right in phase, once refine the regulatory mechanism and we're there. No—wait a bit! Ask yourselves, who's got the upper hand at the end of the day? We have! The buck stops with you, yes? If you say so and so—then those ignoramuses have to agree so and so. If your formula stays in the family—the three of us—what can they do or say if our reports vary by an iota—?'

Quarrier sat forward, intrigued by what he took to be Rem's Machiavellian drift.

'You mean we scramble the issue?'

'Do we deal in feet and inches—or angstroms? Do we weigh in pounds and ounces for Pete's sake? Where's the problem in overbalancing and undercalculating? We push ahead with the original projection, if necessary we'll practise double entry—one set of figures for our legitimate purposes, another for theirs—'

'Our European confrères aren't stupid, Rem—'

'Nor are they starting from your base-line—they can puzzle over your duplicates till hell freezes over under red-hot skates.'

'And when it does?'

'Once we have the solution, you call the shots.'

Quarrier's spirits soared; there was no way he could glimpse the irony that Rem had both cut the Gordian knot and laid the foundations for a Faustian tragedy-to-be. Now, they had a genuine pretext for pressing on, keeping integrity dry under a red, white and blue umbrella patched with scraps and rags of national security directives and devil take the hindmost.

Even a lugubrious Alladyce showed signs of well-being, barring a reservation or two.

'If Dysart has a watching brief how much will he understand of what he sees?'

Quarrier thought it a point worth considering. 'I'm not sure . . . he seemed glib with thymine and Bromouracil, but I imagine these people have nous enough to bone up when there's a need.'

Alladyce nodded. 'And he wants to know who has copies of your paper—why?'

'So he'll know who knows, surely,' Remington suggested. 'Though I don't see how it helps him—you weren't specific on the base-line as I recall, Q?'

'Credit me!' What Quarrier meant had to do with the politics of scientific enquiry. Any innovation first sees the world with the lusty incoherent bawl of the newly born; it simply doesn't spring fully articulate from Minerva's head. In other words, the scientific pioneer leaves out enough data to protect his investment.

Everything seemed as reasonable as apple-pie order could be. Yet Dysart, even by his mere existence, was to cast something of a shadow over the lives of this trio. As the months passed this simulacrum of darkness would lengthen, reach insidiously into every nook and cranny of the collective consciousness, tainting each with an indefinable stigma to advertise the existence of marked men. Nothing so crude as a glance over one's shoulder but turning a corner of the mind in pursuit of some other notion, they would, as it were, stumble over the *idea* of Dysart who might be rooms or miles away.

Later, Rem would admit with the worst possible grace: 'I'll say this much for the horrible little man, he's physically discreet.'

Interveningly the three researchers could console themselves with a genuine sense of false security common to conspirators. They enjoyed priority rating, special privileges and more than usual deference from the lowest computer clerk to Sir Rufus himself. Price-Pearson was their oyster however much philosophers might grieve at the strange places men will get themselves into.

Nothing asked of them except the routine weekly progress report.

R and D is a tedious business; no drama can be founded on endless repetitions, always more of the same with scarcely measurable variables; non-existent the Hollywooden scenario screaming artificial urgency in pursuit of a doomcrack deadline. Their kind of work had a delicacy somewhere akin to copying *Les Misérables* on to a cherry-stone: boring work, the making of an epoch, the shaping of an era.

A year passed . . . and another . . .

Before Helen, waking to the fact that Quentin never surfaced at six in the morning, came down to find him in the den, dead to the world in his armchair facing the window, an untouched milk shake on the desk he'd unpredictably made himself long ago. Dead to the world . . . she viewed that simple, serviceable construct with a vague aversion born of a long-standing whim. 'When I die I've planed planks enough to provide my coffin. Don't forget.'

She'd laughed at the time. 'But why?'

'Because it's a part of me,' simply.

'You're strange—in parts,' meaning she could still wonder at the occasional quirks which seemed to go against his more or less natural grain.

'Strange—because I respect an ancient ordinance? In the midst of life, what else are we in?'

And now, years on, she'd discovered the man she loved—rather as one treasures a precious memento—eyes closed, head high to flaunt a matutinal pallor to the rays of a long risen sun. Sleeping not by his desk, but beside his unfinished coffin . . .

She closed her eyes merely to renew perception, opened them to find the same, different idiot who'd lost his way back to bed hours before. Smiled, filled with love for her precious memento but, hesitant to wake him she looked about her at the familiar objects, 'blood relations to my duster', an eighteenth-century microscope, a sublimely beautiful ammonite, the case of technicoloured tropical butterflies, brought back from Simpson's auctioneers in his

Cambridge days, round which he would still weave tales of his lepidopterous trip up the Amazon, the framed scraps of Mendelian notes and, above all, the prized letter written by Darwin, framed— on the desk . . .

> Dear Huxley . . . I agree entirely, we cannot doubt Nature has it in her power to perpetrate wonders beyond the limits of our comprehension. For my part, I am insufficiently sanguine to hope mankind will not, in some distant age, arrogate to itself some of that inceptual power to perpetrate horrors such as I could have no desire to conceive.

A thousand times over she knew it by heart, but fell into the trap and read it once more; this time, with a deeper disquiet, the slightest of frowns displacing her vague, early morning smile as she registered a connection between Darwin's apprehensions and last night's sensational news from nowhere, formerly the village of Wentworth Magna.

She reconsidered the sleeping man unaware of her deepening frown . . . so often she'd found him thus, at his desk in the small hours, sprawled across pages of foolscap covered with weird and wonderful hieroglyphics, suffering himself to be led back to bed like a recalcitrant, unrepentant child.

In Helen's eyes, he was not so much a genius as a master of mysteries beyond her understanding; she conceded the freedom that title implied, but never doubted the need of a gentle, albeit firm touch of the reins, if only to remind a rare and wayward spirit of the real world . . .

A mentionable fact, because she viewed him at that precise moment in a less complacent light. Laymanlike she suspected the scientific mind, the hedges and barriers sheltering incomprehensible errors, lethal mistakes, the runaway experiments, all seeming to mock her ignorance—no less the Wentworth Magna tragedy, which surely had some connection with Price-Pearson, with the laboratories in which Quentin, her husband, conducted genetic research . . . an almost eerie light, shed on a sudden stranger, asleep in Quentin's ancient and disreputable club chair. If sleep is darkness, to gaze on a familiar figure at slumbering time is to guess at the far side of the moon.

Loath to stay with an unresponsive lay figure, subduing some uncharitable reflection not easily defined, Helen sought sanctuary and black coffee in her domain. The kitchen, she said, was her *cordon solitaire* where she now sat, smoking a rare cigarette, and meditated on seemingly inter-related things while waiting for Radio 4's early news.

Before the children tumbled out of bed . . . she never allowed them to listen to the news, or watch it on the screen, convinced that a daily catalogue of modern horrors must first bruise and then brutalize.

Remembering the kitchen clock was slow she hurriedly switched on the radio.

'. . . disturbing evidence of a major ecological disaster centred in this secluded Hampshire village confirms Gerald Hopkins's graphic account televised in last evening's "Eye-to-Eye".

'Our science correspondent Richard Ogram has on-the-spot details.'

'I arrived here around midnight to find several journalists already congregated, an odd atmosphere predominated, not exactly a typical gathering of newshounds chasing the story of the moment.

'In fact we went nowhere near the village. It's strictly out of bounds from either end.'

'Richard, "not exactly typical"?'

'Well, I suppose I mean that newsmen on assignment are fairly boisterous, take a relaxed attitude when they're simply waiting around for something to happen. These were tense and justifiably nervous, I think. You see these things advance suddenly and then retreat just as abruptly—it's like a great expansion and retraction—'

'What could you actually see?'

'Most of the ground activity was visible only by car headlamps and a few torches. The whole area seemed to be alive with them—pretty spine-chilling.'

'Were they inclined to attack?'

'As one reporter said—they have a discipline—never break ranks.'

'So you could get near—'

'Not really—there's a kind of no-man's land. No one's anxious to cross it.'

'And you have to retreat continuously?'

'Backing and filling much of the time. In daylight it's possible to go forward, if you have the nerve, though one reporter on the *Mail* said he was going through to the village come what may. He drove on against police advice and—'

'Has he returned?'

'Nothing's been heard from him since—that was two hours ago.'

'From what you say, Richard, there appears to be a *modus operandi* with these animals.'

'It's hard to tell on the ground, but we do have an uncomfortable impression of a rapid gathering of forces before an offensive . . . just now, I'm at the main road turn-off waiting for a helicopter to give me a hover view of the scene—'

'Richard, we'll cut you in later in the programme when you're airborne—hopefully you'll have a clearer idea from up there just what *is* happening.

'Not surprisingly, all other news is given the back-burner treatment judging by the lead stories and hyper-headlines in this morning's press. "Supermice Takeover" and in *The Scotsman* "Mice Gang Amok" tend to give a little pause for thought. But how serious is the problem before dust finally settles? We turned to Professor Carl Harberd, Head of Biological Studies at London University, for enlightenment on a none too natural phenomenon.'

'You're quite right to describe what's happening as "none too natural", Brian. I watched Hopkins's graphic demonstration on the Box last evening and I'm bound to say I found the whole business extremely disturbing.'

'But need we be too concerned? I mean, mice are those creatures one shoos back into their holes or catches in a trap, after all.'

'That's the conventional and accepted wisdom for ordinary mice. These, plainly, are not.'

'Why not?'

'To answer that comprehensively I'd have to look a bit closer at one of the brutes. I'm hoping to arrange an acquisition later in the day.'

'"Brutes" sounds vaguely emotive from a scientific scion?'

'Perhaps so. But if I admit to a sleepless night after Hopkins's show, you'll gather I'm more than a little concerned.'

'Should we all be—or is yours the anxiety of a professional taken unawares as it were?'

'Something of both I imagine.'

'Why?'

'The quite phenomenal breeding rate to begin with. Mice are notoriously fecund as you know, but on the evidence it's plain these things are reproducing at a rate unheard of in Rodentia or indeed in any order. To end with, they exhibit certain features quite inconsistent with the species.'

'The eyes and the hand-like fore-paws?'

'Odd, extremely odd . . . but you'll also recall how one of them bared its teeth in close-up—I feel we may have something intractable on our hands.'

'Yes?'

'The canine teeth were disproportionately large—even for what appeared to be very large mice.'

'Is there a conclusion to be drawn from that?'

'Only the inescapable one, that we're not dealing with a new species so much as an artifact.'

'A cause for concern?'

'The short answer is "yes"; those teeth bother me . . . and the obvious question I leave to you.'

'Where did they originate?'

'Quite. They didn't drop from the skies, did they?'

As the radio team moved on to more ephemeral items, Helen might have sensed its evident preoccupation with rampaging mice had she not strayed into a frame of mind filled by a still shot rather than a moving picture.

Part of the maze was visible from her standpoint. Unconsciously she studied it; consciously she tried to think out possibilities that came to nothing because they were too vague and formless. Nor could she decide how to tackle Quentin on a burgeoning issue which she no longer doubted had to involve him—totally.

The phone in action killed conjecture. She hurried from the kitchen, stopping almost as abruptly as the thing itself which had shrilled no more than three or so. A misdialled connection.

She returned to the kitchen in time to catch the 'Today' programme's second report on its uppermost item.

'—as we go over to Richard Ogram reporting from somewhere above the Hampshire/Surrey border. Are you with us, Richard?'

'Yes indeed, Brian. We've just lifted off from a field adjoining the

A315 and heading for the village—I can see the squat church tower little more than a mile distant.'

'Much activity thereabouts?'

'It's a quite hectic scene viewed from aloft. The main road is crammed with cars, police vehicles mostly, ambulances and so on. There's a very strong police presence at both intersections effectually sealing off the winding country road—we're approaching the village now and, as we drop to eighty to a hundred feet altitude . . . eighty to a hundred . . .'

'Richard?'

'. . . it—has to be seen to be . . . this is Richard Ogram reporting —an utterly fantastic sight—a withering spectacle. There's an air of nuclear winter over this place in spite of a drenching summer sun—desolation, systematic destruction—the trees are bare, and there may be vegetation over an enormous circular area . . . except it's hidden by a rippling grey mass, like a breeze brushing over a furry landscape . . .'

'The mice?'

'. . . everywhere. Numbers are meaningless.'

'Richard, is there any sign of life at all?'

'We're flying slowly along the road—what looks like an abandoned car—another could be a police vehicle—an earlier casualty—'

'Are these things—?'

'What we can see is almost indescribable, this enormous mass seems like one great palpitation—as I say—a dreadful expansion and contraction of a single monstrous creation—'

'From your description, Richard, a controlled movement—'

'It's hard to say—a rhythmic discipline with a central authority may be fanciful—I can only tell you how it looks . . . we're going back . . . no—wait!'

'Richard, are you there?'

'I'm taking a chance—one of the houses. We can't leave without trying a rescue—there may be survivors still . . .

'We're almost at the end of the village, an overturned fire tender—a grey movement superimposed on red—in the road I can make out something sprawled under a living mass of . . . nothing much left . . . we're about twenty feet above dereliction, what must surely have been the spacious garden of a house—'

'Richard, it might be wiser to—'

'Ten, eight feet. There's no touching down or we'd be crawling alive with the damned things. As it is, they're being scattered by the noise and turbulence and we're just ten or fifteen yards from the door—I'm jumping—now!'

'Today' had seldom chronicled a more dramatic moment, further intensified by Ogram's snap decision compounded of a need to discover the worst, to satisfy curiosity, to help a fellow-creature or two.

It's a part of the media's paradox that listeners who were totally awake to the situation, were safe and remote from danger, could also share in the horrific novelty. While breakfast preparations and other mundane chores went unheeded, the barrier to reality, first raised by Hopkins, was still being created.

By accident or design a news summary followed. Of significance it had none; nor did the item that came after—some sort of government panic over leaked documents—funnily enough, recovered from a civil servant's mother's laundry basket.

'We have a not unnaturally breathless Richard Ogram on line from the helicopter—Richard, we gather you're safely aboard—what happened?'

'. . .The house door was open—people had tried to escape—I raced across that living carpet and went in—at least—a large hallway swarming with—I couldn't go further—they were everywhere—on the stairs—a woman I think . . . covered, I watched them fighting to get at—at whatever it was. I felt more than one climbing up my back as I beat them off my face—I turned and ran—couldn't do anything else—the pilot came right down and I scrambled on somehow bringing some of the hideous things with me—they're in the cabin—fighting to get at us—God how they hold on—I've got to kill them or we'll not make it back.'

Nor did they.

Ten minutes later reports came through that the contract helicopter had crashed a mile or more from Wentworth Magna. Whether the pilot had panicked as the mice multiplied spoiling his concentration or he'd struck out involuntarily so deflecting the controls will never be known, but Ogram earned a place that day in radio's annals.

'He has courage.'

Helen started from total absorption as, minutes before the crash,

Quentin delivered a touch of epitaph from where he stood at the open door.

'You heard?'

He nodded, hesitated, eyes averted, before slumping on to a nearby chair, merely a dressing-gown filled with rearguard truculence scarcely held together with a length of cord.

She heated and poured coffee in a lengthening silence. The silence was Helen's. He must deal with words.

'I've met Ogram—that interview in "*Science Forum*" two or three years back.'

Not worth a commonplace response, that snatch of trivia. 'I've met him' rang false, an irrelevance adding nothing to the overwhelming issue.

'Quentin,' with deliberation, 'people are dead or dying. What does a scrap of reminiscence have to do with—?'

'Prisoner at the bar, is there anything you wish to say before sentence is passed upon you!'

Angrily, and so, clearly, on the defensive.

'There has to be an accusation, not to mention a trial before we get that far,' as she might gently upbraid young Michael for wilfulness.

'Last night.'

'I hardly asked if you were in any way involved. Presumably others are working on mice and things at Price-Pearson?'

Obliquely she watched him sipping and fumbling about in his mind as if for something mislaid. He found what he was looking for as she handed him a second cup.

'I'm sorry, Helen. There's really nothing much left to hold back. You've seen practically all there is to know.'

Unfeigned surprise rounded her eyes. What could be worse than an apparent confession cleverly masking a denial?

'More to it than that, surely.' Words intended as a private and personal thought; but the tongue has a way with petty considerations.

'Well, yes,' meekly enough, 'two years more, I suppose.'

'They kept you awake last night?'

He closed his eyes, ran hands through already rumpled hair, offered a distorted impression of the man she thought she knew.

'I worked at finding just where I—we had gone wrong. I still don't know.'

She felt annoyed and bewildered, unsure of what exactly he was trying to convey. Bitterly she conceded he might have it in mind to clarify, justify a ghastly mistake with some anodyne, abstruse formula beyond her understanding.

'Is it only a question of rectifying a terrible error?'

'What do you mean?' he seemed genuinely puzzled.

'Quentin, people are dying.'

'Or are dead already, as you said. Can I deny it?'

Surely he could see her point. It seemed more immediate, more urgent than a narrow view about what had gone wrong in his scientifically, hermetically sealed world where retorts couldn't answer back.

'What happens now?' that seemed innocuous enough, yet he was plainly irritable and ready to react when the phone rang once more.

Chapter 7

'QUENTIN? WHAT THE hell's wrong with your phone? Have it checked! And get here immediately! I'll expect you at eleven sharp. The government's breathing down my neck and its science wallah wants to breathe down yours. Eleven!'

Thus, the headlong answer to Helen's question.

Faced with less than a choice Quentin drove at speed into London's hurly-burly arriving in time to catch a suddenly vacant parking place hard by the HQ, stormed its portals at the eleventh hour and cursed the lost opportunity to have a private word with Mathieson or even Sir Rufus before the government turned up.

To his surprise Mathie was waiting for him in the reception hall. It struck Quarrier for the first time, and forcibly, how Mathieson had survived and prospered after the Bromouracil débâcle; a silver-haired alumnus, shaped like a diplomat, who'd drunk himself out of a brilliant career as a research chemist and talked his way into a high-grade position as Sir Rufus's scientific adviser—a sinecure, if one's not too particular about the cure for one's sins—to paraphrase a man who concealed bitterness and a continuing drink problem under a suave, unpleasantly ironic exterior.

He had the ram-rod stance of one who dared not bend to the wind. But, for once, the sardonic air emphasized by the fleshy protuberance of his lower lip was less evident. A tendency to hover suggested unease, as did the pallor in one of a more florid complexion. Things, he seemed to convey, are more serious than you think.

'I've had a hell of a time and you've got yours coming,' was all his greeting. 'They're waiting for you in the Star Chamber.'

'Brief me, Mathie.'

They talked rapidly while a security man riffled without conviction through Quarrier's briefcase.

'First, I must hope you brought sandwiches in that thing. If you care for the rack it promises to be a long drawn-out session.'

'Come on, Mathie, there isn't time for idiocy. What's the opposition?'

Mathieson gave a pithy run-down on the comings and goings, the non-stop intercontinental calls and counter calls since Hopkins's *coup de théâtre*, he ground out the gallicism with excessive venom, adding that *Mr* Hopkins was ripe for tar-and-feather treatment.

'In short, my dear Q, the thing is no longer chemical but political—and there's nothing more lethal outside a test tube—even the genomes of Zurich are disinherited. Just choose your words.'

Quarrier stared blankly: choose his words?

'Comfort yourself, not only you, but your team, Sir Rufus and others could be for the chop if this wee timorous beastie goes too far. So for heaven's sake don't put his lordship's back up or there could be—'

'His whatship?' Quarrier's incredulous response as the lift balanced on the law of gravity and the brushed steel door purred aside. Walnut panelling, flawless carpet and a row of Company portraits still clinging to their positions on the walls defined Price-Pearson's international standing very nicely.

'Lord Betherton. I've got Sir Rufus. *He's* got the Prime Minister. I don't know which of us is the more pitiable but be warned, Q, he's as tough as old boots under the Cherry Blossom.'

He's talking too much about too little, Quarrier's instinctive thought. At the door to the atrium he wondered: 'Are you in on this?'

Odd, the reaction . . . 'What do you mean?'

'What I say. You're Sir Rufus's technical guru. Who else reads his tea-leaves for him?'

'I see . . . well probably not. Betherton says the fewer the better. When the stakes are this high who wants a kibitzer? I'll be off to my hole and await the call that never comes. Good luck.'

A pensive Quarrier watched Mathieson's noiseless retreat into a diminishing perspective of corridor. Time was when he'd felt deeply for a has-been who'd declined, at his worst, to double-distilling vodka in the Company alembics. Now, he could wonder how much sympathy *he* presently needed.

Some, at least, to judge by the wary smiles of typists, word processors and the minor-domo receptionist. Between two offices and an ante-room Quarrier had time to take a drowning man's stock of his position. His last thought before entering: they mean to hold me responsible—and why should Mathieson distance himself unless—?

The lord, a common or garden life peer, sat at Sir Rufus's right hand. He had never been known to give a favourable first impression, and a second was scarcely helpful. To an extent, appearances were against him. Middling in years, niggardly of features, except for governess-grey eyes distorted by pebble-thick glasses, but suggestive of a wieldy authority not otherwise evident in a lack-lustre personality. Vanity oozed out in carefully oiled hair of which little. Vocally he had a tendency to melisma and, as he played on it, one was tempted to toss a coin in his hat—if he'd affected one.

Neither the best of scientists, nor the worst of politicians (although he'd failed his constituency selection exams) Betherton had set out to become a politicized scientist, studying how to make himself indispensable to the prevailing power bloc by interpreting the increasingly complex language of technology into terms comprehensible to an idiot. And, because he was right loyal and capable of being formidably unpleasant, Downing Street made use of him on bullying missions—not necessarily connected with matters scientific...

This particular affair threatened to call forth all his talents.

Sir Rufus briefly introduced, and commanded Quarrier to the usual chair.

'I've heard of you, Quarrier,' apparent flattery, *legato*.

Quarrier had the sixth sense to stay silent.

'Bromouracil, wasn't it?'

Just as instinctively Quarrier took up the snide challenge. 'I didn't come all this way to have ground cut from under my feet—and if you think oneupmanship is a parliamentary prerogative I can assure you the labs are rife with it and I also treat it with the contempt its authors deserve.'

'Steady, Quarrier,' Sir Rufus rumbled, his scissors working overtime, as became a badly worried man, caught between his European overlords and a seething First Lord of the Treasury who was feeling very sick and looking very tired because of all this.

Besides, truculence was a province. His.

'Only speaking as I find, Mr Quarrier.' Unprepossessing too, his use of lower-middle class phraseology. 'I can't possibly keep up with every development but I'm bound to remember the, shall we say, notorious ones? To the point, you'll realize I'm here *ex officio* from the Cabinet Office simply to establish the grounds for an official enquiry into the origins of this outbreak and, of course, to ascertain how best to contain it . . . I hope you'll forgive my putting as many statements as questions.'

'Go ahead.'

Sir Rufus relaxed visibly. He knew Quarrier's reputation for acidic eccentricity, doubted there was alkali enough at hand to neutralize the fellow's pH value.

Quarrier noted his lordship had come well briefed. Papers were piled neatly between elbows resting on the desk. Almost certainly his lab reports were among them.

'Of course,' Betherton conceded, 'I have to proceed on the strong assumption that these creatures are fugitives from Price-Pearson's premises.'

'Why?'

Betherton shrugged, sketched his second best smile. 'The nature of the beast, its proximity to the only chemical complex for some miles—the thrust of your research. Difficult, in a court of law, not to convict on circumstantial evidence of such quality. You began work on this project about two years ago?'

'As you know.'

'We have copies of your reports forwarded by Sir Rufus over that period . . . would it be true to say that, if they are correct, your efforts have been singularly unavailing?'

Beootifully elocuted, but rather too much emphasis on the 'if'. Cautiously, Quarrier. This man has all the fleamarks of an amateur prosecuting counsel. Answer *now*, but keep an eye on *then*.

'We've advanced the reproductive rate by a factor of three. I don't call that unavailing.'

Betherton leaned forward with an expression that did nothing to correct those first impressions. 'But you got precisely the same results two years ago—that is, before Sir Rufus gave you authority to recreate the project.'

'I'd quarrel with "precisely the same".'

'Your own admission to him is on record, a runaway experiment. "I had to abort the lot." Why?'

'For obvious reasons. The irradiated chemical input produced a consistent and persisting high degree of cancerous off-growths. Practice wasn't equating with theory.'

Betherton thought hard about this; the message in his naturally disbelieving stare was plain. A stand-off response. Abruptly, he shot two words at the accused. 'It works!'

It appeared to make no impression. Betherton was forced to expand sufficiently to destroy the dramatic impact. 'That was your reply to Sir Rufus's suppositious "if it works".'

Giving Quarrier time to prepare an explanation. 'I don't have to tell a scientist of *any* calibre, one experiment with a positive tendency doesn't make a breakthrough. I mean one highly qualified success is no more than a failure with possibilities. The hard graft comes later.'

Betherton's frank disbelief equalled Sir Rufus's puzzlement.

'Enlighten me, Quarrier—success and failure on the same level?'

'It's very difficult to fit new clothes on an emperor with St Vitus's Dance.'

'Ah! that's very good. I understand exactly.'

The life peer scowled at the knight who looked elsewhere. A baronetcy or better could be at stake on this one.

'Your colleagues would no doubt take the same line.'

'Not Remington. He's dead. In any case they all agreed my conclusions—'

'And this Indian woman?'

'Which you'll find in the report,' Quarrier insisted on finishing.

'Very much on the periphery,' Sir Rufus felt he could risk an assertion on a point of no importance. 'She joined your team much later didn't she?'

Quarrier nodded.

'Let's come to the break-out—if that's what it was. I imagine you checked all your specimens were accounted for when this broke?'

'No. Why should I?'

Lordly *and* knightly astonishment. One frowned, the other shifted uneasily.

'Didn't you,' Betherton urged, 'assume these things related to the Price-Pearson laboratories?'

'Suppose I had? People are paid to stop everything from mice to isotopes going abroad.'

'You're saying your responsibility ends at the gates?'

'My involvement ends there.'

'Presumably you know what's happened?'

'I saw the TV item if that's what you mean.'

'No recognition that these mice were—different?'

'That was obvious.'

'Perhaps I should make that clearer. Did you *recognize* them?'

'. . . No.'

'And you were so "uninvolved" as not to make a phone check?'

'I've said already! It's not our patch.'

'Did anyone ring you?'

'No—not even Dysart.'

Quarrier's was an inspired answer because it combined a lie loaded with consequences and an important truth. He thought briefly of Helen, not missing an exchange of significant glances. For the first time it occurred they might already have grilled Alladyce.

'According to your reports these female mice are irradiated or otherwise processed in batches almost every working day.'

'It's an assembly-line procedure.'

'You mention injections with specifics from human foetal tissue.'

'It's one line of enquiry.'

'Following which, in the X700 series, and I quote: "S-35 ad heterochromatins positive. Increased ovulation significant. Subsequent fertilization accelerated. Offspring atypical." That was dated 10th April—four months ago.'

'I remember—what we call a flash result. It's the hit-and-miss principle—'

'What I'm getting at, Mr Quarrier, no other laboratory in the UK is undertaking experiments giving this kind of result.'

'I'm not in a position to say as much.'

The spectacles glinted with the rudiments of an austere smile. 'Can you still assert, in face of the evidence, these animals are not from your laboratory?'

'To the best of my knowledge—yes.'

'. . . Why?'

Quarrier explained that strict standards of health and safety, not to mention the need to consider the animals' welfare required every quota of affected creatures to be incinerated at the earliest opportunity. In this case there was the added impossibility of coping with a prodigious birthrate in practical terms.

His lordship listened non-committally as he searched through the papers before him.

'You'll understand I'm sure, the need to press a little on the leakage aspect . . . it's a safe assumption you don't take your work home with you?'

'Calculations, yes. Guinea-pigs, no. The rules are as strict as the spot checks.'

'Espionage is rife in the pharmaceutical world,' Sir Rufus dispensed a lot of information on the world-is-round principle.

Betherton nodded impatiently. 'Quite so. We have to consider the possibility of competitor interest—smuggling out some of these creatures—even vital information on your activities.'

'I don't see it. The animals in themselves prove nothing and for information they'd need access to the central computer and *then* learn to break down the encodes and *even* work out irradiation dosage which is so unproximate we don't always read it into the software.'

'Is that wise?'

'No. Laziness.'

Sir Rufus's snigger quickly converted to a cough.

'Alternatively, Mr Quarrier,' Betherton continued, 'could not someone, an employee say, with a grudge against society, or his salary scale, or Price-Pearson itself, set out to wreak havoc for its own sake?'

'. . . You're pointing so many fingers I'm beginning to lose sight of your hand. What the hell concern is any of that to me! I'm paid to get results, not catch mice. And more importantly—where was Dysart when the light went out? Every other time we look over our shoulders, there's Dysart. If we sneeze, Dysart blesses us. For the last six weeks—if we jot down notes and leave them around, Dysart's there, if we plot a programme Dysart's ahead of us in the computer room. He's particularly fond of men's toilets—what d'you want me to call him?'

'. . . An accredited Government monitor, Mr Quarrier. Are you objecting to his personality—or his position?'

'I'm objecting to an awful lot of pointed innuendoes which don't take a free-lancing stranger from an unidentified Ministry into account! How do you know *he* doesn't take some of 'em home to play with!'

'Because I have your explicit assurance that every quota is incinerated. I can make allowances for your annoyance, Mr Quarrier, but I must warn you, the questions will be far more penetrative when official investigations begin prior to an inevitable Committee of Enquiry.'

'I have nothing to hide, nothing to fear and nothing to add to what I've already volunteered.'

'Are you sure, Mr Quarrier?'

Another musical hit. Thus, Q explained the minor phenomenon to Helen, to his friends, to himself. 'Any sensational event, personal, affecting me crucially—it comes disguised as a gust of music—I mean—I'm hit musically—an outsize blare of trombones, raucous, climbing to a high note, then *staccato*, over a roll of tympani—that's it—premonitory—a musical hit—redder than a traffic light.'

He heard it then, listened with the slightest welcoming smile to that highly personalized bleep advising malfunction in the workings of the Universal Mechanism's sub-station.

Betherton, uncertain of himself for once, seemed puzzled by Quarrier's sudden blankness, his lack of reaction to a deliberately loaded question.

'Are you quite sure, that is, that you have nothing to add?'

'I beg your pardon—to add to what?'

Undesignedly it came to a beautiful example of reduction to the absurd. No end nettled was his lordship.

'Pull yourself together, Quarrier. We've got to get this mess sorted out y'know.' Sir Rufus might have been a paternal CSM seeing a private through his first 'on report'.

Quarrier nodded, still listening to those eerie remembrancers on their way *diminuendo* to rejoin the music of the spheres.

'I'm sorry, but I'm really not sure what I'm supposed to be adding.'

'Your reports are monitored by our analysts—naturally. We have to be sure of what we're protecting.'

Quarrier glanced sharply at Sir Rufus who had the grace to look elsewhere.

'Well?'

'Almost invariably they're baffled. Some of the figures—and most of your reports—are labelled "inconclusive".'

'They would be wouldn't they? It's delicate work tampering with Nature—she tends to over-react.'

'If you've no objection I'd like to go through the papers seriatim.'

No blank shot in Quarrier's regard this time. It was level enough, and deathly as a view from within a skull.

'Are you, one of the government's custrels, daring to put me to inquisition?'

'That's uncalled for, Quarrier.' But Sir Rufus was grinning hugely. Betherton could afford to leave his defence to the hirer and firer in chief, never knowing Sir Rufus was cudgelling his brains over the 'custrel' bit.

'What is this *about*!'

'You seem to attach importance to heterochromatin as it concerns the decidual cells,' Betherton affected to ignore Quarrier's outbursts, 'but the glycogen and lipid content—'

'I discuss nothing until you, or Sir Rufus preferably, clarifies my position vis-à-vis a situation which has sod all to do with me yet appears to concern no one else!'

Betherton seemed highly gratified. 'Terse and to the point. The PM would be the first to approve, Mr Quarrier . . . by the way, are your political opinions much as they were at Cambridge?' Bland as blood pudding.

'. . . Are we talking of mutations or motivation?'

'. . . Both, if one accepts the terms are interchangeable. Now, I'm sure Sir Rufus had other more pressing business. Perhaps we could commandeer a small room big enough for the two of us *and* these reports?'

Chapter 8

SOME TWO HOURS later a figure, its countenance set hard as cement, left the Price-Pearson block, turned, and to the passers-by's amusement, solemnly raised two fingers to that opulent façade known to its personnel as 'Headache House', a fitting soubriquet for premises founded on Price's hundred-year-old formula for megrims and morning sickness. An undeterminable number of sufferers, mainly women, appear to have passed away on account of very quicksilver side-effects—mercurial poisoning—and Dr Price's fortunes faltered somewhat until Mr Pearson, the company apothecary stood the recipe on its head and created a wildly successful cure for corns, bunions, verrucas and other human hardpad ailments.

The price was high to the public—and exorbitant to the good doctor. Pearson demanded, and got, his partnership. The golden handshake had to do with silence. Other times: same times.

Mayhap some of the firm's early history turned itself over in Quarrier's mind as he went at an angry gait to his car in Clarges Mews ... and checked at sight of the familiar figure leaning proprietorially against the bodywork, arms folded on the roof, content to watch the world go by and Quarrier's approach.

'I looked in at your office, but I couldn't wait,' Quarrier lied without conviction.

'That's why I'm here, dear fellow—instead of there.'

Unmistakable, the furtive glances as he spoke; absent, the usual composure; unheeded, Quentin's annoyance.

'Then why the hell didn't *you* wait?'

'My lunch hour.' Cryptically.

Quarrier thought he'd guessed at his meaning and was about to suggest the nearest pub if hunger so threatened his usual thirst. But Mathieson's sudden and inexplicable sense of urgency got there first.

'Open up the car *pronto*, Q, there's a good lad. We'll troll round the park for a bit.'

There was enough in his tone to give substantial pause, to prompt a blare of those too prevalent trombones. Catching Mathieson's wary mood, Quarrier glanced involuntarily about him, unlocked the car door and slid into the driving-seat. Mathieson was beside him the moment he'd slipped the off-side door catch.

Nothing of consequence passed as Quarrier followed a Theseus thread through a one-way labyrinth which brought him to the park at last.

'Why not in the office?' again, but mildly.

'Because the whole place is bugged to the eyebrows, laddie. Private conversation died with Dysart.'

'Come on!'

'When he isn't in your pit he's swinging on our pendulum; practically commutes between me and thee. Your air-cooling system is not only under, it's counter-productive.'

'Open a window. You must have an idea what's going on.'

'All I know is, he has the Ear. He's got Sir Rufus by the hearing-aid too—tuned in to hints on everything on internal security—even the bloody office cat get's a monthly clearance check.'

'You're joking of course.'

'Our Ruf is progressing from normal business precautions to bloody paranoia—one only has to whisper Official Secrets Act and he dribbles like a Cruft runner-up stuck with a signed portrait of Pavlov.'

'Because—?'

'Because you threatened to make a breakthrough of unmanageable significance. Gene tech is getting out of hand that's for sure.'

'That isn't what the furore's about.'

'No,' Mathieson conceded, 'it's not the troops we're worried about—it's the deserters.'

'Mathie, leaving aside your mortgage, are you with me or against me?'

'I'm fully paid up, so I'm my own man . . . just tell me what happened.'

Quarrier glanced aside left, frowning the measure of his surprise. 'But you'll have it all on tape.'

'I'm still the Daniel interpreting your dreams to King Rufus, but

I'm *non grata* for the rest. He doesn't trust his own shadow on this escapade.'

Quarrier considered this demonstration of a man cleverly distancing himself with a growing sense of helplessness and much anxiety. He decided to quote the whole exchange with every circumstantial detail, omitting nothing. It might draw from this conscious Pilate some useful speculation if not the ray of comfort he'd missed so far. His account rendered he drove in silence leaving Mathieson to digest it at leisure.

He all but stalled at what came of it.

'When I said "Tell me what happened" I meant, what happened at the plant that put some of your ugly customers out into the night—and into Wentworth Magna?'

'I've just told you!'

'You've told me what you had to say to Betherton—'

'Now look here!'

'I'm sorry, Q, the nub is, how did the things get out, and you're the man with a finger on the button.'

'I'll drive you back!'

'All I want to know is, do you have *any* idea how they got loose?'

'None!'

'Then you've nothing to worry about.' He chuckled, became something more like the Mathie remembered from the long ago days before the booze went to his head.

'I envy and pity you your knack of total recall, Q. Can spell salvation—or martyrdom.'

Quarrier relaxed. Contact re-established. 'I had an English master once—used to mark my essays—invariably obiter: careful but unhelpful.'

'Sorry. I must've had his brother. His version was much more destructive: unhelpful *and* careless ... but I had to use the needle—to warn you, I suppose. Something's in train I can't put a finger on. I smell a rat—'

'Can you give it a name?' Quarrier had Dysart in mind, but Mathieson shook his head pensively.

'Mouse or rat or whatever, something on-going has gnawed its way out of Pandora's Box, Q. I'm not blaming you, but you've started something—'

'I can't finish—is that what you mean?'

'It's a pretty slippery slope to the top,' Mathieson to Mathieson seemingly. 'What you're doing—even if I don't care for the trend I'm scientific enough to recognize inevitability.'

'Of what?'

'The quest. Simply. But what I really fear is the sequel. The big cover-up. The propaganda exercise—"altogether now, we *like* being gassed, irradiated, CO_2 asphyxiated, contaminated". Chemistry is good for us—it gave us plastic buckets—physics is better—it loves us to death!'

Another Mathieson, or the same man deep down, viewed from a passing bathyscope.

'We—live very nicely with the advantages.'

Mathieson ignored that. 'They're already putting the squeeze on Fleet Street—that much I know—and Hopkins has been *warned* to keep his mouth shut. No more references. Ogram's opus was the last straw.'

'By now it's on a thousand videotapes.'

'Aye, but they've sequestrated the TV company's mastertape—not to mention radio's a.m. recordings with the pundits.'

'Uninformed precipitancy.'

'Maybe. When events move that fast how do you put your finger on them—you can't, because meantime they've waved the wand—hey presto! a non-event. They're awfully good at it.'

Back to their starting point. Not a satisfactory outing. Nothing resolved because each appeared to favour a different version of the mystery needing a solution. It crossed Quarrier's mind that Mathieson seemed to be enjoying the total situation with a bystander's complacency.

This unpleasant impression of a man carefully washing his hands in public alerted Quarrier again, and more forcibly, to his predicament. His opinion of Mathieson, never high, slithered lower as he watched another parade of furtive glances, like a ham actor drumming up conspiracy.

'We're not that important.'

'That's the botheration of it,' solemnly. 'Means we're less indispensable.' Transparent, the pause, apparent, the afterthought: 'I meant to ask you . . .'

'Well?'

'Do lower your hackles, Q, if I don't know all the facts, how can I help? I just wonder why, since you first heard about this, you haven't been to the labs—checked out the population, so to speak.'

What else could this be but rapid softening of the brain?

'Did you hear *any*thing of what I said? Betherton put the self-same stupid question. For the second last time, I'm not in the business of vermin control. Let 'em ring Rentokil.'

'. . . Marie Antoinette in jeans and a sweatshirt. A lot of people died in that village. Now what *was* it Shakespeare said about conscience?'

Fortunate Helen, not to be there when Quarrier, all guns blazing, rounded on Mathieson.

'Stuff your conscience! You and the rest make me sick with your tawdry displays of ragged hypocrisy! No one shits on Henry the Ford because his brainchild kills *in perpetua*, who blames the Wright brothers for Dresden? Was Logie Baird a killer because children hang themselves aping TV crap heroes? Rutherford, Einstein, Pauli, Hiroshima. Price-Pearson—Bromouracil! Me? Mice! I'm remote too, because science is monastic—Mendel, monastic, isolated—stimulated *my* interest. Put me on another planet and I'll still seek answers, but don't tax my conscience while some are devising better ways of killing people simply because they're people!'

Conceivably, the word 'Bromouracil' stuck in Mathieson's throat. Possibly, it figured in his long, reflective appraisal of Quarrier's tirade.

'Dedication—to the death—like Remington.'

'Yes! And yes again.'

Leaving Mathieson, like the curate's egg, dedicated only in parts, to conclude with a social nicety or two.

'How's the divine Helen?'

'Fine. She's fine.'

'I must come and pay court soon. It's been a long time.'

'Yes. Do that . . . and I'm sorry.'

'About Rutherford—or Bromouracil!' Viciously. 'Don't spoil a hundred per cent dedication with anything so scientifically vulgar as an apology.'

With these last words Mathieson went his ways and Quarrier drove home in a mood alternating turbulent resentment at seventy mph, with sullen pensiveness at fifty.

★

REPORT

Top classification, for Cabinet Office use only

PRELIMINARY FINDINGS ON THE WENTWORTH MAGNA AFFAIR. Prepared immediately subsequent to my interviews with the Chairman of Price-Pearson (UK) and Doctor Quarrier, of some eminence in his particular fields of microbiology and experimental genetics.

In accordance with your directive I at once obtained Sir Rufus's absolute assurance that no material relevant to the Accelerated Pregnancy Programme could have gone missing between the pharmaceuticals production centre and the London head office. All data relative to research is computer coded with mainframe transmission only.

I then questioned Dr Quarrier in Sir Rufus's presence.

If I may mix metaphors I have to say that my impression of Quarrier was hardly to his advantage in that he conveyed a holier-than-thou air of devil-may-care.

He would, I feel sure, take it as a compliment to be recognized by his manifest conceit and arrogance as a member of the élitist scientific community. In my opinion, this indication of a pragmatic attitude of mind seldom allows such a man to concede error, obvious as it may appear to the eye of reason.

He emphatically denied all prior knowledge of, or responsibility for this matter, yet it must strike the most disinterested observer that the problem centres on Price-Pearson's complex and one or more of those engaged in R and D.

In parenthesis I must stress we are faced with a gigantic assumption, nothing more. There can be no 'pressing charges' or sanctions of any kind until it is conclusively shown that from nowhere else could these creatures have originated.

But, it is important to keep this in mind, because I feel sure Quarrier himself has it in mind; his reactions indicate a total disregard for the consequences precisely because there is presently no cast-iron evidence to prove his personal involvement.

Nor was I impressed by an aggressive posture bordering on insolence not only to me but also to Sir Rufus who, later and unnecessarily, explained that latitude must be allowed to men of high intellectual calibre even where it appears in some as eccentricity. To quote the Chairman's pithy observation: half the stinks wallahs down there are bloody mad.

Quarrier accounted for certain inconsistencies in his progress reports with a candour leaving much to be desired.

In short, I have to confess that our unofficial vetting procedure is so far from being satisfactory in this instance that we should consider means of increasing surveillance of and pressure on Dr Quarrier to determine his motivation and possible objectives. In my opinion, the 'outbreak' leads to him alone.

The lesser members of his staff have a loyalty to Quarrier which, on my information, cannot be easily breached, but we are hopeful that a Mrs Chandrasakar, on short-term assignment to Price-Pearson, may be co-opted to the investigative process.

I have instructed D to question Dr Quarrier on the routine aspect of departmental security.

In conclusion, this affair is bound to raise voices in the House, calling for a Committee of Enquiry. The Animal Rights people and assorted environmental groups will generate further publicity with their usual spurious emotionalism.

I strongly recommend therefore that every means be employed to limit all knowledge of this affair (if it be not too late). The slightest hint of government involvement in the APP could be attended by incalculable consequences domestically and, perhaps, internationally. I need hardly remind you, we are already in breach of our undertaking to the US government to provide scientific information as it relates to defence potential.

Chapter 9

AFTER A NOTHING-VERY-MUCH lunch Helen took a novel to the garden, settled herself in an ancient wooden deck-chair and spent five sybaritic minutes thinking of all the things she should be doing.

A natural solitary, she scorned the idea even of a 'daily', delighted in the round of shopping, cooking and cleaning, which seemed to her historical interpretation of femininity a perfectly adequate lifestyle. To her odd professional friends' jibes she would counter that, at least, she was her own boss, was well paid by her husband, who never set production norms, never demanded employees' contributions, never talked of making the workforce redundant and only dared to pinch her bottom if the soup was cold.

Didn't she ever feel like striking?

No. She simply took time off.

Helen suspected a wisp of envy under the sophisticates' sneers. Her recipe for a perfectionable marriage might be old hat, but it made hash thrown together by working wives look the marriage of convenience food they affected to prefer. Quite inedible to a healthy palate.

So, on a hot day in late August, she thought of items unpurchased, the need to nip nasturtium pods, left-over ironing and an already postponed visit to her parents some twenty miles distant, but, under thoughts mildly stirred by conscience, ran a deeper current, ice-cold and intractable.

Items of news culled from radio bulletins both placated and disturbed. A tragic loss of life in deliciously bizarre circumstances but wasn't it too anodyne to talk of a little local difficulty as the latest commentator had suggested?

Could it be that simple—that easily dismissed?

If these things multiplied in geometrical progression how long before they spread thickly, inexorably, devouringly, over the entire country? She had listened for the question no one seemed disposed to ask.

Juggling the three adverbs in her mind she realized at last where her true apprehension lay. With Quentin, of course.

Hindsight—the conscious product of a subconscious review of the past year or more—revealed the none too subtle change in him, how he'd sealed off, double-sealed the door to a compartment in his inner world where none dared knock and enquire. (Were all husbands Bluebeards?) She recalled the snatched glimpses of untypical preoccupation, the same but different, unlike those brow-furrowing bouts of abstraction which such men's wives must learn to live with.

What it meant and whether it portended, she couldn't resolve, but the idea was anyway rooted and wouldn't go away. Quentin's affliction had to be acute dilemnitis; Bluebeard stood outside a self-locking door and the key was inside. . . .

Wentworth Magna, people dead and devoured—*very* local difficulties. Price-Pearson. Mice. Quentin trapped in a double helix. DNA, the new Laocoön, writhing print-out of life—engineered, links severed and replaced . . . genetics. . . .

She woke with a start as the book slipped from her hand, but the dream persisted, creating a stuporific fantasy behind a barrier of eyes merely closed.

Through the red and black haze she could visualize a section of the maze, a seven-foot wall of green, herself wandering through it in search of Quentin though unaccountably calling 'Martin'. To no avail, and that annoyed without terrifying because it was hardly more than a kindergarten conceit—they knew by heart its ingenuous twists and bends. But terror came as she rounded a sharp inward turn to find a gigantic mouse-like creature padding towards her—smiling. Then it reared, waving with an ironic flourish of its forepaw as it—strolled—through her gaze and out of sight by the way she'd come.

Wide-eyed now, she sat erect, staring ahead like a probationer sybil exploring an horrific vision for signs of meaning in a moment of drowsy madness.

A comforting analogy of Alice. White rabbits and gold watches would not serve.

The everyday phone's jarring bleep delivered her from chaotic musing, brought her thankfully to her feet. She smoothed her warm hair, thought of mild sun-stroke and resolved to sport her disreputable straw hat after she'd dealt with the caller. She hoped fervently it would be Quentin.

'Helen! For heaven's sake where have you been?' A querulous voice scant of preamble. None needed. 'This is Mother' sounds ridiculous forty-three years later.

'Sorry, darling. I've been asleep.'

'All day?' a shrilling crescendo. 'I've been trying to get you since eight o'clock.'

Helen made no immediate reply. She was thinking: I flicked a duster over Quentin's desk not two hours ago; the phone wasn't set right—these slim-lines need to be replaced exactly. Accident or design? Had Quentin deliberately cut off incoming calls by a simple artifice?

Why? To avoid awkward queries—the press perhaps? to evade unpalatable discussion—to protect *her* from curiosity she couldn't and he wouldn't satisfy?

'Your phone is a disgrace,' Mother again. Not surprising from one who'd been used to mentioning top buttons undone, agonized over ties askew, all but crossed herself at dyed hair and three earrings to an ear. In her fraughter moments she tended to address everyone as if they were 'comprehensives' from a deprived area.

'I'll get them to look at it,' vaguely.

'Don't pay the next quarter's bill till they do. Have you heard about the mice—they were on TV last night.'

Helen said she made it sound like a new comedy series.

'Don't joke about such terrible things, Helen. Didn't you know they're carnivorous? *Did* you see them?'

'They always have been—so are we—and yes I did see them, Mother. In that order.'

'And do you realize Wentworth Magna is only twelve and a quarter miles from our front door?'

'Well no, actually.' Other times her daughter might have giggled at that, floored by a vision of poor old mum trudging along the high road pushing a way-wiser before her from A to B, twelve and a quarter miles, give or take a few inches.

Quite calmly she assured Mrs Creedy there was no cause for alarm.

'No *cause*?' frankly *falsetto*. 'Do you imagine we retired and came all this way to be near you only to be devoured in our beds?'

The answer was so obvious Helen forced herself not to say 'yes'. Through an impressive silence wholly stage-managed by Mrs Creedy, she fingered, in a few seconds, the terrible razor-line between horror and the ludicrous. The fact *was* grisly, but the manner of its telling made such a fate sound like jolly hockey sticks bound with black crêpe.

'Surely you heard? "The situation has been contained. No cause for alarm." Robin Day said so.'

'If you haven't lived long enough to know that when "they" say such a thing, there's *extremely* good cause to believe otherwise—then I'm prepared to wait till you have.'

'Mother dear, they show no signs of spreading at the moment. Listen to your local radio station. If they advise evacuation all you and Dad need do is jump in the car and come over, or ring us and we'll fetch you.'

'That's all very well, but how do we know *you* haven't got them already?'

'. . . what, exactly, do you mean?'

'Your father feels sure they escaped from Price-Pearson. Quentin works there with mice and things doesn't he?'

'He doesn't bring his "things" home with him, and he always changes out of his dungarees before he rides home on his bicycle.'

All gentleness vanished. Not her mother's predictable acerbity, but a genuine surge of resentment on Quentin's account sharpened her retort and Mrs Creedy, chastened by the rare outburst, replied with what Helen called a Surbitonian act of contrition.

'You must make allowances, dear. We're worried silly by this dreadful business—for your as well as our sakes.'

Helen found a platitude to satisfy both and hung up with a sigh of relief. To say she found her mother trying at times is to add: those times were often and critical.

As with the string of useless pregnancies.

'Are you *quite* sure the fault isn't with Quentin, dear?'

Almost certainly she would have broken with Mrs Creedy if Quentin hadn't been so understanding.

It rankled, and it rankled just then, especially. Once again her mother, a veteran of staff-room intrigue, was tentatively putting a finger on the man she blamed for Helen's miscarriages; who else could be responsible for the deaths of so many people?

Who else?

She wandered about the house in a vagrant mood, or like a Phidias masterpiece come to life excepting the eyes, window-shopping in the *galleria* of her mind, but sifting her thoughts as carelessly as a child with a handful of sand.

Longed to be able to freeze the thought process for sheer respite, not understanding a penalty had to be paid for preferring a solitary's existence till Quentin returned home and made her smile herself back into the pleasure of his company.

'Are you at home, Helen?'

Six sudden squeaky syllables jolted her back to the real world, to Quentin's den, to Darwin's prophetic letter, from Down, 23rd March 1882. She'd been studying it as if to prove that even mindless meanderings have their source and significance.

No sign of Nick from the study window. For, of course, that voice could belong only to Nick Alladyce—or possibly H.G. Wells and *he*, she knew, had been dead for years.

She'd reached the kitchen door as Nick's anxious face appeared at the half-open garden entrance. As a close friend and workmate he had right of illegal entry by back doors, open windows and drainpipes in an emergency.

'If it's an awkward time, I can—'

'Come in, Nick. No, better still, stay out and park on the garden seat. I'll make some tea and—'

'Is Q home?'

'No.'

He cast about him like a rabbit at bay. 'Ah! In that case, not to bother. I'll come back later and—'

'Nicholas. You will take a pew in the garden and I shall make tea for the two of us.'

'Oh . . . all right.'

'Unless you prefer iced coffee—or something stronger if your need is as much as you look.'

'Er—tea would be fine.'

Good grief, I must've sounded like Mother on dinner-duty. She prepared the tea things convinced she'd never before spoken so imperiously to the poor chap. But why?

Between the kettle and the pot she found the obvious answer. She'd got to talk privately to one who was nearer Quentin in this matter than she could ever be. Perfectly understood the small f in freemasonry, but there were times . . . and this—with or without sugar—was one of them.

Somehow, she had to get more definition into the blurred background of an affair in which Quentin stood too clearly in the forefront.

Alladyce, still dithering on his feet, seemed anxious to help. She stifled refusals and encouraged him to discover what it must be like to be mother; behind her banter was cunning intent. Juggling with sugar, milk jug and a plate of Digestives he might say more than he would with a mere cup and saucer in hand.

'Have you seen Quentin?'

'Not since yesterday. *Then* I'm told he's in town for a high-level meeting.' Mildly aggrieved, she decided.

'But you just came by to see him.'

'Well I assumed he'd be back by now.'

'Who told you he'd gone up to head office?'

'Mathieson rang, early this morning. Told us not to expect him back today. Sugar?'

'Lots. Well—two. That's odd surely? I mean Mathie doesn't usually—'

'It's an odd situation—weird. And worse not to know what's going on.' He handed her a half-empty cup tilted on a saucer full of tea. She smiled. Two in the same boat and all at sea.

'*You* rang last evening. Why?'

He stared at his floating tea-leaves and looked belatedly for the strainer.

'Wentworth Magna. It has to be our mouse . . . I couldn't believe it—Hopkins making the big pass and revealing the secret. Ours.'

'Quentin thinks otherwise.'

It never occurred that Helen might just be goading him—gently.

'Then he's living in another world where facts are cleverly fictionalized.'

'He could be right. Isn't it a matter of proof?'

He leaned forward to the limits of propriety, cutting in before she'd quite finished.

'Helen, no one but your husband *could* have produced that strain. He'd isolated the regulator—its structure. When it went haywire there was no problem identifying just what had given us the wild swings.'

'Are you talking about the inhibiting factor?'

'That's right. The messenger that tells an organism when to slow down and stop.'

'Or speed up . . .' She too had forgotten tea neither really wanted. 'But these things are aborted every day?'

'No—that's not strictly true—it depends—' he ran a hand through wildly disordered hair reminding her of the short sharp breakdown not so long ago.

'The survival time isn't the point . . . there's an unwritten code, Helen. You do *not* let these creatures, *any* of them, get into the outside world. You just don't. No way . . .' and again, 'no way.'

She pointed out the contradiction. 'It has to be ours.'

'Right! Why shouldn't I deny the impossible?'

'Isn't that what Quentin's doing? He's working hard to show a lack of concern.'

Still he failed to see how she'd cleverly created confusion and sheer illogicality in his mind.

'That's what I can't fathom. "Price-Pearson's nose is clean," he purrs down the phone, "and if it isn't, it's not our job to wipe it".'

She registered that, but turned to another troubling aspect. 'Nick, the size of those creatures—'

A responding smile or the grimace of one standing at the frontier dividing the incredible from the unacceptable.

He nodded, like a sage in his dotage. 'Half as big again as the species . . .' he faltered, still nodding, still with an idiot's fixed regard.

'Well?' fear sharpened curiosity, gave a cutting edge to her sixth sense.

He explained that Quentin and Remington had done some incredibly fine work with nuclear magnetic resonance techniques, talked of radio waves tuned to hydrogen—all of it over her head but necessary for him to explain: 'It was breathtaking—Nobel Prize stuff—a new strain, an altered time scale of embryonic growth—it reproduced itself perfectly, and of course we had them under constant observation—then the regulator went erratic—it took a month for the quantum leap in growth—quite fantastic . . . we meant to keep this particular series going, reducing on an inverse ratio to the multiple increase . . .'

'When was this?'

'Almost—no—forty-two days—surely I mentioned that? I wasn't there for some of the time—we were all feeling the strain. Sheer slog around the clock, monitoring, tissue analysis, metabolic rate, stimuli testing . . . then, one night, Remington phoned. I remember the panic in his voice "Get over here fast". That was all.'

She vividly recalled Quentin's two a.m. curses. They'd been to a dinner party with a Price-Pearson executive and his wife. A chess game between the husbands had taken it beyond midnight. He'd dressed hurriedly and dashed off saying unkind things about Rem.

'I got there after two,' Alladyce continued. 'They were both shaken, Rem of all people, especially. It wasn't surprising . . . no, not surprising.'

In that low register the words told all about a former state of mind, the sudden crack-up; time off to come to terms with time past.

'We walked down the long passage, Q looked stern set I remember. All my questions just rebounded . . . cages either side—the smell of that place . . . at the end was a desk, a chair, a blood red Thermos, Rem's records, the photographic apparatus and a cage, in isolation, by the fire exit—red . . . the sweep hand of the wall clock above, blood red, passing through two thirty-seven . . . and the cage . . .'

'Yes. The cage, Nick. What about it?'

Certainly he considered her, not dreamily, but drunk on a bad dream as it seemed. Lines creasing his forehead, so many stigmas impressed by the unacceptable; more than thirty-nine years of mere living could excuse.

'We kept the P_1s and a pair of F_2s for breeding and observation—had to destroy the rest. The female dropped her young at almost hourly intervals—'

'How many?'

'Eighty or so—in any one period of twenty-four hours.'

'. . . Good God.' Half a blasphemy is no less than half a prayer.

'That we were used to, were fascinated by—this was Q's unique triumph—he'd cracked the code controlling the con-gest period—

speeded it up to unacceptable limits, that was no problem—but . . .'

'But?' Was he quite unaware of a hostile note in her abruptive query?

'The foetal hormone implant—and I'm putting it simply—was compatible, but we knew it could be a shot in the dark—the parents showed human characteristics and features . . . it was uncanny . . . they became inherited factors—but worse than that—these things had suddenly doubled their size—'

'From what point, Nick?'

'Exactly. We knew it was the forty-second day after the HFH input . . . it's no use, Helen—it's all a damned sight more complicated than that—and it was worse . . .'

Had doubled their size . . .

She read the few scrawled words writ large in the eyes of a witness to his dying day of a double or quits calamity he lacked layman's terms to describe. Alladyce's expression pleaded: you had to *be* there. As I was. As *he* appeared to be under her not particularly merciful scrutiny, however much that rent in the veil of oblivion haggared him to a semblance of Alladyce.

Helen now understood why the link with a village called Wentworth Magna was indissoluble. And unforgivable. For the moment that was all she knew.

'If you recall, we held back on the X700 series,' Remington explained to the still convalescent Alladyce.

'But that's been dormant for weeks,' he objected.

'It's the X700—no argument. Q's made his point about methaglione—abstract that and exponential growth has nowhere to go but up. It's *the* inhibitor.'

'Should we discount erythropoetin entirely?' Q wondered.

Rem shrugged. He seemed ill-at-ease. 'Hard to tell. I'm inclined to think it got written out earlier in the sequence—it's another evidence of heterochromatin's function.'

'And the HFH insert?' Alladyce tried hard for matter-of-fact.

Rem's gesture lacked conviction—even vitality. 'It worked. Just look at the perishers.'

'Let's drop it,' Alladyce's badly troubled eyesight shifted from the cage to Quarrier.

'What's bothering *you*?'

'I'm not bothered, but this demonstrates the hormone insert was—gratuitous. Let's just verify methaglione and scrap the lot.'

'Why?'

'Because we're not in the business of raising freaks!'

'My dear idiot, we can't prove methaglione unless we follow through, right Rem?'

'You stumbled on it two years back, but this time I think you've proved it . . . if we let these grow at present rate we might find we've caught tigers by their teeth.'

Impressive and very nearly improbable, Remington's subdued air. Both men were regarding Quarrier much like appellants faced with a hanging judge.

Lost on Quarrier. Would the gods, summoned to an immense spherical laboratory by distraught contractors, care tuppence because their formula for a new *in vitro* species had produced a sport dying to dignify its ludicrous self as *homo sapiens*?

'You talk as if we're running a safari park—' a judge, what's more, in contempt of court.

'Accidents,' doggedly, 'can happen . . . and sometimes do.'

'We've touched a vital spring—clumsily, yes, but exactly what we've worked for—the inhibitor—'

'Accelerant pregnancy! Not uncontrolled proliferation!' Alladyce bellowing. Of all people. Alladyce.

'We've got both.' Messianic the flaw in Quarrier's eyes. 'We follow this one through. No Dysart, no company records. None but ourselves.'

'You can't be so—'

'Can't?' Below zero scorn. 'Go home, Nick. Rem and I can handle this.'

'He was wrong about Rem. I bawled a lot of nonsense before I left. Incredibly, Rem didn't say much though I'm convinced he was on my side. Maybe hysteria flourishes best in silence . . . *maybe* Rem smashed his way out of it in the Volvo.'

She listened, retroversion fixed on a familiar stranger, steadfast and stockstill in the pursuit of knowledge, rapt in contemplation of his creation. She felt lost, at a loss, utterly at variance with thought, things, all men, even with the apparent innocence of nature's studied beauties surrounding her. Nothing could be so—central—in her mind as that image of mysteries knitted from a pattern designed by one she dimly suspected she knew.

Everything, the flowers, birds, trees, sun, shrieked of malevolence, hostility scarcely camouflaged, tranquillity was a lulling pretence in league with a whoremongerish sense of false security.

Paradox compelled her to find a new kind of courage to take a different path. The maze she must explore had nothing in common with the green box hedge nearby—a simple pleasaunce negotiable to a safe and uneventful end.

Courage? Well, yes. To beat new paths through one's mind is a dangerous imperative.

The same Helen then, as perception cleared, but another woman, sombre as the dark side of a two-dimensional moon, watched a snivelling urchin recounting the Ph.D. antics of a gang led by a gene-bashing thug who was no other than her husband.

She had never lacked stature, an indefinable aura was hers by right; but now, Alladyce finding himself eye-to-eye, as if drawn by twin lodestars, faltered into silence, troubled by received impressions not easily defined.

'You're blinding me with science over which you have no control, Nicholas. That makes us level.' Dismissive as a queen to a custrel. 'Histones, blastulation, the sigmoid growth curve . . . are you initiating me into the mysteries of your craft, or building a wall high enough to make climbing it not worth the while?'

Petulance frowned at the unexpected. 'I'm trying to fill you in on what actually happened. Isn't that what you wanted?'

'If I put a finger to the ground and spun the world a little faster, would you ask for a straightforward explanation or demand a mathematical formula which must be over your head to start with or you could have turned the world yourself?'

Puzzled he looked for some sign, a twinkle not rare in those very beautiful eyes betraying humour, but he saw none, smiled doubtfully to supply the deficit.

'Really, Helen, you're an extraordinary person, like Quentin—not noticeably predictable.'

She recognized a pleasantry borrowed of Q, and returned his smile, but bitterly. Just now she felt herself to be the most predictable of God's creatures.

And yet . . . 'Is it unpredictable to be disgusted by minds emulating the heartlessness of computers? And whoever said thou shalt have no other gods but the supreme and ultimate piece of hardware?'

It might have been a quote from Eleusinian mysteries, powerful enough whatever to give Alladyce a hang-dog aspect.

'Helen, you asked me.'

'I'm still asking: what happened in words recognizably from the King James' version, after this great discovery?'

A wasp whirred angrily over the sugar-bowl. They watched its irritable plunges till it went elsewhere forcing Alladyce to concentrate his attention though he finically avoided a penetrating, specimen-on-a-watchglass regard.

'I think they ran through the computer programme, made notes of certain calculations and procedures. They probably erased a lot of related material.'

'Why?'

'Credit us. We didn't want them getting interested in way-out side-effects.'

'Was that Quentin's idea?'

'He's in charge of the project—but a consensus sounds better I suppose.'

'Even though he—'

'I've already told you—yes! *He* wanted to follow through, but privately, speculatively if you like.'

Because they were scientifically fascinating. Quite. A certain type of woman seldom curls the lip. A small matter of respecting symmetry. But yes, in their terms she understood.

'What happened to them—the wonder mice?'

'They—were transferred to a small cage . . . you knew Rem had his own vivisectorium at The Bowery.'

'I'd heard of it . . . and Rem died only days after . . .'

'. . . Yes.'

'Everything taken out of Price-Pearson is checked and logged.'

'We don't have to follow that procedure.' Indignantly? The very idea! 'Anyway, the cage easily fitted into Rem's old Gladstone.'

'So they were smuggled out?'

'I'm telling you exactly what I was told. There was no problem.'

'I'd have thought otherwise—if this comes to an enquiry.'

He blinked, like an owl snared by a sudden beam of light. 'I don't follow.'

'It's notable—and notifiable—if Grade 1 scientists go helter-skelter back to their place of worship in the small hours—isn't it?'

Plainly, it hadn't occurred. Just as plainly, it disturbed Alladyce to the verge of stunned silence.

'Tell me about Rem.'

He glanced at his watch reflexively. Time can be an attractive alibi. 'Nothing to tell. Look, Helen, if Q isn't—I mean he may be delayed—'

'What happened to Robert Remington?'

'You know perfectly well—!'

'*Before* he crashed.'

Unwittingly, she had asked the single, almost vital question setting her on that dangerous new path. For the moment Helen's surprise equalled his astonishment, and this time his silence was absolute.

But she did see at last, it wasn't her lack of knowledge but their knowledgeable ignorance that had shone like fools' gold, blinding her with misconceived glory.

Wryly it flashed across Helen's mind how Alfred must have yearned to award himself the Nobel blown-to-pieces prize for pioneering the Big Bang theory . . .

Chapter 10

ALLADYCE GAVE THANKS for Quarrier's timely return. Not possibly, to the point of incivility, could he have satisfied Helen's need to know. To detail the final horror leading to Rem's death was to relive the unpalatable. Hadn't Quentin himself avoided all mention of that other night saga; a *bal macabre* in which one of their number had taken leave of his senses *and* mislaid the will to live?

Quarrier looked for Helen in the house, tried the kitchen last. Hearing voices from the garden he took avoiding action with a muttered oath or two, unwilling to share her company with God knows who. Not stealthy by nature, he went a circuitous way to the main shrubbery and so to the back entrance of the nearby maze where he might, with luck, forget much of himself in its green recesses. He'd wandered like a contemplative, practising to shed thoughts and images born of events, until a powerfully projected mention of Rem brought him to a standstill . . . perversely a sudden craving for company of any kind drove him in search of the exit. That he had trouble finding his way out of a simplistic situation tells something about states of mind.

Surprise mingled with relief greeted his unexpected appearance from the wall of green to their left, true to his reputation as an 'allrounder', who came at one from every point of the compass, mentally and very nearly physically—Quarrier's former tutor's celebrated but ambiguous view of his and Fortune's favourite charge.

Better described as a virile lurch that rather ungainly stride but, at any distance, women sensed the approach of an exceptional man, perhaps not conventionally attractive but exuding confidence, building dominance with every thrusting step.

To Helen's critical eye it was less evident by a margin of hours. She saw that Alladyce had made a quick change to the role of a totally loyal subordinate. Not the wildest of horses would drag mention of Rem from his lips in Quentin's presence.

'What are *you* doing here?' the hostly smile just saved Quarrier from seeming boorish. He knew Nick too well, brilliant, but a bit of an old woman, fond of gossip . . . not to be encouraged just now.

'I was just going,' the moustache drooped despondently as if it knew it was inflammably caught between two fires.

'You came in order to go,' crisply. 'Logic lives yet. I could do with some of that tea, Mrs Q.'

'I'll get you a cup,' she rose on a lighter note, almost as relieved as Nick that she could stop grilling him.

'Women's logic,' he smiled, softening as always to her incomparable tranquillity. 'Helen,' a musical friend once observed, 'moves through life in the mood of a Satie Gymnopaedie.'

'Helen's logic,' he corrected. 'She doesn't say I'll fetch you a cup *and* saucer because it's the *container* that matters.'

'It must have been *very* hot in Town,' she said with mock gravity, went reluctantly, fearing to miss something of importance.

'Well, Nick?' Quarrier slumped down in the garden seat shaking them both.

'There's bloody chaos in the labs, Johnson's threatening resignation, there's general depression about the calotropin tests and Dysart's questioning everyone into the ground.'

'Including you?' sharply.

'He would have if I'd been around. I took your tip and made myself scarce—spent most of the morning with Coombes in the production area.'

'And here you are,' pointedly.

'Confucius says the horse's mouth is where the horse is.'

'Ah, but back or front? What did *he* know of Western civilization?'

Quarrier summarized what had passed in London.

'They *are* blaming us!' Alladyce was looking pretty terminal long before Quarrier had finished.

Quarrier shrugged. 'Mathie's reaction disappoints—otherwise one sees their point on the two and two principle.'

'Yet you persuaded them it's nothing to do with us?'

'Nor is it.'

'Oh for heaven's sake! They got out—I mean, you took them to Rem's.'

'Well?'

'Then it *has* to do with us, and I don't see how lying helps us out of the shit.'

She returned in time to hear her husband defend himself against manure and mendacity. So many things happening for the first time.

'A controlled takeaway isn't an escape.'

'The fact remains—*we* know they disappeared.'

'Am I interrupting something crucial?'

Enter stage right, the sprightly little woman, trying not to sound significant but dear me, their combined expressions did rather suggest juveniles with stolen jam on their faces.

'As the Americans mouthe it, "we have a prahblem".' Quentin affected levity but eyed her intently as she poured his tea.

'Theft?' to coin a Cartland—that adorable widening of the eyes as she handed him the cup.

'No saucer,' he bantered, heavily Victorian.

'You've spoiled the joke.'

The briefest extract from a shared and uncrackable code, externalizing inmost thoughts.

Alladyce listened glumly. So many questions were on the tip of his tongue he seemed to have his mouth full to his lips.

'We're going over to Wentworth Magna tonight.'

'Why? If it's none of our business?'

'I didn't say I wasn't interested.'

Alladyce glanced at Helen plainly at a loss as to what and how much he could safely say. 'They've evacuated a large area,' he muttered.

That seemed nice and nondescript; much like his features, badly worn with anxiety. 'Always were,' the late lamented Rem once said. 'Most of us get over falling out of the cradle—he's still looking for somewhere to land.'

'They' had indeed.

A lot had happened since Hopkins opened the proceedings. First, the pea had to be removed from his whistle. Then the Fleet Street burners had to be turned low and preferably out; news editors were discreetly advised to comply with appeals heavy with reference to the national interest.

A number of Junior Ministers were recruited to pour oil of unction and heap *gravitas* over the vocal few who'd suffered and survived a first-hand experience.

Three biologically bent scientists seconded from government establishments set out to investigate the scourge. Scientific overlord Betherton would collate their findings with other relevant information and prepare a digest for Cabinet consideration.

Many holiday plans were completely wrecked.

First observations suggested a curious hiatus keeping the colony concentrated in the village and environs. Few, if any, of these inquilines were breaking a mysterious and seemingly arbitrary circle. Either a superior intelligence was at work, holding them in check, or herd instinct operated, to generate a prodigious mustering of energy for the next onslaught.

The powers-that-were used this breathing space to plan, mobilize, and take all possible counter-measures. For example, the area could be ringed with troops as the PM demanded, but what then? Top brass dressed as Action Men from MOD had run a quick recce over the scene and reported back to the Bunker, appalled by what they saw.

Major-General Slingsby Arrowhead Norton haled from Nato's emergency base camp in the grill of Brussel's Hilton Hotel, growled something about a nuclear tactical strike, but that was too alarming to contemplate. Waste nuclear energy on *mice*? was heard by the neighbours in No. 11.

Besides, the Falklands Factor had to be nursed, not blown out of existence. Why else fifty Officially Secreted cameramen and radio/TV reporters already gripping the tools of their trade or rehearsing extreme vocal tension while they waited for gung-ho-ho against 'the enemy within'—worth a few quid to some of them in I WAS THERE royalties.

Official photographs in the pipeline showed two thousand assorted troops 'standing-to', guns at the ready, to repel *mus domestica*. An accredited journalist wrote of 'a ring of steel in which the four-footed foe (sic) was inexorably contained', but when a subaltern pointed with pride to a cunningly deployed battery of mouse-traps he tore up his copy and lit another cigarette instead.

They were part of a seventy gross consignment urgently requisitioned from an almost forgotten store-room formerly used by the old Min. of Works. But the thrust of a perfectly logical counter-attack was somewhat blunted at three that afternoon when a dumb-as-they-come private in the Royal Army Sanitation Corps wondered 'where's the bloody cheese then?'.

In double-quick time a squad from the Royal Army Catering corps was ordered into civvies, issued with Army Access cards and told off to scour the area for cheese.

How much?

Oh Christ!

In less than half an hour the Royal Army Computer Corps calculated that, at half an ounce per trap . . . thus, the foragers, or 'fromagers' as some francomaniac dubbed them, set off to find 2 cwt 7 stones 7 lbs of the stuff before the shops closed.

With two hours to go the men drove around in desperation and a pick-up truck and returned mutinous and stinking of every variety of cheese from Brie through Stilton change at Camembert to Marks and Spencer's best Cheddar.

Most supermarkets in a large area were cleaned out and mystified because the men—strangely enough, members of the Cheshire Regiment, were under strict orders not to mention mice.

Against the blood red thread of any campaign a black thread of comedy reads welcomely.

The serious nature of the problem could not be lost on anyone staring it in the face. The scientists, for example, took a long look at the phalanxes from the highest vantage points to the lowest possible bird's-eye-view in helicopters and returned to brief the GOC and deliver the same conclusion.

'You're wasting your time.'

What, exactly, did that mean? They stressed the overwhelming numbers, the impossibility of dealing with them during the hours of darkness. We'll set up floodlights. Yes, but if they decide to break out . . . bullets against millions?

The GOC tried but just could not bring himself to mention the mouse-traps.

Foresight claims the lid was firmly on a seething situation; hindsight proves it would never be that simple.

A dead village is sealed off by the authorities with apparently decent intent; to contain the pestilence and ensure the safety of the vicinity population. But, to sow secretly in the interests of national security is to grow more questions than available answers. Thus, the reaping of whirlwinds.

How the millions, alerted by Hopkins' scoop, must have wondered at the sudden black-out on the present goings-on. Pity the ghouls at a barmecide feast, fangs sunk into nothing more substantial than TV snacks, waiting for the cameras to range over half-devoured corpses. Didn't he say they *ate* people? What do we pay all that license money for?

Bland assurances: nothing too immediate about the problem. Like a gadfly—ignore it and it *might* go away . . .

She'd cobbled together a lobster salad for three. Alladyce was too full of other things to do it justice; Quarrier ate steadfastly, looking straight ahead as if repelled by the sight of food, while Helen toyed with hers waiting hopefully for some significance, an enlightening word from Quarrier to dispel the murkiness that thrives on mystery.

His brand of silence told her something; not just a fixed determination to stay mum—to give nothing away, but a tacit command to Alladyce—do as I do.

Not in front of the ladies! Keep it for the nuts and port! Helen could simmer beautifully, apostrophizing deep down her indignation that she should be treated like a delicate houseplant, no draughts, no burst of hot air. She all but banged refrigerated mousse under their noses and sat again, drumming her fingers as she eyed them in turn.

'Alpha, beta, gamma, delta . . .' a studied recital of the Greek alphabet to the final omega startled them both.

'*What* was that all about?'

'I'm trying to vary the level of silence. I do think it does better for a little contrast.'

'Yes. Try it backwards.'

She obliged.

'Good. About all that was what?'

'Proof that Aristotle couldn't have been scientific without the most elementary symbolic knowledge.'

Please, not a camouflaged family tiff. Nick's appealing glance bounced off them both.

Quarrier merely smiled—aggravatingly. Signalling, clever, but not clever enough. I know your game.

To his friend's relief the word play ended there and he was ready to go at Quarrier's very nearly polite suggestion. 'Leave your car. I'll bring you back to pick it up. We shouldn't be more than an hour or two.'

Alladyce agreed but said he must call Erica first. It gave Helen time to hope, he, Quentin, would do nothing foolhardy.

'I'll look and leave,' he sealed the promise with the wisp of a kiss on her cheek.

'If Dysart rings . . .' he paused, frowning at an unsavoury supposition.

'Yes?'

'Tell him to go to hell.'

'It's a big place. Where shall I tell him to meet you?' Nick appeared at the door. 'How is she?'

'Sick of waiting.'

She nodded, understanding. Seven months. Once only, she'd got that far. 'I'll give her a long ring while you're away.'

'Do that. She'd love it.'

'If you've done playing father-to-be,' Q, sourly.

And they were gone.

Leaving the old stain, faded from bright red to a dingy brown; no more urgency, too late the desperate desire to perpetuate a form of love between passionate conspirators. The dead ending in the anguished smiles of a failure—the womb an icy sepulchre and six, and six, and then seven months' tenancy terminated, wasted . . .

'Doesn't he mind, darling?'

The incontinence of curiosity—the female kind. From seven years' distance she could still hear the frisson in Erica's cruelly harmless question. Put it down to youth—immaturity. Erica would always be some years junior—even to her juniors.

A neighbourly cat ran low across her line of vision, disappearing into the thickset. It carried something in its mouth. One of those. Somehow the word evaded her and she remembered with relief the voles were plentiful this year.

Tired, defeated and utterly defenceless against a league of wild conjectures she sat at the kitchen table and, like an Open University undergrad she studied an exercise in domestic futility; recap, a pile of dirty dishes. Make notes and discuss heuristically.

Hot. Too damned hot was partly the trouble. A storm should be in the offing to judge by the premature twilight and a silence grown stealthy. Even her favourite evening blackbird was cowered into cancelling his recital.

Not noticeably bursting with enthusiasm she acted out her promise to ring Nick's wife.

Chapter 11

QUARRIER DROVE WITH the shutters down. Alladyce assumed a foul mood. Clichés like 'flying off the handle' and 'at the drop of a hat' fitted Q very nicely, he thought.

Alladyce was wrong: a brown study can as well contain a worried man as a thoughtful tiger.

His mention of an obviously imminent storm brought no response so he rough-timed the intervals between flashes in the blue-black sky to the south-west.

Until Quarrier swore softly, dropped into first gear and crawled painfully behind the last of a long tail-back—and so to a stop.

'An accident probably.'

'How far to the turn-off?'

'About four miles.'

Alladyce took his courage, not between two hands, but pincered delicately between thumb and forefinger. 'It's an opportunity to sort things out.'

'If you like,' milk and watery for Quarrier.

'Hadn't we better agree an alibi?'

'On what?'

'You told Betherton *and* Mathie you've no idea how these things escaped.'

'If you recall, we didn't know at Rem's—we don't know now.'

'That's hair-splitting! They're querying how anything could get out of Price-Pearson's—no one's asking about the Bowery.'

'Repeat: they didn't escape from the labs—and I haven't a clue how they got away from Rem's.'

'Helen isn't so sure.'

'Helen can speak for herself.'

'She can also ask the kind of questions the rest haven't thought of yet.'

'Can you?'

'Yes . . . I can wonder why we didn't inform the police—a toxic substance gone missing is notifiable.'

'If you widen the definition—'

'Wentworth Magna defines it!'

'Charmed I'm sure! You want me to supply the ammunition before they hand me the gun to shoot myself.'

'Have it your way, Herr Doktor Frankenstein.'

Quarrier frowned, more puzzled than angered by the bitter levity. This was Alladyce Mark II. He easily preferred the original.

'Is that how you see it?'

Alladyce didn't bother with a reply. 'You blame Mathie for a stand-off, but he can't help without the facts.'

Quarrier shook his head. 'It goes deeper than that.'

No explanation offered, none demanded. The traffic had begun to move briskly once more. Quarrier with broken continuity repaired, slipped into gear and eased forward into an impenetrable silence.

Extract from the Report compiled by an All-Party Select Committee following the first phase of its enquiry into the origins of the Price-Pearson affair

On day 2 the Chairman, Charles Folson, M.P., Q.C., Cons. Abingley, questions Professor J. Hammond, Senior Lecturer in Genetics and related subjects at ——— University.

FOLSON: Professor Hammond, before this committee proceeds further, it feels that some understanding of the mechanism by which these creatures were bred and developed might give a clearer picture of the events under review.

HAMMOND: I understand.

FOLSON: I shall request you use the simplest language commensurate with our near ignorance of what we take to be an esoteric subject.

HAMMOND: I'll endeavour to do so.

FOLSON: I'm obliged to you . . . we know that Doctor Quarrier had persuaded the Price-Pearson executive that a drug might be successfully developed and marketed which could accelerate pregnancy, effectively reducing the gestatory period by a third.

HAMMOND: Yes.

FOLSON: Clinically, may we, for example, speak of an insult to the brain?

HAMMOND: Beneficently—not pejoratively—if you mean a controlled procedure.

FOLSON: What I'm getting at is the phrase that has gained currency in the Press and some sections of Church opinion. Would you agree that Doctor Quarrier's concept is 'an insult to the womb'?

HAMMOND: . . . I'd prefer not to get involved in an ethical appraisal of his work. A partial explanation of the mechanics is as far as I'm prepared to assist.

FOLSON: I take your point . . . what then, is the base-line from which such a revolutionary proposition takes effect in the geneticist's mind?

HAMMOND: Several highly complex options would suggest themselves. The subjects evidence a remarkable degree of negative imprint accounting for the high growth factor. Particulate hormones of the Adenohypophysis would certainly figure in the replicate, particularly STH, the somatropic hormone stimulating growth.

FOLSON: This may be artificially increased, induced?

HAMMOND: Yes, given NMR techniques, the avoidance of extracellular distortion, and preserving the relative values of other genetic factors.

FOLSON: So the variations in development sought by the researcher depend on infinitesimal molecules rejigged to provide a materially inheritable template?

HAMMOND: Er—that is roughly the position.

FOLSON: If this was a conscious search for the growth factor, how do you account for Doctor Quarrier's alleged denial of seeking monstrous developments?

HAMMOND: Easily. He was known as a highly respected and responsible worker in his field, he had no possible incentive to engineer abnormalities as an end in itself.

FOLSON: He was concerned then, if I read you correctly, to isolate the growth mechanism for more careful study?

HAMMOND: Oh much more than that. In doing so he revolutionized bio-genetics by further isolating glutathione, a crucial determinant of growth. Truly remarkable.

FOLSON: Would it be fair to say that a price may be paid for 'remarkable' discoveries, that laboratory experiments on animals may, like a nuclear experiment, run away, get out of hand?

HAMMOND: . . . much research of this nature abides by the rules of trial and error. If problems were instantly soluble investigative science would scarcely differ from applied science.

FOLSON: You would agree however that gigantism would be an unwelcome distraction in this instance?

HAMMOND: Unwelcome—and inevitable.

FOLSON: But hadn't Doctor Quarrier already succeeded in his primary objective—reducing the gestation period quite substantially?

HAMMOND: As I understand it his earlier attempt was accidental, a one-off achievement of no great validity. From his later reports—

FOLSON: I was coming to that. Much publicity has been given to doubts cast on Doctor Quarrier's calculations. Did you find them misleading?

HAMMOND: That charge is often made to cover imperfect understanding. It's also worth remembering that in a prodigious series of papers intended to chart the course of any such project, there will be errors.

FOLSON: Why?

HAMMOND: Because the researcher is always at risk of *being* misled by his preceding observations and calculations. The questing path is both narrow and bedevilled by twists and turns.

FOLSON: Like a maze?

HAMMOND: Exactly so.

FOLSON: I understand the numbers of tests involved would be staggering.

HAMMOND: Thousands. Most of course would be contracted out to the junior staff.

FOLSON: For clarity's sake I would put to you, Professor, that we are concerned with three separate strands: abnormal post natal growth, abnormal parturition rate, abnormal syncope of embryonic development.

HAMMOND: I might quarrel with the use of an emotive term applied to those procedures.

FOLSON: I leave the definition to you.

HAMMOND: Neoteric preferably.

FOLSON: In passing, I believe Doctor Quarrier was deeply concerned with the inadequacy of language as an aid to scientific understanding?

HAMMOND: We all are.

FOLSON: Is there not evidence of failure here?

HAMMOND: I don't follow.

FOLSON: His object was to cut the gestation period by a third, not to increase the number and size of newborn subjects?

HAMMOND: You talk of strands which in fact create a spun thread. Were you to attempt to unravel three filaments of a spider's web you would have *some* idea of what he achieved.

FOLSON: But what he achieved—accelerant embryonic development was surely balanced if not outweighed by what went wrong?

HAMMOND: Nothing went *wrong*. In a particular construct Quarrier had simply obliterated the inhibitor built into the chain of command.

FOLSON: Simply . . . this would be messenger DNA?

HAMMOND: It touches on that, certainly.

FOLSON: Wasn't that rather careless of him?

HAMMOND: Facetiously speaking, perhaps it was. Scientifically speaking we're talking of an invisible particle of unknown content, the function of which is crucial to the whole of evolutionary history.

FOLSON: Not visible—even to the electron microscope?

HAMMOND: Scarcely apparent to highly sophisticated MNR techniques.

FOLSON: Then how can I—we—know what we're talking about? (Laughter)

HAMMOND: Deduction, induction, inspired inference and, to the layman unsure of the laws of thermodynamics for example—plain common sense.

FOLSON: Presumably, without this elusive regulator nature would go mad?

HAMMOND: She would—exaggerate.

FOLSON: What would you say to the unscientific argument that all is ordained, that a moth as large as an elephant is as unthinkable as an elephant the size of a moth?

HAMMOND: The argument in terms of nature is perfectly scientific. Much *is* ordained by nature—but some is commanded by man.

FOLSON: I applaud your humility. But what is the demonstrable proof that this regulator or inhibitor is existent?

HAMMOND: First, in the fact that you and I are not twenty feet tall and still growing to an early death. Second, deductively from the fate of the giant Sauria. Third . . . in the incredible development of mice to the proportions of a small dog for which Doctor Quarrier is responsible.

Like a war game; one of those delicious Rambo extravaganzas with meat deployed for killing the enemy in imagination and more beer than blood spilt either way.

They came to signs of military activity long before the turn-off. Sight-seers were being turned back in both directions. Those who could prove urgent business were allowed through the barriers.

'Name, sir?'

'Quarrier.'

'You're the gent they're expecting?'

'I suppose so—this is my colleague.'

The burly NCO waved them on.

They passed a long line of military trucks and jeeps. Knots of troops in combat gear merged with the thickening twilight but showed up plainly enough by lightning flashes. A motion of red dots from myriad cigarettes gave a touch of tension to an uncannily quiet scene.

Quarrier rounding the bend into that fateful country road was almost immediately halted by a windmill masquerading as a junior officer.

'You can't go further, sir. The beggars're only a hundred yards away.' Young, fresh-faced, frightfully *keen*.

Quarrier shrugged and both men got out. Noise enough thereabouts. Some of it the distorted, scarcely intelligible cackle that comes from delectable gadgets for instant communication. The rest was familiar—a massive sonic background of squeaking . . .

He listened briefly, closed his eyes momentarily. 'I went to the Covent Garden opera once,' he confided to no one in particular, then, to the nonplussed subaltern, 'who's *your* leading man?'

'Leading—oh, you mean Major-General Norton.'

'If you like.'

The officer led them to an overgrown caravan in a much trampled field. A snapping to attention, salutes as positive as old railway signals.

'Dr Quarrier and Mr Alladyce, *sah*!'

The newcomers had time to gather a single impression: a large desk-table, a few chairs, a smaller desk, with a computer plus word-processor plus an attractive corporal person handling the softer ware. Civilians—government scientists—and military types were crowded about the table in a Wellingtonian huddle, peering at a blown-up section of Ordnance map 185.

A strong-featured officer detached himself slightly from the group, jutted his jaws through the haze of cigarette smoke, adjusted his beret and shot at Quarrier: 'You're the author if not the authority on these pests I understand?'

He missed.

'I don't have the advantageous pleasure,' casually.

More adjustment of the beret. 'Norton, Major-General. All right?'

'If you say so.'

Instant antipathy. Science and the martial arts at odds. Alladyce looked anxious, as if visions of drum-head courts-martial had crossed his mind.

Quarrier nodded to one of the civilians, a slight acquaintance, transferred his attention to the officer. 'You'd better brief me or something.'

Or something! Not noticeably losing his grip, Norton did so, with a workmanlike summary of troop dispositions plus the various opinions offered by the civilians.

Quarrier nodded. 'And what exactly are you waiting for?'

Further taken aback the officer re-readjusted his beret and looked pensive, like a man who'd lost a vital forward position and was still standing in it. Then he had an inspiration.

'The Minister of Defence is due any moment.' Impressively.

'Wouldn't the cast of *The Mousetrap* do more good?'

The corporal sniggered. The others smiled.

'It's no joke, Quarrier,' severely.

'I agree, but what, in practical terms, are you waiting for?'

'*They're* waiting! We're here simply to contain the brutes.'

'Really? I saw one lolloping along the main road verge on our way here.'

'. . . That's impossible. The men have orders to shoot on sight anything breaking the cordon.'

Quarrier's smile was grim. 'You're not dealing with enemy troops. Today they're thick on the ground—tomorrow . . .'

'That isn't too helpful, Doctor.'

'I'm giving you facts. Numbers no longer count. . . what matters is aftermath.'

This was not the cut-and-dried language favoured by military men. The scientific types listened with more interest. They could read the small print below Quarrier's concern; but the CO was bound to question a last word seemingly fraught with God knows what consequences.

'These things have obvious genetic defects. They breed fast and erratically. Several generations show an apparently normal growth pattern—but there's a ratio leap of about 42-1 . . . a leap of 42-1 . . .'

Alladyce watching the general reaction glanced at his companion. Q—of all people—faltering, trance-like and beyond present company, as if an unpalatable truth had taken form and scampered across his very own visual display unit before he could depress the key for 'cancel'.

'Is this relevant, Quarrier?' Tom Foolery never served under the Major-General's command.

Awareness returned and with it a disconcerting regard travelling way beyond Norton's immediate presence.

'It's not a curve—a definite and inexplicable leap in the metabolic rate . . . quite suddenly a litter will grow by geometric progression—in the space of a week they can reach the dimensions of a medium-sized dog.' His hands shook uncontrollably and all too plainly. He bore the faintest resemblance to the genius many supposed him to be, dragged his words behind him like a down-and-out with a bundle too big for his shoulders. 'No—consistent pattern of development . . . they *have* to be destroyed after a week or God knows . . . it's the ferocity, the hands—there's no question—they could leap at a man and strangle him—as they strangle each other . . . but I don't understand how they could possibly—'

Quarrier broke off, confused by parallel, but unspoken thoughts on a symbolic track in which exponential growth expressed as

$\log \frac{N}{NO} = Kt$ clashed with $\log \frac{N}{NO} = (\log 2) Kt$ but how could K be a constant?

Merely an avenue of escape to a comfortable world of abstract formulae. Sooner or later such avenues lead back to the bleak arterial of *now*. Like some Hamlet caught soliloquizing in a public toilet he reverted to his everyday self, paler but less irresolute; still badly chastened by what he could no longer deny, a majority shareholding in a growth industry threatening untold misery.

Someone, his vague acquaintance, seemed to be asking for more information about the ratios. He ignored the question and told them what had to be done—and quickly.

It was common knowledge even before the Enquiry's report, that Quarrier urgently proposed a scorched earth solution which, as Major-General Norton explained to Aaron Selby, Labour MP for Telstone, he'd insisted was the last and only resort.

SELBY: Just a few questions . . . as the officer commanding did you feel bound to take Quarrier's advice seriously?

NORTON: I was surprised certainly but yes I was required by the highest authority to take his opinion very much into account.

SELBY: Why were you surprised?

NORTON: Frankly, he struck me as being somewhat unbalanced. Then and now I had the impression of a man in two episodes.

SELBY: Can you explain that a bit?

NORTON: He began with a certain arrogance, and some contempt. He could even make the kind of facetious remark no way suggesting he took the situation seriously. Then, as we all agreed later, he seemed to change—transform completely—as if he'd wandered into an artillery duel somewhere in his mind and came out badly shell-shocked.

SELBY: Yes . . . it's said he was present at his own request. Do you know anything about that?

NORTON: I can only doubt it. If I had a specific brief from the Cabinet Office to take his proposals on board I can only assume he'd been ordered to the scene.

SELBY: That appears to clear up the matter without reflecting credit. Let's consider his proposal. How did it originate?

NORTON: Certainly not immediately, but then, in the middle of some unintelligible stuff about growth rates and ratios he began to tremble. His friend Alladyce didn't look much healthier. I had to cut in and ask him—Quarrier I mean—to be more specific.

SELBY: And was he?

NORTON: Not really. Kept repeating, almost shouted, that our measures were totally inadequate against creatures that could grow to ten times their size or something of that order.

SELBY: You were sceptical?

NORTON: I think we all were—then.

SELBY: What was your response to his insistence that you place a cordon of fire round the entire area?

NORTON: Frank disbelief. On the other hand we couldn't ignore the evidence of our own eyes, and we knew what had happened to the village. I decided to seek clearance backed by a signed order from Downing Street.

SELBY: Your orders were clear enough surely?

NORTON: Not for a scorched earth policy of such magnitude. I couldn't take that kind of initiative on his say-so.

SELBY: You got immediate clearance—no question of discussing pros and cons?

NORTON: That's right.

SELBY: The logistics were no problem?

NORTON: Not once the decision was taken. In less than an hour we had five oil-tankers on the scene. We sprayed the whole circumference to saturation point.

A mortar bomb did the rest. That night there was fire over some of England. Troops, journalists and scientists watched in silence as a posse of flames tore a great hole in the night sky. Smoke climbing beyond the fireglare seemed to promise a threat reducing to ashes. Surely nothing could survive within that comprehensive wall of flame?

But, respite is another matter. Calamity would strike again—differently.

Ignis fatuus played tricks at a juncture. The storm broke with a torrential downpour, not killing but dampening the fiery spirits so that, when troops protectively clothed, moved in to shoot survivors, they found more than they'd expected. Many more.

Cornered, desperate, much like ferocious rats at bay they fought,

fought back, killed, injured and broke the nerve even of the toughest veteran.

'Guns,' one sergeant testified, 'were no bloody good against things that grappled and clung to you with those horrible hands.'

When this had been said—and more than once repeated—what shall we say of these things? Do they compare with God's own creatures? Or are we returned full circle to the realms of myth furnished with fabulous beasts, each with a handful of characteristics filched from other species? And if so, were the ancients, powered by imagination moving at one-tenth the speed of light foreseeing a kind of genetic cocktail, as if they sensed how the Quarriers of a golden technological age would give their fantasies some form at last?

Just one of many speculative questions being asked in the present febrile atmosphere breathed by a slightly endangered species—ours.

Of course, the lid has long since vanished, but the cauldron still boils over and over, not least because everything written or taped about that nocturnal barbecue was impounded for the duration. Adroitly or not, the totality of a drastic solution was played down to the point where it very nearly appeared never to have happened at all. That too, would prove to be Morgana's own blessing; short and illusory.

Chapter 12

ANTI-CLIMAX AND NAMELESS misgivings followed them home in the small hours of the next morning; persisted long after mental imprints of the night's work had faded.

Not till Quarrier dropped Alladyce at his cottage were a few words exchanged.

'At least you solved the problem.'

Quarrier looked dubious. 'And created others . . . I also gave myself and the game away—but which self? Which game?'

'They wouldn't know what you were talking about then—and I haven't the faintest now.' Lugubrious perhaps, but all he could manage to make them both feel better at a depressive time of day.

Three in the morning and home again, Quarrier was amused—and touched—to find lights burning.

'You should've gone to bed.'

'Yes, I know. But the storm was so exhilarating—I hadn't the heart to ignore it.'

She looked regal in that golden dressing-gown; but not just for the enhancing poise he thanked his lucky star once more. Rather, for her tact, exquisite and comforting beyond all. No 'what happened?' or 'had a good time at the fry-up, dear?' Just—presence, and a little silence in the right places.

He gazed almost humbly at the firelight, savouring the moment . . . which lasted longer than most.

'It got quite cool after the rainstorm, so I thought we'd be extravagant.'

Coffee percolated on a spirit stove—there were sandwiches and things on a small table. After washing the smokiness out of his eyes he came downstairs repossessed of a sense of well-being she never failed to contrive, even in the uncritical moments of his life.

Like all things, good or bad, it couldn't last. She remained true to her well-formed nature, kept silent, served his wants, helpfully, but the need to confide had Quarrier bantering his way to a beginning.

'No curiosity?'

A miraculously fresh, early morning smile. 'Yes, always. But it depends.'

'On what?'

'On you, my love. The importance you attach to what you feel inclined or reluctant to share. If you don't need, I'm neither more nor less the wiser.'

'And so, you wait.'

'That's what an awful lot of wife is about.'

He smiled. 'Once upon a heyday, a lady set out for Cliché.'

'Yes?'

'And very nearly missed her way.'

'Well bowled, sir!'

Remembrance broke in, sent him packing back to what life, clichéd or no, threatened really to be about.

'I think I'm in trouble, Helen.'

She nodded, carefully, not the faintest hint of 'I know'.

'It's grounded in a dream, I suppose. Every man has one—maybe keeps it in a tumbledown shed at the bottom of the garden—in a bottle—a shoe-box. Something—somewhere, d'you see? Mine had to do with cure-alls—the ills of mankind; socially at first, by physical means at last. Taking the biological clock to pieces for example—putting a new face on poor ticking humanity—betterment intended—not Quarrier's greater glory . . . it became personal—you know that—make life easier for other women plagued with your problem—what you called the nine-month cycle—punctured . . . statistically it's more prevalent than most people realize—fine, I work on it and I begin to get somewhere. The mice respond, but they overdo things. Litters on the double—but litters almost *ad infinitum*, uncontrollable fertilization my God it was uncanny. We try to put on the brake and there's another shock—the growth pattern goes haywire—unacceptable—fascinating but disquieting.

'Then the State peers over our shoulders. Splendid fellows! This thing you're doing is a very good thing, but while you're doing your own thing, why not do ours. This has immense *potential*, betterment of our species and all that crap, but quicker mothers equals faster manpower—and by the way, we could drop a few of these vermin behind the iron curtain, so they need to build more mousetraps and fewer SS20s. So the gags are passed round with coffee and sweeteners, pats on the head, thank you very much—next please.

'It wasn't good enough. We took a decision on a matter of existence. Way out mutations were off the record. We saw the possibility of mice approaching the size and ferocity of wolves and that couldn't be good for the human race.'

'You say "we".'

'Yes . . . that's not strictly true. *I* saw clearly how it could happen—and, of course, it did. We deleted a section of the series and that's where the trouble began.'

'Why?'

'Because, if we destroyed the litters, how do they come to exist in droves only weeks later?'

A rhetorical question—or was he in the process of deceiving himself? She must either soothe his conscience—or awaken it. Scarcely thought of the consequences before committing herself to the future, come what may.

'You needn't finish—I had a long talk with Nick . . . didn't he tell you?'

Quarrier glanced, very nearly scowled at her. 'He hinted as much, strongly for him,' he recalled the rebellious note, the jibe, 'Doctor Frankenstein', but his eye veered from her too strait regard.

'What he said is unimportant, but I was bound to overhear "a controlled takeaway". Your words.'

'My words, yes, my words, what then!'

'We can talk of other things or retire gracefully if you prefer. You must be exhausted.'

'I'm sorry. There's magnanimity for you—yes—at the end of the day I have to apologize to someone. I'm not sure you see, whether I'm avoiding the issue or struggling in a web of circumstance. But yes, we took the things to Rem's place.'

'. . . Yes.'

'. . . From which they escaped.'

'Who knew,' Helen wondered, 'who could possibly know they were spirited out of the Complex?'

'Rem, Alladyce, myself. No one else.'

'What about Mrs Chandrasakar?'

'She worked on low-powered, delegated experiments, filed her reports, informed us of any interesting abnormalities—and that was all . . . except that she . . .'

Extract from the Report (Part 1) of the All-Party Committee. Mrs I. Chandrasakar replies to questions from R. Sedgemoor, Liberal MP for Corley.

SEDGEMOOR: Mrs Chandrasakar, I gather you were party to an exchange scheme whereby scientists from government or private establishments overseas work for a fixed period in the UK and vice versa?

MRS C: Yes.

SEDGEMOOR: Plainly your qualifications fitted you to work in a highly specialized sector of the pharmaceutical industry.

MRS C: My Ph.D. was obtained at Delhi University.

SEDGEMOOR: You choose not to be addressed as Doctor Chandrasakar?

MRS C: Yes.

SEDGEMOOR: What is your practical experience in the field of genetics?

MRS C: Basically five years' research at the Gaharatta Institute—and most of that evaluating the chemical factors informing the gene complex.

SEDGEMOOR: Would mutations be covered by that line of research?

MRS C: Inevitably. One is studying recessive factors to find or even induce a homozygous condition where a recessive gene from both parents shows in the zygote.

SEDGEMOOR: I can't pretend to understand that, but you've made it clear that you're cognizant of the work undertaken at Price-Pearson.

MRS C: I hope so.

SEDGEMOOR: Doctor Quarrier's programme was well advanced by the time you arrived?

MRS C: It had been running for eighteen months I believe.

SEDGEMOOR: Did you know before joining Price-Pearson precisely what the project entailed?

MRS C: No. I understood that I would be assisting in evaluating the chemistry of certain regulatory mechanisms in foetal growth.

SEDGEMOOR: Exciting from a scientist's viewpoint?

MRS C: Not particularly. The definition is too wide to be intriguing.

SEDGEMOOR: But you *were* interested enough to accept the post.

MRS C: I can't deny it had a prestigious value.

SEDGEMOOR: The Committee has heard suggestions that your appointment was considered a blunder.

MRS C: I'm sorry. I'm not sure what the question is.

SEDGEMOOR: My fault. I mention the fact on your behalf. The concern had nothing to do with your professional standing, everything to do with your position under the Official Secrets Act.

MRS C: I believe there was some agitation when it was realized.

SEDGEMOOR: Did you—were you made aware of the anomaly?

MRS C: On my first day. Oh yes. And I would like for the record to disagree with those who say Doctor Quarrier ran his department in a 'slovenly' manner.

SEDGEMOOR: That will be noted.

MRS C: He informed me that my 'alien status' would preclude me from high-powered research under his direction. I would mainly be concerned with routine monitoring and evaluation.

SEDGEMOOR: What was your response?

MRS C: I think I made a poor joke about our being all Commonwealth members under the skin, but I determined to make the best of things, as I told him.

SEDGEMOOR: Did he explain the true purpose of the project?

MRS C: Not immediately. And this is the odd thing. I was told by Mr Dysart—something quite different.

SEDGEMOOR: Mr Dysart?

MRS C: He led me to believe that Doctor Quarrier was engaged in hush-hush work connected with national security.

SEDGEMOOR: . . . he told you that?

MRS C: He also led me to believe that Doctor Quarrier was politically suspect.

SEDGEMOOR: How did you answer him?

MRS C: I told him it was none of my business.

SEDGEMOOR: So you remained in ignorance of their declared aims?

Mrs C: Not at all. As the days passed it filtered through. In fact, Doctor Quarrier and his team did not attempt to hide the nature of—perhaps I should say, the specific thrust of their research.

Sedgemoor: About which you were enthusiastic—?

Mrs C: Oh yes! Privately I had doubts, but it was innovative in a way I had never dreamed of. Oh yes, quite a thrilling concept.

Sedgemoor: In spite of doubts?

Mrs C: Another woman would better understand my meaning. The female instinct never quite dies in the most scientific of our sex.

Sedgemoor: Yes . . . so you were satisfied to fill a minor role?

Mrs C: I could not expect more. The data output was colossal. All previous experimentation simply could not be absorbed in a brief period.

Sedgemoor: Now I'd like you to think back carefully to what appears to be a crucial day in this affair—July 7th of last year. The information on the screen to your right may assist.

7.7	12 irrad 3-35. B_3-2mls form hydrol guan 1.5 mils
D.64/42	ISO134. 20 sec int × 6 inj plac at 12C. $CH_2 NH_2$
X700	COOH. 6-4 control P_1-F_2. Nil con.
DIF 6:0:411	

Sedgemoor: You will recognize this?

Mrs C: Only in general terms, as one of hundreds of specifics.

Sedgemoor: How would you interpret the left-hand column?

Mrs C: The date of the procedure, the batch number and X700 represents the current series. The following digits give the computer encode on Data Interchange Format.

Sedgemoor: And the rest is a formula?

Mrs C: Correctly speaking, a trial variant of a very protracted and tedious process—the tip of a considerable iceberg.

Sedgemoor: I see . . . Mr Folson points out that you made no mention of stroke 42.

Mrs C: . . . I'm sorry. That is day 42—terminating the referred procedure.

Sedgemoor: So it's a recapitulation of a six weeks old 'construct' as I think you call it?

Mrs C: Yes.

Sedgemoor: I assume 'nil con' to mean the test was inconclusive.

Mrs C: Oh yes.

Sedgemoor: At first glance does this data strike you as puzzling?

Mrs C: . . . it is outside my experience and so I would prefer not to comment.

Sedgemoor: I understand . . . you would agree every experiment or procedure is recorded—computerized—if you wish.

Mrs C: That is so.

Sedgemoor: By whom?

Mrs C: Invariably by those responsible, Doctor Quarrier or his senior colleagues.

Sedgemoor: Invariably?

Mrs C: Perhaps that is exaggeration. I was sometimes asked to process the data.

Sedgemoor: Do you recall doing so on the 7th?

Mrs C: . . . yes.

Sedgemoor: Although you state you have no recollection of the specifics?

Mrs C: That is true. If I may explain. A note had been left on Doctor Remington's table in the monitoring section of the vivarium. It contained nothing more than a few scrawled words—much like those on the right-hand side.

Sedgemoor: In his hand?

Mrs C: Yes. The note simply gave the left column reference, the specific and the terminal phrase 'nil con'. I had only to recall the preparatory data and relate it to that reference.

Sedgemoor: Does that support the accusation of slovenly conduct—or a casual approach?

Mrs C: Neither. Such men carry a thousand items in their heads—they are human, lacking the cut and dried deficiencies of the computer.

Sedgemoor: But how do you—?

Mrs C: An important part of my job was to tidy any such loose ends. That is what I did.

Sedgemoor: No offence was intended, I assure you. (Pause) Did Doctor Quarrier or any member of his team know you had tidied up in this instance?

Mrs C: I saw no reason to mention it—and they never asked.

Sedgemoor: Were you at any subsequent period reminded of your entirely proper action?

Mrs C: Very much so.
Sedgemoor: By whom?
Mrs C: . . . Mr Dysart.
Sedgemoor: Go on, Mrs Chandrasakar.
Mrs C: He informed me on the following day or perhaps two days later that I might have placed myself in an untenable position as an accessory to a breach of security.
Sedgemoor: What was your reaction?
Mrs C: As I did not like him I told him I had not the faintest idea what he was talking of.
(Laughter)

Quarrier broke off, startled and perplexed by some abruptive thought that set him frowning.

'Yes?'

'I—we'd agreed a compromise. Scrub the experiment but follow through with a pair from the litter—get them to Rem's place and lose the paper work!'

'How did that concern Mrs Chandrasakar?'

'I'm not sure.' He lurched to his feet and wandered head down through some intricate pattern of his devising, stopped and glanced about him. 'This business of doing that which one shouldn't, leaving undone the things one should have done.'

'Please adjust your thoughts before leaving the laboratory.' A poor attempt to lighten his sombre mood, scarcely deserving the wan smile.

'I'm searching for those whys and wherefores they call clues. How did they escape? That's all I really care to know.'

Lame, unconvincing. She went her own way, starting from the simple premise that every disaster spawns a scapegoat. If the state was involved, if a man is called to account by the Lord High Executive, if one man dies and another lies, she *must* go against the grain and follow through.

'Quentin, what happened this morning? With Sir Rufus?'

Strangely, it wasn't what Quarrier most wanted to talk about. The session with both had been predictable; Mathie had bothered him far more; his manner, his behaviour, like an angler playing a fish for spectator sport.

Yet he told everything, with alacrity and in detail, portrait of a man floundering in deep waters of anxiety, touching bottom long enough to walk tip-toe, his head just above the surface of consciousness. An accurate catalogue, it shed light on everything but cumbersome scruples not wanted on a voyage of discovery by this intrepid explorer who, before he embarked, had filled her life and made an otherwise world acceptable.

She made no comment when he'd meandered into silence, was content to wait for dénouement still in the making.

Which came at last. 'Accountability is a figment most of us have to live with in a dangerous age. I could accept the Bromouracil punch below the belt because that's part of the game. But when someone exhumes the past—your past—it's worse—as if they'd handed you the spade to bury the rest of you.

'It's true—in the Cambridge days I belonged to a Marxist study group. Nothing wrong in that. Dons, lecturers, all kinds were involved down to the first year riff-raff. Milsom, distinguished Professor of Sociology—he came along sometimes—enthusiastic madrigalist—used to drop in after rehearsals. Well they killed him long after he died—last year I think it was. Maybe you remember how they wiped the gutter with that "communist subversive". Waited fifteen years, and when the climate was right of centre enough—they got him, the bastards. If they could they'd have dragged him from his coffin and strung up his bones outside the Odeon, Marble Arch . . .'

'And you?' not loud but clear, a warning against digression. But Quarrier would have none of it.

'I'm talking about dear old, inoffensive Milsom with the atrocious stammer who could sing "Now come, welcome, all ye maidens" beautifully *and* care about the mechanism best suited to make life a fair offer for all . . . if they could do that to him would the powers-that-are hesitate to string up me and my reputation on the strength of this—mishap?'

Mishap . . . but 'dear old Milsom' hadn't let things go bump in the night.

'Those are the facts. I never thought them consequential enough to mention,' he concluded.

'All these years,' she mused in a kind of wonderment, 'I'd taken it for granted you had no interest in politics.'

'Nor had I, after that first fine reddish rapture. Eight years in the cloisters infects and cures one at last. Hadn't been out in the big wide world six months before I realized the farcical nature of politics—democracy! Thanks but no thanks.'

Understood, at last: his adroit change of subject whenever others mentioned politics, the closing of eyes and mind if items political were aired on screen or radio; newspapers largely unread, scarcely conned. She'd felt an odd sense of pride that her husband was an apolitical animal.

Also understood, that he was, or believed himself to be in danger imperfectly defined, the fate of most scapegoats, which was what she'd first thought of. Her attempt to reassure sounded thin to at least one of them.

'If you genuinely have no idea how those animals escaped nothing can be held against you.'

They had only to prove he'd engineered a break-out and what good would be his insistence on a controlled take-away? Buy him a dress, clap a bonnet on his head, introduce him to the public as Aunt Sally! Set her up to knock him down! Discredit him and let someone more reliable continue the good work—someone less influenced by pseudethics, hogwash and Pugwash peddled by fellow-travelling, card-carrying, pillar-box coloured ideologists!

So much invective signifying nothing much more than a mere human being after all, tired out at the end of the beginning of another day.

Time to switch off lights, bolt doors and minds against the almost incomprehensible arrows of the night, those shafts of thought that *will* persist in the waking darkness.

Quarrier slept, all passionate resentment spent, while she watched over the congenitally restless sleeper.

It's not uncommon between bedfellows for one to chatter coherently or otherwise, somniloquently so to say. Quarrier was an incorrigible somnatterer as Helen termed it, but, exceptionally, she was able to respond, waking, to his slumbery monologue, easing him by carefully chosen words over problems of incredible complexity brought home from the laboratory. Much of it passed over her head but satisfaction would come next morning.

'Helen, I think I've got the answer to that SRS-A problem I mentioned—er—sorry, slow reacting substance of anaphylaxis. Incredible what a good night's sleep does for the grey matter.'

'Yes, darling.'

She especially relished the mumbled witticisms, most of them at his colleagues' expense. Wickedly she'd egg him on to the limits, discovering more about the unfortunates than ever she could have at a dinner party. Even Mother came in for some stick.

'She lives in a Sunday supplement world, that woman. Not surprised your father lives on the golf course. No room for both of 'em in that house *and* a 385-piece cutlery and dinner service *and* 15 bestsellers a month at 30p each, not to mention—'

'Now I'll tell *you* a mother-in-law joke.' She dared not giggle because that tended to wake him and the fun was spoiled.

Incredibly, he never faltered, seldom lost coherence or a train of thought however involved; and never did he remember the *fact* of holding these nocturnes. In her wisdom she hoarded the secret that they happened at all.

Nights there were, of course, even long periods, when she could sleep through the hours and no word passing between them in that odd fashion. But not this early morning time, when dawn almost saw them to bed and Quarrier asleep at the first touch of pillow . . . leading her, by chance and through the veil of his oblivion into another world, shaped like a labyrinth—stupidly finger-posted: This Way to Wentworth Magna.

'It all centres on Rem.'

'. . . Of course.'

'We hijacked them to his place—it's about four miles from that village . . . beautiful stone barn—makes an ideal vivarium.'

'And Rem?'

'He's a microbiologist.'

'I know.'

'Well, he keeps a collection for his own pursuits.'

'Dissection?'

'Among other things, naturally.'

'. . . Naturally. How long were these mice at the Bowery?'

'But you know. That's the point. He came into the Complex next morning in a hell of a state. The damned things were still growing, but the litters stayed normal on the log phase. It was a Friday. I rang Helen, said we had a weekend's urgent work ahead of us.'

'I remember.'

'The originals doubled their size in twenty-four hours, then the growth rate slowed . . .'

'Did you record all this?'

'Rem must have . . . when I left his place that Sunday night they were the size of young rabbits.'

'What was Rem's reaction?'

'I had to . . . persuade him to keep it going. He wanted out.'

'But—you persuaded him.'

'We couldn't lose this! The HFH procedure was showing up—a masterpiece . . .'

'But they escaped.'

'I keep telling her—I'm not sure—I just—don't—know.'

'. . . What happened then?'

'We'd arranged, Nick and I, to meet at The Bowery, on our way to the Complex.'

'When?'

'Monday, of course.'

'The day he died.'

'We—got to the house about eleven. No sign of his car . . . and the gate was smashed . . . the house was closed up. We tried the barn behind the house, again the door was open—lights still burning . . . the mice were gone. Nick and I just stared at each other.'

'Was there any one circumstance that—?'

'Good God yes! The cages were open . . . deserted.'

'All of them?'

'That was the oddest thing of all. Every one. We couldn't begin to work out what had happened. Nick went to pieces and—I suppose I wasn't far behind. We—had to agree something . . .'

'Silence—for example?'

'About those animals . . . yes.'

'You told the coroner you rang the police.'

'From the Complex. We had no choice. If Rem was over the top he needed help. Nick insisted.'

Nick insisted. She thought about that in a lengthening silence. Mistakenly she supposed he'd talked himself out.

'They rang back. The gentleman we'd reported missing. Found in the early hours by a farmer who rents Rem's field for grazing. Seriously injured, in ——— Hospital's ICU. He died before we got there.'

But Helen found herself on the brink of an idea, blurred and indistinguishable from the morning greyness. Tired but determined she wondered further.

'Did you enquire what was found in the car?'

'What would we expect them to find? Anyway, questions of that kind could only mean complications.'

'So you assumed—'

'Rem cracked up. That's not assumption, it's a fact. We knew why he'd acted in a frenzy—opening up the cages like that . . . he'd spent too long in their company.'

'And then killed himself—because he'd had enough of your creation?' Hesitantly she added: 'Is there another explanation? One you could live with?'

'They escaped—or he let the damned things go free! I can't—I told Nick—I *won't* be held responsible for another man's brainstorm—it's a risk we all take in a hyped-up profession—I can't.'

He whimpered some nonsense about a maddening blare of trumpets and rolled away from her taking his conscience with him.

But the fact at her side remained: Quentin Quarrier, a ranking employee of Price-Pearson, head of a research department with unlimited finance and facilities, director of a team researching one of the century's most explosive ventures, transforming metabolism, reorganizing the gene sequences, groping in the unseen entrails of endocrinology: all in the name of hastening the pangs of labour months before nature's own ordinance . . . not responsible . . . she came as dangerously close to hating the man she loved as her balanced nature would allow.

And fought to stay awake, desperately clutching at a slender thread spun from his meanderings, concerned to keep a prime strand clear in her mind against a future need. One broken phrase . . . a smashed gate. . .

A smashed gate . . . why should that—?

Thumb and forefinger rubbing together, a childhood habit, but old as Eve who span, they say, when Adam was a gentleman dead to the world after a hard day's delve.

She too slept at last.

Chapter 13

'You're listening to the "Today" programme, Wednesday August 29th. The time, ten minutes past eight. Now, what are the things you're *not* supposed to know? Could the reports of a major conflagration in a remote part of Hampshire be one of them? If I mention Wentworth Magna as the epicentre you might put two and two together and come up with a four-footed reason—mice.

'Someone who must remain nameless at his request actually witnessed this firestorm. I *can* reveal he's a scientist of some standing so objectivity without literary flourishes is guaranteed.

'First, let me ask you, the authorities are reluctant to allow discussion of this outbreak—why did you decide to tear aside the cotton-wool curtain?'

Mr X: Possibly for the same reason that your policy engineers agreed this was far too important—not too newsworthy—but too crucially important in the public interest.

R.H: So the die is cast, and we find ourselves at risk as being in breach of what?

Mr X: I haven't the faintest idea . . . National security *has* been mentioned but I do think it sometimes pays to remain seated *and* be counted.

R.H: Fine. So what actually happened?

Mr X: The countryside immediately surrounding the village was quite overrun by these creatures. All access to an area of about one and a half square miles hardly needed to be evacuated—the residents thereabouts had already fled.

R.H: Are we talking of thousands? Mice I mean?

Mr X: In this case the numbers game is meaningless. It was certainly beyond my experience.

R.H: The measures taken plus the secrecy do suggest a serious threat surely?

Mr X: That's not in dispute—hence a military operation to contain it.

R.H: Is it possible we have a sledgehammer and nut situation here? I mean, it's hard for most of us to see mice as having more than nuisance value—some people even like them.

Mr X: . . . to my knowledge, eight men died and forty-seven were badly mauled in the follow-up operation.

R.H: I see . . . and how would you judge the success of this—?

Mr X: If you're asking was every last animal destroyed, the short answer must be no.

R.H: So there's every likelihood they could pop up again elsewhere?

Mr X: I can't say categorically. I *do* know these are no ordinary mice—that they fought back with appalling ferocity.

R.H: Which brings me to the point. It's unlikely anyone could forget the Hopkins exposé—the shots of those things at close quarters. Is there any indication as to where they came from?

Mr X: I can confidently assert they were bred in laboratory conditions.

R.H: Why?

Mr X: Manifestly, they're a particularly unpleasant mutant—or genetic construct.

R.H: So one might legitimately wonder how they come to be wandering about the peaceful English countryside?

Mr X: One might.

R.H: And who is responsible presumably?

Mr X: I know who's responsible.

R.H: . . . yes?

Mr X: I was in the same—confined space with him not eight hours ago. I can say no more.

R.H: In the public interest—or your own?

Mr X: . . . you know to your cost the risks involved in interviewing a man who says too much, Mr Hardcastle.

She'd been up and about for an hour or more; bathed, dressed and cleared of 'nightwebs', her euphemism for the definable ravages late hours can inflict on any woman's fourth decade. Breakfast and minor chores were done with before she turned to the news and caught the item that followed. Hearing Quarrier's heavy tread on the stairs she switched off what he called 'that irritating joker with the "mock-mock who's there?" intonation in his maddening voice'.

She gave him time and silence enough to get through two cups of tea and toast, made a pretence of tidying the kitchen, her thoughts right-angled to their nocturnal talk and the morning's news.

'I must've bored you with a lot of rot last night.'

'At least you talked it out.' Ambiguously. And it seemed wiser to warn him of things as they now stood. 'It's back with the media. Someone gave an account of last night's goings-on.'

'I'm sure he couldn't wait.'

'It takes courage to defy a government ban.'

'And hounds were born to bay for blood.'

'He talked of the public interest.'

'Of course. That covers a multitude.'

'And eight more dead.'

He felt rather than saw her point. And it hurt.

'. . . eight. Yes.'

Almost brutally she added, 'He thinks they could resurface.'

'I—can't argue with that. Endangered species discover incredible powers of survival . . . there's a stream runs through Wentworth —some will swim their way out of trouble.'

Of mice and men, she thought bitterly. 'Too big for a cover-up, surely?'

'It's too big not to play down.'

Does he *really* understand? She might nod perfunctorily to his logic but her irrational knots of reflection, of visual images, seemed more valid—things like a smashed gate.

'Questions were asked but—'

'Naturally. Where they come from, who bred them?'

'I was about to add—they know the answers.' Exasperation very nearly betrayed itself.

'But won't say. Play down, play for time. It's part of the ritual—phasing in the sacrificial victim in truly civilized fashion.'

This is my husband Quentin's talking about. But does he know? The idea, so strong in her mind, somehow leaped the difference between them and he reacted as if to a stillborn accusation.

'Helen, it's obvious to the meanest intelligence, I'm involved, but not to the point of criminal negligence. I stand by what I said—I'm not responsible.'

How, she wondered, should the caring wife respond? No, dear, of course you aren't. You couldn't possibly know the naughty little creatures would steal away into the night and eat up everything they could lay—hands—on; as for eating people—it's a question of upbringing isn't it?

She still read *The Tale of the Two Bad Mice* to her youngest but, on reflection Helen saw what a horror story Miss Potter *might* have written after a sleepless night and half a bottle of brandy.

Quarrier, like a Brutus wrapped in Burton's best toga for self-righteous people, passed through the security system, ignored meaningful looks from other departmental heads, went straight to his office and cleared away the correspondence always reminding him of his administrative role in the total structure. Laura, thanks be, had learned to cope with most of it though it vaguely spoiled her lunch-break knowing he signed her letters sight unseen.

Mrs Chandrasakar's arrival with results of long-term 'ancillaries' interested him more, though now as ever he found it hard to relax in her company. Especially now.

Having laid the reports on his desk she hovered and hesitated quite without artifice, the fingers of a now disburdened hand plucking at the sari he could never quite come to terms with. Definitely incongruous under an open white lab coat.

He watched the performance long enough to memorize it before enquiring a touch impatiently, 'Well?'

'I wanted to say, Doctor Quarrier, that slide 27 from the M81 series—you have the details there—is quite excit- promising. It suggests some validity in the mitogenetic ray theory—at the metaphase stage particularly.'

He relaxed a little. 'I'll note that with care, but don't read too much into it—the electron microscope, by its very nature *can* contribute to and so distort the picture. Anything else?'

She rarely smiled, but inclined her head to register gratitude that he should make an obvious effort to put her at ease.

'I—could wish more was known of the protein hormone in the fifth series.'

'Relaxin?' At another time Quarrier would have dealt curtly with 'wishes'. 'I couldn't agree more. But until we do we'll have to make a hundred inspired guesses, which is what much of our job's about.'

'Yes, Doctor Quarrier,' submissively. She started towards the door, but turned positively, a mind made up to the hilt. 'I think I should warn you—Mr Dysart is very much in evidence this morning.'

So, it had been smattered verbiage, bits of bazaar haberdashery screening deeper intent.

'Warn me? I don't understand.'

'I do not think a microscopist would understand the specimen that stared back at him.'

He chuckled at the hint of humour. 'I see.'

'He is in a very ugly mood. Characterized by the many questions he asked concerning you and Mr Alladyce.'

'Yes . . . what, if anything did you tell him, Mrs Chandrasakar?'

'Very little, amounting to nothing. I explained that, as an Indian citizen, I was not subject to the context in which he put his questions.'

'. . . Thank you.'

'And I think you should know that he asked particularly about July 7th.'

He said nothing. When words are inadequate an exchange of intelligent appraisal tells all.

'I would like to add that I cannot explain his presence here at all as he appears to be scientifically deficient.'

Amused by indignation trailing echoes of the Raj, Quarrier apologized for not informing her exactly what Dysart was about. 'The truth is, I hardly know myself, but when I said he was connected with the Personnel Department that's a high percentage of fact.'

Her display of loyalty touched him somewhere near his conscience. After all, he'd shown her no especial consideration; a transient, eastern exotic transplanted for a mere nonce. So long as she equated with the job polite condescension would do.

He made a mental note to invite her for dinner some time and, in thoughtful mood, applied himself to the neat and legible notes she preferred to write long-hand.

Minutes later he gave up pretence of interest in the electrifying effects of increased bromocriptine dosage to suppress GH secretion, and fixed his peripatetic thoughts on the dove-grey door.

Why, he wondered, had she made not the slightest comment on a phenomenon currently on everybody's mind—at Price-Pearson's, if not the rest of the UK? Peripherally maybe, but she had enough involvement in the programme to prompt at least the question even Laura had timidly ventured: are they ours?

He felt sufficiently curious about her total lack of curiosity to think of ringing her when a knock at the door neatly cut the thought from the action.

Dysart's appearance crystallized the fluid situation, not for the world's sake, but as between two poles apart. Had this encounter been a climactic set piece in a novel, or a grab-'em-quick scene from a JR pseudocrudographic, some might have been enthralled at sight of these two protagonists, inimical as hell on ice, facing each other, probing for weaknesses, circling for openings the size of a dagger thrust.

In short, we're eye-to-eye with the concentrated filth belonging not prehistorically, not mediaevally, but squarely in the twentieth-century flowering of peccable, maculate middle-class animalcules sweating value-judgments. Their sky-high stench scarcely beats the sky-high sales of deodorants . . . that's the trouble.

'May I take the chair you were about to offer, Doctor? This could pre-empt some of your time.'

'I've a lab project set up for eleven—'

'Your secretary has instructions we're not to be disturbed.'

'She takes her instructions from me.'

'. . . sometimes perspectives are more important than priorities.'

Dysart took a letter from his pocket, handed it to Quarrier. 'If you'd just glance over this.'

Quarrier did so, looked up at some thought high over Dysart's head.

' "All those involved in this unprecedented situation are charged to give unqualified co-operation to the bearer of this—" travesty,' he returned it between two fingers. 'You fit your boss admirably.'

'I do think insults are the "rhubarb-rhubarb" of the sweaty masses don't you? We're not trained, but we are encouraged to wear a mental Burberry against mud-slingers' throw-outs, so let's be civilized and avoid wasted effort, eh?'

No response and a blank stare was response of a kind.

'In a sense,' Dysart continued, 'you've put your foot in your mouth badly enough to catch swine's disease, as an old Czech proverb has it. A potentially lethal strain of mice goes missing from *your* department—not days, but weeks ago. Why they didn't show up publicly till now I don't pretend to understand; but someone must know. It follows, I need to find out exactly why you failed to report the circumstance and why, when the facts *did* become public, you made no effort to clarify the situation.'

'I've explained that adequately to *my* boss. There were no "circumstances" to report so what was I supposed to clarify?'

'Yesterday you were urged—had to be persuaded—to advise those given the dirty work of clearing up your mess.'

'Now look—'

'When everything's done and blustered, Doctor, you left it crystal clear in their minds the damned things were of your creating.'

'Where does that get you?'

'Back to your persistent denial of responsibility for their safe-keeping.'

'They did not escape—not on my authority.'

Dysart weighed this with some care. 'I suspect a semantic nicety hidden somewhere . . . so what happened in the early hours of July 7th, Doctor Quarrier?'

'No idea. You tell me.'

'Let's try a kick-start . . . every incident out of the ordinary, every visit, is entered in the night security guards' log-chart. We know Robert Remington burned midnight oil monitoring an experiment connected with your work on Accelerant Pregnancy.'

'Nothing unusual.'

'As you please. What was unusual as far as security's concerned was your and Alladyce's pell-mell arrival less than an hour after Remington's mayday call. What so urgent that you should both turn out at 2 a.m.?'

'. . . The strain looked promising. Showed positive for rapid foetal development—our objective . . . unfortunately they presented with symptoms of equally rapid tumorous growths.'

'A big man like him—couldn't he handle the crisis?'

'We worked as a team—our disciplines are interdependent—which means making tri-valent decisions.'

'What "decision" did you make at that time?'

'To scrap the experiment.'

'Semantics will undo us yet. Why?'

'To avoid unnecessary suffering—'

'Admirable! But if the experiment promised results why not necropsy—that's common practice isn't it?'

'We knew what had gone wrong—over-exposure to radiation.'

'So they were incinerated?'

'As I believe.'

Dysart leaned at his quarry, too intent on pursuit to care about expressions of repugnance, eyes filled with abhorrence and all such nonsense.

'Then, if X700 held the importance you all attached to it, why no record, nothing on the software except a meaningless negative to show it was planned and conducted at all?'

'It must be on file.'

'We ran it through three times at Head Office, three times here. Nothing.'

'What does it matter!'

'High fly research—an experiment goes missing and it doesn't matter?'

'. . . I can't explain it.'

'You make much of the fact of having total responsibility down to the most detailed instructions to your secretariat . . .'

A statement of fact or a query on a taunting note? Either way, Dysart waited politely for some reaction. Waited in vain; was forced to continue.

'It may be you're fortunate in your triumvirate: Remington's dead, Alladyce denies everything and admits nothing, and the dusky rose of Shalimar pleads diplomatic immunity.'

Not worth the bat of an eyelid. Dysart smiled briefly with that tiny jerk of the head characterizing a lawyer's sneer.

'Three out of four leaves you, Doctor.'

'If you've finished—'

'Realize and reflect. I'm letting you down lightly. This is a preliminary "seek-out" as the Yankees have it. Later, if there has to be a later, my back-up team—a pair of heavies—will put you through the mangle so delicately you'll hardly know you're only dripping information.'

'All right. You win. As a humanitarian gesture . . .'

'Yes?'

'I'm prepared to work out which amino acid went missing in the polypeptide sequence.'

'. . . what are you talking about?'

'Genetic renovation. Yours.'

'Quarrier, *you* put yourself on the track of a world-shaking discovery—we didn't. I'm not even saying you could foresee the consequences of its success, but "no government could allow such a formula to reach the open market" and I'm quoting the writer of that letter. Which puts us all squarely within the meaning of the Act.'

'Betherton made that plain enough.'

'What I'm coming to is what he only hinted at.'

Quarrier needed no blaze of trumpets to warn against the punch he saw coming.

'Of course we researched your connection with a political study group active in the careless latish Fifties. Professors Rockley and Milsom, Saunders, Lostein, Sempill, Perez—names you'll recall I'm sure . . . two or three issues of what for want of a better word I'll describe as a magazine were actually printed—a collection of papers contributed by the more ardent members.'

Again, the conjurer with a nostalgia for old tricks reached into his pocket to produce a faded copy of the pitifully meagre, badly printed magazine.

He intoned its title: '*Di grado in grado*, a typically neat and donnish conceit, eh? By degrees . . . and towards what? Apparently, a post-graduate, tipped for a brilliant career, had some of the answer . . .'

Dysart delivered the scrap, opened at page 3, into Quarrier's reflexively outstretched hand.

'You'll recognize this as your effusion.' A plain statement of fact.

SCIENCE AND SEMANTICS

★

Before we go much further along the technological road to an old Utopia or a new Valhalla, I suspect we may have to reconstruct a host of terms which are multiplying with the speed of makeshift to create a *lingua arcana* not easily intelligible even to those scientists necessarily concerned with neighbouring and highly specialized disciplines.

Possessed of a pioneering spirit I might have gone further, positing the need to create a whole new language in the Esperanto mould. A pioneer indeed! To end as a raving lunatic tearing a million contributions into confetti.

It's comfortable doctrine to deny the plea even for a modest restructuring of the scientific vocabulary. '*I* understand hotchpotch, therefore *you* must understand', is everyman's besetting humour, the very basis of his failure to communicate, more so in this paradoxical age of plethoric *means* of communication.

Which brings me conveniently to the sociological point I want to make.

If science is to function at its best, privately or publicly, purely or appliedly, it must surely merit not the uninstructed fear but the informed respect of a world it claims to serve. Service to mankind is the point. Man is not required to reverence science *per se*. But already there exists an uneasy perception that science has displaced religion, exercising in its stead an equally ambiguous influence on a fairly comprehensive and suggestible mentality. This not unconscious exercise of mumbo-jumbo and unintelligible jargon which threatens to cloud judgment, depreciate understanding, devalue ethical principles, may end by demoralizing the strong-headed and captivating the weak-minded.

In other words, the ground is preparing for a new phase of the class struggle in which an élite (more sizeable, more ramifyingly influential than any historically identifiable body of aristo theo or plutocrats) may well emerge as a powerful contender in the pyramidal power structure of late twentieth-century society.

Doubly potent, with possession of a grossly inflated and coded language undecipherable even to the odd B.Sc. straying into politics. Is it fanciful then, to predict a subtle transfer of real power under the noses of, but beyond the comprehension of, the scientifically illiterate guardians of the democratic process?

Indiscriminate terminology, borrowing from every dead and

alive tongue as occasion requires cannot compare with a highly structured mode of intelligible expression devoid of symbolism (the merest shadow of the substance while the sun shines).

I stress, science cannot benefit from worship without universal understanding; lacking clarity, condemned for its obscurantism, science may well labour into the future like a grotesque mountain, bringing forth in the eyes of the multitude a ridiculous mouse.

'Written,' said Dysart, 'before the era of bytes and technosquelch. Well, Doctor?'

'. . . if "well" means do I disown it—the answer is no.'

Dysart leaned forward and relieved Quarrier of his flimsy burden; his oddly compelling eyes never left its author.

'Researches into a lost past, to parody another master of the negligible. But you can't be less than fascinated by an obvious irony.'

Quarrier, pensive, stared blankly at his inquisitor.

'I mean the allusion: *mons parturient et nascitur ridiculus mus*. Doesn't that disturb you—even marginally?'

Very likely, or it's hard to say why Quarrier reacted—marginally—to the Latinism. He recognized one of those dangerous moments thereabouts when the past is inescapably impaled on the present.

'I can't pretend to—'

'It almost looks, doesn't it, as if you'd projected, for an instant, into the future, *your* future, in some part of which you were destined to produce—a ridiculous mouse.'

Perceived or not by Quarrier, a process of depersonalization had begun. The first stage had much to do with banter: humour in skilled hands can be a deadly weapon of depreciation.

Perhaps the fact wasn't altogether lost on the neo-alchemist, transmutor extraordinary, not of a philosopher's pebble, but of flesh and blood, molecule by molecule, gene by gene, to produce at last—a laughing-stock. Uncertainty showed. He failed to respond and so proved that his tormentor had made his point. Which he drove home.

'This matter of preparing the ground for a new phase of the class struggle in which technocracy emerges triumphant. Where, in this usurping white-coated hierarchy do you choose to place yourself?'

Quarrier glared at a man with so many last straws up his sleeve. 'Who the hell are you to burrow into my past like a bloody parasite! You're the living proof of a cancerous growth spreading through the body politic . . . you typify the evil all men fear.'

'. . . I'll accept still more bluster as a reasonably honest expression of anger, but let's stick to the facts shall we? Whatever the colour of your politics it remains that you're engaged in research elevated to the highest level of national importance. By whatever means the fruits of your labours escaped you know and I know these things pose not only a domestic threat but, suppose them to fall into the wrong hands—dead or alive—is it unreasonable for the guardians of *status quo* to sound the tocsin? Or that they should wonder at the significance of a high-powered experiment missing, presumed dead, according to almost non-existent records?'

'That's your problem!'

'The problem, as always, is cause and effect—echoes of the class struggle and an apparent liberation of monstrous propagators gnawing away at a society that refuses to wither away.'

'. . . You're going too far.'

'I hope so, but I can't—in an uncertain age aggravated by hi-tech—be absolutely sure.'

'I'll tell you what it is—you people are *infested* with the Berlin wall syndrome. Spies and dissidents in your underwear—I'm surprised you don't write novels in your spare time.'

Dysart smiled pleasantly; abashed he was not. 'We use professionals for literary disinformation. But as a matter of fact you're wrong . . . our besetting syndrome stems from classical history and a better chronicler than all the spy-thriller hacks lumped together. The Trojan Horse is seldom far from our thoughts . . .'

It marked an end to questioning for the time being. Much like exploratory surgery—Quarrier's wry reflection—not too painful, but some grounds for apprehension. He recalled the promise to return and a hinting threat of henchmen less delicate in their methods of finding out moonshine . . .

Quarrier that day appeared no different to those about him. He made his customary rounds of the labs in his fief, discussed progress with teams of earnest young researchers, teasing them out of their gravity with his usual microtomic wit and, if they noticed anything untoward, it may have been the length of time he spent over lunch with Mrs Chandrasakar.

'But,' a more than usually observant staff member recalled long after, 'she did most of the talking while he seemed to be listening intently to something else—the clatter of cutlery maybe.'

Chapter 14

HELEN DROVE HER little Fiat out of the small market town suburb and on to the by-pass connecting with the main Winchester carriageway. She was reminded how Price-Pearson had drawn a whole colony of workers into its gigantic new hive set in rolling Hampshire countryside.

Many of the 'desirable residences' lining the M31 from Alton to Alford were mortgaged to employees under the company's paternal scheme designed to give home ownership to all. Most of those who'd first joined were now muttering something about tied cottages, but let that pass.

In time she reached the turn-off leading to Wentworth Magna—noted the scatter of police cars, army lorries and an ambulance, the road barrier still in place and a straggling plume of smoke in the south-west distance rising sullenly to a clear blue sky beyond blackened spectres of trees.

About three miles further on, a narrow lane, one of the longest in the county, led to The Bowery, a once derelict farm-house, home of the late Doctor Robert Remington, a distinguished research biochemist, much loved and missed by all who knew and worked with him: thus, the still warm obituary in *Alembic*, the house magazine.

A woman, on her way to visit Mother somewhere beyond Alford, follows an impulse to turn off the main road and bump along the scarcely made-up lane lined with massive beeches arched to give a cathedral hue of grey-green, a cool and remote nave almost two miles in length.

To view an up-for-sale house, to call on ghosts lately moved in; to still that familiar tingling sensation between thumb and forefinger?

Strange compulsion whichever—even for Helen.

She well remembered the housewarming, could it be nine years ago? Linda still alive, atrociously humorous, advertising her urban distaste for Rem's truly rural choice by welcoming the guests at the front door sporting a wrapround overall and Wellington boots, one hand grasping a dolly-stick.

Poor, dear hospitalized Linda 'atrociously tumorous' as she'd weakly quipped to her friend from the old London days. 'Southwark'll never be the same without us queuing outside the works on Friday nights, beautifully manicured hands stretched out for the old man's wages, darling.'

No more hilarious evenings, no more Linda, no Rem, and Jeremy their son dead from drugs.

She drove slowly, weighed down by a feed-back of memories, quite aware how much she longed for five minutes of Linda's unerring common-sense. Aware, too, of her What-on-earth whim. What, exactly, had driven her off the usual Tuesday afternoon course of duty? Surely a senseless exercise to go roundabout simply to court nostalgia? Unless it has to do with a doubt.

About a gate . . .

Which was there, almost under the front wheels, forcing her to brake hard. In a new frame of mind she sat staring at the smashed set of timbers still sprawled across the entrance, scarcely barring a determined passage to the house just visible behind a squat of ancient sycamores.

She left the car and stood in thought before the pathetic bits of lumber; wasted not a glance on the house, showed no desire to visit the barn, cared only to study the five-barred ruin under a compulsive impression that that was what she had come out of her way to see.

Unawares a finger and thumb rubbed gently at some invisible filament, coaxing it to immaterialize into an idea, an answer to the why.

Because: violence is *not* a meaningless exercise. Violence, especially perpetrated by a highly intelligent man, trained and formed by experience to the delicate touch, has to mean more than a superficial loss of reason, abdication of all the senses. She remembered him too well to nod at the coroner's verdict: death by misadventure, delivered with a knowing eye to evidence given as to his mental state: stress, overwork.

A simple bolt had, more or less, secured the gate. The ring into which it shot was torn from the stout wooden post. On the outside . . .

Finger and thumb rubbed steadily as in the childhood times spent poring over adult mysteries.

Had it been on the inside, a car driven at speed would have ended the matter, recklessness paying the penalty there and then. The converse was true. A frenzied driver might well crash a gate bolted on the outside in order to save time.

But why should he want to save one of the first bits of impedimenta a man in turmoil lets go hang?

Just an inch from what had been the top bar her eye caught a gleam of blue-black, alien in its dun coloured surroundings. She bent to finger it, to lift and examine what had to be a flake of paint. It was little enough but, at that moment she felt the thread forming quite palpably, in her grasp. Two visions, one concrete, the other notional, spliced into an harmonious whole.

A smashed gate, and a car containing a badly smashed human being. And why stop to open those cages when he couldn't stop long enough to open the gate?

Agitated by some train of thought she paced about the neighbouring stretch of ground and, inevitably, found what she hadn't particularly been looking for. A large clump of cow parsley, broken, crushed and already dessicated suggested the impact of some large and impersonal object, the wheels of a car in the act of turning for example. Not Rem's of course. Could be anybody's. Or someone's.

Someone besides the only three men who knew the mutants had disappeared . . .

She looked unseeing towards the house, spell-bound, transfixed by a burgeoning make-shift vision of what *must* have happened on that night of all nights.

SIGHTINGS

Preston Candover: Wednesday. A farmer reports three strange-looking creatures on his land. Like those mice on TV. But these were bigger, size of a small dog. They stood their distance—not thirty yards off. Never took their eyes off me. Then they sort of looked at each other—that's how it appeared, seemed to be deciding their next move—they turned all at once and took off into Seven

Acre—a cornfield. Didn't much like it. Thought as you oughta know.

Same day: The curator of the Wakes museum phones police, reports an odd-looking animal, much like those seen on TV, but considerably larger. Several visitors had brought it to his attention. One swore it had picked a large rose, sniffed it and thrown it away. Over-heated imagination. I saw it briefly—seemed to be examining everything with great care—then astonishingly, it leapt a high wall and disappeared. Oh, this was bigger, much bigger.

Same day: A distraught lady in Haverstoke rings to report an animal devouring her Sealyham—even as I speak, officer. It turned and actually snarled at me as I tried to drive it off . . . in the garden of course . . . the most horrid-looking creature in my long experience of local fauna. Like which animals on TV? No idea—I do not possess a TV. Large? Well, no bigger than poor Tranter, but undoubtedly more anti-social.

Same day: In the Cheriton area a small-holder reports several chickens massacred by four really vicious brutes. Three of 'em went for me—I retreated to the tool-shed. They were killing the hens—I watched from the bit of window. It's the way they did it—seemed to strangle 'em first and then—what I want to know is—what are they? No—they're not like the TV ones—these are bigger.

Same day: AA patrolman, reports on M3 near Basingstoke: queer-looking rat-like animal streaking across motorway, swift, like a panther, quick enough to dodge a lot of traffic. Greyish. Something like those jokers they showed on TV. No—definitely bigger.

Same day: A retired naval officer from West Meon admitted to Petersfield Hospital. Multiple lesions. Badly bitten about the legs while out walking in the neighbourhood. Fought them off with walking-stick. Treated for shock. Talked obsessively of an animal outside previous experience.

Detective-Superintendent Whitfield, Hampshire CID, 'placed' his visitor with the automatic in-depth regard of his kind. Middle-class, past first youth, but the second not doing too badly at all, the sort of fine hazel eyes that don't know how to age; poise enough for a duchess.

'. . . And you wanted to see me about—?'

'Remington, Robert Remington. He died in a car crash about a month ago.'

'Ah yes . . . Quarrier—you wouldn't be the wife of Doctor Quarrier?'

'I am, yes.' She suspected a quickening of interest, thought of paludinous places where first footsteps squelch and it becomes obvious: wise not to go further, wiser not to have come at all.

But there was no going back, however forcefully it occurred that her enthusiasm might mean trouble for Quentin. Misplaced enthusiasm was something else.

'You live at Alton or thereabouts?'

'Yes.'

'I'm quoting from what I recall of the inquest. Your husband gave evidence.'

'He doesn't know I'm here.'

He smiled—carefully. 'Is that significant?'

'I mean, I didn't expect to be here—I was on my way to visit my parents, they live at Alford, but I came straight to Winchester—I had this idea you see.' Unlike Helen, this almost childlike impetuosity—not much sign of a duchess after all.

'How can I be of help, Mrs Quarrier?'

'These mice—mutants—he's worried—the responsibility for their existence.'

'I saw some of 'em last night. He's got a bit to worry about on the face of it.'

She ignored the ill-concealed accusation.

'Superintendent, I'm here to question—perhaps that's not quite—to wonder at the verdict on Doctor Remington's death.'

'Misadventure,' evenly.

'Yes—if he wasn't going anywhere.'

'Oh,' plainly he was enjoying this. 'And if he was?'

She took a deep breath. 'Murder, perhaps.'

Amusement went to the wall. Senior police officers tend to take such matters seriously.

'He crashed his car, Mrs Quarrier. It was made clear he'd been under stress probably from overwork. It happens. The medical report listed injuries consistent with high-speed impact. Two and two don't make more than we need.' As gently as he dared.

She floundered, slightly awed, but badly irritated by men's

insufferable logic. If she'd retorted that one and one *in flagrante* could make more than two he'd probably have been disgusted. Wisely she swallowed the retort.

'I'm certain he was driving with a purpose. However suicidal a man might feel in the dead of night, he doesn't smash through his gate and drive safely almost two miles without a reason.'

'He had a purpose right enough, but his state of mind explains the rest. The theory is he wanted to reach the main road.'

'But why?'

Whitfield shrugged off annoyance. 'Obviously to go at speed reckless enough to destroy.'

Annoyance returned at sight of the slow gesture of denial. Such a beautiful head under its coil of brown hair—and nothing in it.

'But the cages were open—and the animals were gone. He would never have done that whatever his state of mind.' Not a contradiction, so much as a last attempt to persuade her illogical self. Whitfield saw that, and made due allowance.

'People do odd things none of us can rightly account for.'

She might have heard but seemed busy about something in her shoulder-bag.

'I almost forgot.' And suddenly she was offering him God knows what, and he was taking it, gazing at it, and looking for words. 'What's this?' seemed too rude.

'A flake of paint. I found it almost under the gate—it's cellulose isn't it?'

He nodded gravely, carefully concealing astonishment that Sherlock had married after all. Better late than never. 'Navy blue,' he murmured, for want of else to say. Doodled with a pen for a thoughtful moment, then pulled himself together.

'From his car you see—as he went through the gate—'

'His car was grey.'

'. . . I'm afraid it'll have to remain an accident—unless you have a motive in mind, Mrs Quarrier.'

She started to speak, conscious of the snapping thread, too slender to bear the weight of cast-iron conviction *and* a sliver of paint.

'I'm sorry, Superintendent. I've wasted your time with foolishness when I should be discussing recipes with Mother.'

He smiled, mollified by her retraction and yet, intrigued suddenly by the odd quality of her reasoning. Another glance at the inch piece of cellulose.

'It's an interesting line you draw, though a house of cards isn't stronger for having more aces than jokers . . . I'll confide that I did wonder a bit . . . the usual appeal for witnesses, but you can't expect much at 2.30 in the morning—an unlighted stretch of lane . . .' but he was thinking hard, out of all contact with his tongue, weighing the value of adding fuel to her unextinguished conviction. 'The speedometer stuck at twenty.' Brusquely.

Well, yes, it had been worth it for the widening—almost the flowering of those extraordinarily lovely eyes. Filled with recognition of a throwaway significance—as if it strengthened her tenuous bit of theory. After all, twenty hardly suggested driving with a death wish. Yes, he *had* wondered.

'It doesn't fit, Superintendent.'

That was worth a hoist of eyebrows. 'Oh?'

'You'd have to hit that gate at more than twenty to get through; why slow down to crash at last if dying is your purpose?'

Whitfield grew thoughtful without missing the feminine touch, sudden timidity, as if she were appalled that a supposition could transform into hideous reality. Helen tailed off, not daring to add a word that might demolish the teetering house of cards; not knowing how much more interested the professional in Whitfield had become.

His sense of humour returned at her expense. Serves you right for playing the amateur detective. Too reminiscent of those ghastly 'crime-writers' who used to make chintz, blood and disposable curates the main ingredients in their Surprise Puddings. Yes, better go and swap recipes with the Old Lady.

Very nearly the end of the matter—if word hadn't just gone out from the topmost brass—well, a man called Dysart—odd in itself —to be gone into—investigate anything untoward bearing on the Wentworth Magna business . . . this looked rather untowardwards.

'Of course,' cautiously, 'it's nothing conclusive. Twenty's enough in the right circumstances.' It convinced neither of them, so he threw caution to the winds and a kite after them. 'I suppose the real mystery is in what Doctor Remington had to say after the crash.'

Definitely worth it, the reaction, violent, eloquent, Helen's.

'But—I understood he never really regained consciousness.'

No point in hurrying. He commandeered an interval to remark the curious working of the thumb and forefinger. How would psychology explain it?

Apt, that a detective should unravel the minor digital mystery, inherent and ingrown beyond the ken of Helen's psyche. Threads, following through to somewhere called nowhere—threadbare. Odd from a copper who cultivated gorgeous chrysanthemums but never wrote poetry—even in the bathroom.

He made a decision, just big enough to put her out of her misery. Not chivalry exactly, but enchantment, a knuckling under to her spell not consciously cast but casually trailed, as that fabled lady of the road dragged a mink coat in her wake.

Besides, she might even have a clue what he was talking about.

'"Consciousness",' he picked up where she'd left off, 'there wasn't much left of that I believe. He mentioned your husband's name and something imperfectly understood I suppose, by the medics. "Quarrier . . . $C_2H_4CL_2$ . . .".'

'. . . Yes?' not too comprehendingly.

'That was all. I don't think a lot was made of it at the inquest, if anything . . . odd though.'

'I don't see why. Doctor Remington dealt in formulae.'

'Oh ah—right enough, Mrs Quarrier. But apparently it didn't make sense to your husband—who'd also know about such things?'

She remained silent.

'It's of no consequence. Just a vague curiosity as to what might have been in his mind—enough to link Doctor Quarrier with its—significance. Probably the ramblings of a dying man. Meaningless.'

Helen bowed her head, not particularly to fate and the trick it had played on her urge, out of all character, to meddle; but the better to study those pieces of crazy-paving at her feet, fragments perhaps, of good intentions for a path that leads, they say, to . . .

'I—haven't been much help, have I?' rare portrait of a chastened woman.

It had been a pleasant interlude, but mindful of ever-pressing business, his enchantment had to end. He would let her down—and out—lightly.

'Everything has significance to everything else. Nothing's wasted,' rising from his desk, 'Now I mustn't keep you. Those recipes?'

She smiled her perfect understanding, was quick to respond.

'You've been patient beyond the limits of tolerance, Superintendent. Thank you.'

Time after her pervasive quality had faded from that humdrum office he found himself looking up from a thoroughly boring dossier long enough to murmur: she's classical.

What seemed bad to worse, he had to admit that he hadn't the faintest idea what he was talking about.

Journalism, handed a story on an electron-plated salver, just found time to organize a wet benefit for Hopkins at el Vino's as the likeliest Communicator of the Year before it joined those flocking from much of the world to witness the aftermath of a *cause macabre*. *Floreat* the grapevine.

The authorities still played desperately for time in the key of D: disinform, deny, delay and damn the consequences. Above all, wake not the two sleeping giants beginning to stir and question phenomena they had no part in.

But fe-fi-fo-fum was already at work. Moscow Radio quoted the following from a Tass agency report.

'In the last few days disturbing information has come to light concerning new forms of experimentation in the southern parts of the UK.

'It appears that scientists have created a super-strain of mice of unparalleled fertility—presumably by suppression of the resorption mechanism. The young, we are reliably informed, may grow to the size of dogs, whether of chihuahua or wolfhound dimensions is unclear. These mutants are sufficiently large and numerous to give concern and there are unsubstantiated reports that many deaths have resulted from their accidental release into the environment, possibly from a clandestine research establishment.'

Who, the red giant seemed to infer, do these pygmies think they are?

Washington: The *Post*, faced with the same set of facts, reported thus:

'Britain today is currently gripped by a terror that beats E.T. aliens from another Hell, the death-mask recently discovered alive in the White House and everything you ought to know about the newly constructed maxi-missal silos recently observed on Mars.

'Not thousands but maybe millions of mice are reported roaming

England's countryside, striking fear into the sturdiest yeoman heart. They are economy size, omniverous, omnasty and legion. Entire communities have vanished, eaten alive according to panic-stricken survivors.

'These monsters, uncannily human-like, have made their TV début. First impressions sent shock waves through the nation. Media czar Hopkins' exposé has prime-time on tonight's major networks, and Americans can judge for themselves how far these mutants resemble our very own Michael Mouse.

'Watch out for a clue greasing the answer to a highly intriguing question. What exactly are the Brits up to in their genefactories?'

Resentment clouded the striped and starry-eyed giant's brow. How could these 'Brits' produce the most epoch-making send-up of *homo sapiens* since Barnum mated with Bailey, and not let their oldest allies since tomorrow grab a piece of the action? Bio-warfare could be looking good if half the reports were true.

Behind a blatant appeal to sensationalism lurked the proverbial grain of truth. The poisonous effects of a conspiracy to conceal were powerful enough to stimulate the search for an antidote, a fact underlined by James Stringer, a top journalist with *The Sunday Spectator*, in his evidence to the Committee.

Paul Cherston, MP (Labour) questioning.

CHERSTON: Mr Stringer, you are one half of a two-man team of investigative reporters known in Fleet Street as The Archaeologists?

STRINGER: Mike Hendricks is my partner, yes.

CHERSTON: What was—when were you given the assignment to look at this thing in depth?

STRINGER: It grew out of our involvement in a story concerning the Animal Rights Movement—

CHERSTON: This was just prior to Wentworth Magna?

STRINGER: Yes—there'd been a big scare about contaminated supermarket products.

CHERSTON: Your paper published the first brief item on these mice I believe.

STRINGER: We knew about that naturally, but I don't think anyone saw a possible connection till Hopkins' story broke.

CHERSTON: You were bound to examine that possibility?

STRINGER: Our contacts in ARM had already hinted at sensational developments in their campaign. We assumed this had to be one of them.

CHERSTON: Did you suggest they might be able to throw light on these events?

STRINGER: Almost in those words, yes.

CHERSTON: And their response?

STRINGER: Gleeful I should say, full of biblical quotes 'As ye sow' sort of thing. Just to make sure I understood, their spokesman explained that chickens have a way of coming home to roost.

CHERSTON: What did you infer from that?

STRINGER: Not only that they had nothing to do with the outbreak—they hardly knew what I was talking about. And they're not known for sitting on publicity.

CHERSTON: So you had to look elsewhere?

STRINGER: We went to Hopkins as the only source we had.

CHERSTON: Could that be helpful?

STRINGER: There was a slim chance he'd left out a vital piece of information.

CHERSTON: And had he?

STRINGER: Only that a huge pharmaceutical research and production complex existed almost on Wentworth Magna's doorstep.

CHERSTON: Did you draw conclusions from that?

STRINGER: On two points yes. First, we were investigating in a prohibited area; secondly, we had to keep an eye on possible libel action.

CHERSTON: By 'prohibited area' you mean the directive to the media limiting discussion—?

STRINGER: Yes.

CHERSTON: By which you were undeterred?

STRINGER: Not deterred—it simply lacked relevance. We were being muzzled in the interests of national security. This had to do with the public well-being, public safety if you will.

CHERSTON: Most of the press complied with the directive.

STRINGER: If you mean why didn't we—our editor isn't in anybody's pocket—certainly not the proprietor's. In fact, we had his blessing.

CHERSTON: Anyone else's?

STRINGER: We saw a lot of closed doors at that time. Government departments as well as Price-Pearson's.

CHERSTON: Did you know the company was subject to the Official Secrets Act?

STRINGER: Most of them are for one reason or another.

CHERSTON: I believe your names were excluded from the list of authorized pressmen allowed in to the affected area.

STRINGER: That's right—they knew we were digging into the present, not reporting for posterity.

CHERSTON: You went all the same?

STRINGER: Yes.

CHERSTON: And on the basis of what you saw, you wrote the first of a series of articles.

STRINGER: We learned enough to convince us this was potentially bigger than Thalidomide. We wrote the article in that context.

CHERSTON: 'Potentially bigger than Thalidomide.' Do you mean you had precise knowledge of Price-Pearson's research programme?

STRINGER: I mean that our informed ignorance justified the conclusion. If the press is hamstrung, the public deliberately excluded from all knowledge of the facts, if a government takes the veil of silence, and a multinational turns coy about its extramural activities then it doesn't take a genius to figure out stakes high enough to warrant a smother-up.

CHERSTON: Did the name Doctor Quentin Quarrier come to your notice at that time?

STRINGER: . . . Yes.

CHERSTON: How, Mr Stringer?

STRINGER: We received an anonymous phone call advising us to 'look into Doctor Quarrier's activities—re Wentworth Magna'. That was all.

CHERSTON: We may have further questions on that later. By the way your articles were never published I believe?

STRINGER: Yes and no. The editor arranged syndication in the world press—and simply quoted them at great length.

(Laughter)

Chapter 15

WHAT DID STRINGER'S testimony amount to more than this? I live and work in a fundamentally sick society under the insupportable yoke of a government sick to the limits of paranoia. Not Quarrier, not Price-Pearson, but Britain, is on the verge of a shattering, *world-beating* scientific breakthrough. But, something had gone wrong.

'I am sick and tired of those who seek to destroy our confidence in ourselves by publishing the facts. The public must be protected from the truth. There is *no* alternative.'

Thus the voice of death across the great Cabinet table.

Helen, returning along the Alton road, witnessed all unconsciously the end-result of a criminal absurdity, for the 'secret' manifested itself like an open sewer along much of her route.

Cars everywhere, cars parked in every available space, while happy holiday families disported themselves in the bright August sunshine, busily hunting the elusive snark.

She discovered later that sightings *were* being broadcast by local radio stations, so it had become the instant fun thing to go searching for that rare product of an engendered species, the mutant mouse.

The search would lead further afield as the days passed . . . and it would diminish to zero as they found yet another child dead of a hundred bites . . . or an adult was rushed to hospital in a badly mauled condition.

Not comprehending she weaved her way through this *fête macabre*, thankful to reach home and cool down a little before phoning Mother with a valid-sounding excuse for her non-appearance.

'Your father will be disappointed. He's just returned from the links. He swears he saw one of those rodents on the fourteenth.'

'Tell him he couldn't have. The fourteenth was some time last week.'

'The hole, dear, the *hole*! Just before the green. Really, Helen, you seem to live in a world of your own. Perhaps you'll come out of it when you see my thirty-six piece compatible saucepan set. It arrived today—only £39.70 and £18.35 p. and p. It's too vexing. I was so looking forward to showing you. But then I suppose you'd agree with your father. We've got saucepans he says. There's simply no understanding male logic.'

'But it's true, Mother. You *have* got saucepans,' and what the hell do saucepans have to do with things that go bump in the night and devour people, not fifteen miles from the packing-case world *you* live in cheek by jowl with three dozen extra pots and pans?

She ended on a lighter note. 'And I'm not a male.'

'I know, dear.' Crisply. 'Four miscarriages do tend to bear out the fact.'

She replaced the receiver gently before the Terror of the Fourth noted for its blunt, retractable tongue could stammer an apology. Knew why she infinitely preferred her father who never used cruelty to wound. Knew from bitter experience—the bleeding to death by inches . . .

Badly reminded of a barren world in which a pampered consumer society had little left to consume but itself, Helen turned from the hateful instrument lately dispensing motherly love, eyes closed in search of undemanding nothingness. Strove not to use her mind, but failed to repel sundry images: Quentin and roses, again and again—flowers for consolation, nothing to show for suffering gladly borne. An ergate, an unproductive female ant, a Degas dancer on the wall of a hospital room, sick dreams of coffin-shaped cradles, her father delighting a ten-year-old so long ago, dancing with an amiable butterfly they'd called Fenella Fritillary; at which she could still smile when the ache *in vacuo* grew intolerable.

Thus, one of those maenadic moments not Quentin, not her father, certainly not her saucepanized mother, not anyone, had inklings of—the frantic evasions against insane projections of what might have been, if only four foetal redundancies had struggled whole-heartedly to belong to a bit of the world she shared with Quentin.

She would succumb at last, in secret, sit for an hour or more, playing a dumb-dirge pantomime of feeding, changing, dandling—even reading aloud to a nothing. Nothing but what had once been flesh and blood, galvanized at such intervals into meaning by that kiss of life some call 'imagination'.

The fit would pass.

As now, when there was supper to prepare, broken gates to think of, a chemical formula to memorize. To the ritual of peeling potatoes she debated how much, or even whether, she should tell Q of her fact-finding mission.

Some of the point being in today's isolated pockets of resistance, assuming sentience and a fine-tuned intelligence, there lingers beyond the farce of routine and chore—the changing of light bulbs, defrosting the fridge, feeding the cat and so on—a deep and continuing debate on what, basically, is the meaning of life.

For Helen, Quentin had provided much of that meaning until . . .

She paused from slicing tomatoes for the salad and gazed out at window to join in the vista of beeches and rhododendrons and some of the hedge enclosing the maze, a view she never tired of . . . until . . . and she not entirely aware that a word had brought her, knife poised, into more than ordinary contemplation of a carefully tended idyll.

Certainly, it had to do with life; not hers, not Quentin's; but the principle, the *post hoc, ergo propter hoc* which closed the circle to all argument: without life, you wouldn't be here to discuss the pettiness of destinies—yours and his, for example.

And if it had a transcendental value . . . could anyone escape whipping for tampering and juggling with genes and chromosomes, prestidigitating a travesty on four legs and with distinctly humanoid features? Could Quentin?

'My husband,' she said aloud, 'is a genetic engineer.' Listened intently for the note of accusation.

To shed tears inwardly is proof of true sensibility. Helen wept, not for herself, or even for Quentin, but for a world so ordered that, at the end of any and every day, life must come to some such pass.

It was no less poignant that, unknown to anyone, she'd contrived to prefer existence with her ghostly brood. With dream children there could be no suffering, flesh of their flesh.

★

After a desultory meal they tried that evening's Prom, agreed it wasn't worth the effort. Contemporary music. A Messiaenic mess. 'Tomorrow's composers have a language problem,' said Quarrier. 'Which, in particular?' she wondered. The language of music, apparently. So they lynched Albert Hall when he wasn't looking.

The heat enervated; even to turn the page of a book invited a bout of perspiration. But, importantly, they could talk.

'You hardly ate a thing.'

'I wonder how Mrs Cavewoman got that over to hubby after he'd spent a lousy day hunting Diplodocus.'

'Was your day prehistoric?'

He told her of an hour spent with Dysart, of his better understanding re Mrs Chandrasakar.

'So she has no part in it.'

'In what?' Irritably. 'There's no conspiracy, nothing to cover up.'

'But there *is* a mystery,' she insisted.

'According to Dysart I'm the mystery, and he's out to solve me.'

'Because of the past?'

'It's convenient for their purpose.'

She sensed he was hobbling with a cleft stick along the same wrong path. 'It's too vague—too emotive—and it explains nothing.' She meant the distant, as against the present past.

'I can see their pathological point. There's an inferential gap in the data storage system—information is missing—what have I done with it—and why?'

'Go on.'

'It's complex. He claims the later procedures are on file with reference back to Day 1. If we three agreed to exclude a significant experiment on Day 1 how does it turn up on Day 42 with a negative result?'

'Was anything of the slightest reference on record for Day 1—or even prior to it?'

'Some preparatory stuff naturally.'

'Coded for the series?'

'. . . There'd be an identifying number—yes.'

'Then what more do they need?' sounded better than how could you be so stupid?

He nodded gloomily, almost winced at the bluntness *and* the point. 'All we saw was a potentially fascinating idea going haywire.'

To be followed through at all costs. She wanted to shake him out of obsession with a secondary consideration going nowhere near the heart of the mystery. At least, not yet.

Time to talk of uppermost things, to give some record of her afternoon's odyssey. Which was done—to his obvious astonishment. She blundered to some kind of conclusion badly aware of an error in timing, or presentation, of having spoken at all.

'Why on earth—'

Almost angrily she cut across his feeble reaction.

'I want it to be crystal clear to the whole world my husband is *not* a mad scientist or a complicated idiot who can't keep his mice under control—that's why on earth.'

He apologized, chastened enough to recognize a helping hand at work. Left time enough and silence for ruffled feathers to settle.

'It's just that I'm not surprised your policeman couldn't see the drift—I mean, gates and things.'

She tried to explain. 'My feeling about that gate and his theory based on what he thought he knew had happened, don't add up to four—three at the most. He was sure and I wasn't. But when I left the station I felt I was sure and *he* wasn't. It still made three, so neither of us has a satisfactory answer.'

Quarrier very nearly groaned and said he sympathized with Whitfield. Heartily.

'It *is* difficult. But we owe it to Rem—and Linda—to prove he had more character than the inquest verdict gave him credit for.'

'The idea of an inhuman scientist breaking down ought to be reassuring.' Bitterness was in it somewhere.

'Inhuman or not, a man hell bent on destruction drives faster than twenty.'

'. . . That's true.' Through her mind's eye he caught a glimpse of shapeless apprehension looming into an unidentifiable form of—someone. 'You seem,' hesitantly, 'to be pointing in the direction of a third party . . .'

Finger and thumb, industrious as piece-workers for an Ariadne scheming against time and the Minotaur.

'A *locus delicti*.' Sybilline words.

He smiled at a catchphrase geneticists might use to describe a misplaced gene in a chromosome, but encouraged her to go on, amused and attracted by the total pose of one sifting as it seemed, the ruins of an exploded career. That it *had* blown up in his face Quarrier no longer doubted.

'The computer . . . aren't there as many suspects as those with access?'

'A dozen might have expertise enough to know what to look for—but why should they bother?'

'You'd vouch for them all?'

'Helen, I've worked with most for a long time. Long enough not to have unhealthy doubts.'

As if doubts could be unhealthy! Well, what was sanitary about ignorant certainty? Or grey conviction setting hard as wet cement? But let that pass.

'So it comes down to the formula—does that suggest anything to you?'

'$C_2H_4CL_2$? Ethylene dichloride—what they call Dutch liquid. It's quite meaningless. That was agreed at the inquest.'

'How agreed?'

'Poor old Rem was rambling—it's as simple as that.'

'Or as difficult as trying desperately to convey information?'

A blank regard, before he countered—cautiously: 'Such as?'

'Suppose they misheard. Suppose he was finally struggling to say eight not H, T not two?'

'Giving $C_{284}CLT$. That's *totally* meaningless.'

'Is it?'

'My dear Helen—'

'Why must it be a formula? why not a C registration car licence number—for example?'

Quarrier's smile, a bit superior at the edges, faded.

SIGHTING

It moved swiftly from the front of the semi-detached house to the rear, passing the garage by way of a narrow side alley; stopped to snuffle the air, raised a hand to rub the rheumy matter from its eyes before dashing at the clump of delphiniums visible in the swathe of light from a street lamp almost outside the house. The night breeze was just strong enough to set them swaying. It startled the interloper into a fierce and mindless attack ending in a scatter of floral débris.

Satisfied no danger remained in that quarter it scurried on to the small neat lawn, darting glances all around, searching for enemies, for sustenance, for a reason to live and to kill.

The animal's attention seemed drawn to the pale gleam of windows on the upper floors. There was a hint of indescribable deliberation in the way of turning its head slowly, not viewing so much as studying them, some on one side of the wicker party fence, others beyond it.

The breeze strengthened briefly and the creature's yelp as something flicked the back of its head had a curse-like quality. With breathtaking speed it turned and leapt, rending everything hanging from the circular clothes' drier before scampering about on its hind legs trying to free itself from a torn sheet. It stopped, seemed to examine the problem, then, with the greatest care, detached itself from the entangling strip.

A sudden jerk of the head brought it to the alert; eyes, round and strikingly intelligent, concentrated on the luminous darkness from which some alien thing crept stealthily forward; cautiously it approached, then froze, its back arched, tail upright and quivering. Too late, the newcomer with the instinct of its kind growled defiance at what it could neither fathom nor overcome, then turned and fled . . . too late.

Householders turned in their beds, registered the squeals and screams, sleepily identified a cat-fight before drifting back to where they'd come from. One or two people did, in fact, venture out of bed, startled by the persistence, the terrible severity of that caterwauling.

They saw nothing and were glad of the silence when it came at last.

Mrs Jardine was one who left her bed. She had a particular interest and some misgivings that Pilate was up to his tricks again.

Pilate, the cat, was a relic of happier days when Jim had brought him home in his pocket for young Michael. A kitten with a lovable knack of making people's lives difficult, he'd grown into a pugnacious two-year-old ready to dash at anything on four legs—or two at a pinch—so it be covered with feathers.

Pilate? Because he behaved so biblically badly. Like the original he would distance himself from every outrage of his devising and calmly wash his paws with maddening unconcern, for the dish swept off the table, the mouse dropped into one of Jim's carpet slippers.

Not three months ago Jim had died leaving her young Michael, a mortgage—and the cat. Almost, but not quite, she'd got used to loneliness at night. Michael, a healthy youngster coming up to school age, would sleep soundly through the brawling she knew, so that sometimes, as now, she felt as if no one else was wakeful, or even alive in the whole wide world.

She slipped motherly into his room, reassured herself he'd not been disturbed and returned, glancing at the luminous figures on the radio alarm: 01.49. Bent to her bed and paused as in the act of afterthought. Half-minded to go downstairs and make tea she straightened up slowly and forgot all else as she listened to what had been a total silence.

From outside and below came distinct snatches of rustling. Almost covering the north wall was a long established Virginian creeper that had come, to Jim's delight, 'with the house'. It reached to, and beyond, the window level and she kept a fond memory of his carefully clipping the stray runners neatly to the oblong frame.

But the rustle of its leaves puzzled her. The night breeze had died down or was not enough to stir them that much. The open window gave an inch or two gap top and bottom, and she hesitated to open it wider and look out, fearing the squeaky sash would wake young Michael at last.

With the vaguest sense of unease she returned to bed convinced that Pilate had never tried to climb the creeper at any time in his short life. She'd surely remember if he had . . .

Sleep never came easily after waking for whatever reason. She lay listening, in spite of herself; eyes closed in a semblance of repose opened abruptly with a conviction that the rustling had grown louder and therefore nearer. In the otherwise silence the sound had the quality of life—in motion.

She smiled at her fears. It had to be Pilate, up to a new trick. That creeper wasn't strong enough to support anything bigger.

Quite at ease with an obvious explanation she was about to throw off the duvet and cross to the window on her right when she heard another, more chilling sound.

The window was being stealthily, unmistakably opened, its sash squeaking eerily louder than the thumping of her heart. Surprise, more than fear reduced her to immobility, as if her whole body shared astonishment. Because she knew it had to be an impossibility —the creeper could never support the weight of . . . therefore, the cat.

She called softly on a giveaway note of enquiry, still concerned not to wake Michael.

'Pilate?'

The window grew silent as it seemed to an imagination now wide awake but blindly groping in the darkness. Yet, in another moment it screered again, so that her body was forced to respond at last. Wide-eyed she sat up, listening, listening, conscious of the cool night air flowing in unchecked, conscious of a light thud as of some—thing landing on the carpeted floor—conscious of a snuffling . . . close at hand.

Frowning, too bothered by disbelief to be fearful, she thrust out a hand and switched on the bedside light . . . and there, staring intently into her eyes, not three feet distant . . . such as she'd never . . .

The neighbours heard those catastatic screams; as they told later, screams so unnerving you couldn't ignore them, turn over and go back to sleep. You just couldn't.

Several men, still in night-clothes, rushed to the house while their womenfolk dialled 999. The second shock was to find all doors locked and every window on the ground floor securely fastened. By the time the police arrived, a ladder had been found and placed to reach the lighted back window from which . . .

None of those present in that day's smallest hours would forget what happened next. As the screams diminished and died one of the men clutched a patrolman's arm. 'Look! Look!' a whispered cry of incontinent terror.

A needless command. All eyes were locked on to that luminous oblong framed by the creeper, every one of a dozen men saw head and shoulders appear in silhouette, saw malignancy in the light of torches, saw, as they heard the cries of a child sobbing for mummy, saw, two small hands grasp the topmost shafts of the ladder and twist it till it crashed back to the ground below—and one police officer had already started to climb.

'It's gotta be a dog—' but they knew fine it could be no such thing.

The monstrous ambiguity vanished and, before they could replace the ladder, an incongruous blare of pop music flung itself against the window as if—as if a radio had been switched on, as if, to enliven a scene of grotesque and unimaginable horror the thing had decided on a little night music.

The volume increased till it could be heard all over the neighbourhood.

'Do you recollect what happened then, Mr Edwards?'

Some weeks later, Doctor John Truelove, Conservative MP for a Devon constituency, and a member of the All-Party Committee of Enquiry, gently takes the witness through each remembered moment of that night's horror.

The Committee, overwhelmed by a mountain of accumulating evidence had determined that the fate of Mrs Jardine and her son—the worst of the earlier incidents—should go on record as a pattern of events still proliferating, till the whole country south of a line from Severn to the Wash could match their fate with accounts no less grisly.

At this juncture, excepting the Wentworth massacre and army casualties, 674 men, women and children were listed as victims of the mutants . . . another 1,301 had received treatment for varying degrees of injury.

EDWARDS: You mean after the animal turned on the transistor?
TRUELOVE: Well, that raises another point. Did you agree among yourselves this creature *had* switched on the radio?
EDWARDS: No. I have to say I'm relying on later police evidence. If we thought about it at all, we assumed either Mrs Jardine had accidentally knocked it on during a struggle or young Michael had somehow done so. Mainly, we were dumbstruck—I mean, a sudden blast of pop music in those circumstances . . .
TRUELOVE: There seems to be enough evidence to show these things have a great liking for pop music. Can you recall your reaction to the ladder incident?
EDWARDS: I just went cold—couldn't stop trembling. It was the same with the others. You had to see that evil face lit up by torches

from below—half-human—half-else—like one of those gargoyles on Notre Dame as someone said.

TRUELOVE: The humanoid features were striking?

EDWARDS: They—got through to you—gradually—as if you'd racked your brains to remember something you'd known all your life.

TRUELOVE: Did it not occur, as a general conclusion I mean—this creature must have a connection with those reported by the media?

EDWARDS: I don't think we had time to think about it—although the ambulance people said it wasn't the first case they'd dealt with. The situation was—it was too immediate.

TRUELOVE: I understand. What happened next?

EDWARDS: We heard these cries—not very loud because of the music blaring. George Burrows, our neighbour, shouted 'That's young Michael!'. We didn't hang about then—some of us went to the front of the house. I stayed with the rest at the back. We broke down the conservatory door no problem. The back door wasn't so easy. But the others got in at the front and somebody opened the kitchen door from the inside. We all just fell up the stairs.

TRUELOVE: Yes, Mr Edwards?

EDWARDS: It's—hard to tell of something you never ever want to see again. In the back bedroom—a cor—Mrs Jardine's body—torn apart, blood everywhere—nothing we could do—we ran in a kind of panic—you've got to remember—there was this unholy din—it seemed to fit the picture—we just ran to join the others who'd got there first.

TRUELOVE: Take your time.

EDWARDS: . . . even the police officers didn't go further than the doorway—there was no need . . . the youngster was on the floor —his throat torn out . . . and at the open window the—animal, not at bay, but grinning—triumph you might say—we could see the bloodstained jaws, pink saliva and those fangs—because it was grinning you see.

TRUELOVE: And then?

EDWARDS: . . . Then? I'll never forget it. Never. One chap keeled over in a dead faint—someone else vomited, not so much because of the poor kid, but y'see this bastard thing jumped on to the window ledge, burrowed through the gap to the sill and then . . . and then . . .

TRUELOVE: Yes, Mr Edwards?

EDWARDS: From the outside . . . *it shut the window*. You understand what I'm trying to tell you? It shut the window . . . it actually shut the window . . . I mean, it *shut* the . . .

And disappeared into the night, leaving remnants of former selves alone with two human corpses, a partially dismembered cat and those subcultural shrieks tearing the night to shreds.

Chapter 16

THE HOME SECRETARY, the Right Honourable Vernon Little, Conservative MP for Feltenham, questioned by Gerald Askew, MP for Airdley S. (Cons.). Same day.

ASKEW: Mr Little, you were present during Mr Edwards' testimony?
LITTLE: I was, yes.
ASKEW: Harrowing would you agree?
LITTLE: It couldn't have been a joyous experience.
ASKEW: I hope to show it has relevance to your part in what followed ... first, I understand you were to be informed of all developments and incidents arising from the spill-over of these mutants.
LITTLE: Certainly. It was a domestic matter within my cognizance.
ASKEW: Presumptively.
LITTLE: If I may correct you—positively.
ASKEW: I was thinking of shared responsibility—the role played by the Ministry of Defence.
LITTLE: There *was* an overlap of function, but essentially their job was to clear up the physical mess—Wentworth Magna and so on. My concern was to contain the psychological damage occasioned by this unfortunate business.
ASKEW: Unfortunate ... so it was agreed at the highest level to limit the 'psychological damage' by placing an embargo on all reporting of incidents—?
LITTLE: As far as possible, yes.
ASKEW: With hindsight would you maintain that was the best and only option available to government?
LITTLE: All the reports we were receiving—there was no way we could let the situation become a media fest.

ASKEW: So the media were threatened in entirety with proceedings under your reserve powers?

LITTLE: Not threatened, strongly advised. There was no question of censorship.

ASKEW: The Committee notes your denial of a non-existent accusation.

LITTLE: Your suggestion of a threat implies an accusation.

ASKEW: I think that was Mr Hardcastle's, Gerald Hopkins' and Mr Stringer's reading of official letters and unofficial summonses.

LITTLE: At all times it was emphasized we were not denying publication—only delaying it.

ASKEW: Yet you used journalists 'on the side' to report the containing operation at Wentworth?

LITTLE: On the understanding I've outlined.

ASKEW: Men you could trust to keep a secret?

LITTLE: That smacks of innuendo—if I may add—the whole situation related to national security—that's why the MOD had—

ASKEW: I shall come to that, Mr Little. You see, we're all exercised in our minds as to—I mean, it's a paradox isn't it that you should think a crisis of this magnitude was of such overriding public importance, all accounts of it should be withheld from the very public it threatened—a threat of a particularly horrible and lethal nature?

LITTLE: The confusion is in your court. I've tried to make it clear, we had to pay due regard to the needs of national security.

ASKEW: Perhaps we're both afflicted with misunderstanding. Are you saying, a collective decision was arrived at which, in effect, put public safety and well-being below the need to blanket a disastrous situation in the interests of an hypothesis?

LITTLE: There is *nothing* hypothetical about national security!

ASKEW: You astonish me. I thought billions of public money was spent on nothing more than the word 'If'.

LITTLE: That's a digression if I may say so.

ASKEW: Not quite. Defence capability depends on the suppositious *if* the Russians attack and so forth.

LITTLE: Matters outside my department and irrelevant to this enquiry.

ASKEW: Really? Are you saying that in a time of great national emergency—apart from CND—your department has nothing to do with containing alarm and despondency?

LITTLE: Of course it has. You're making my point. A government would be failing in its duty if it refused to take account of fall-out effects on national morale.

ASKEW: Right and proper . . . but is there not a stage at which the doctrine becomes ludicrous, dangerously self-defeating?

LITTLE: I wouldn't have thought so.

ASKEW: No . . . you see, I have a parallel in mind which makes *my* point in the light of your observations—national security—the operation of the OSA and so forth.

Now, it's common knowledge, *only now*, that the depredations of these creatures have resulted in several hundred deaths over a wide area of the South of England—admittedly a small part of the total UK landmass . . . are you, as the spokesman of this Administration, asserting that none of what has and is happening has relevance to the unaffected populace?

LITTLE: Not at all. We were concerned to protect the remainder population in psychological terms—that is what we attempted to do.

ASKEW: Psychological . . . I see. Then I may confidently revert to my parallel example. Let's say—hypothetically—a hydrogen bomb devastates the self-same area presently infested with these things. Would you in the aftermath, invoke 'national security' etc., to deter what remained of the media from reporting the misery, the squalor, the casualties, the obliteration, to the rest of the UK . . . for fear of spreading alarm and despondency?

LITTLE: . . . I'm sorry—is that relevant?

ASKEW: Yes. I am asking if it is policy or personal preference, given a totally disastrous situation, to protect 'psychologically', to destroy understanding, to immunize by calculated use of ignorance, against the effects of a catastrophe you are powerless to prevent physically?

LITTLE: I must appeal to the Chairman as to relevance.

CHAIRMAN: I think you should answer the question. The Honourable member is making the point which seems to us to be at the very heart of this matter.

Is it agreed government policy to stifle all comment and

factual reporting when the magnitude of a disaster makes it obvious to a degree that concealment for whatever reason, becomes odious, if not insulting to what remains of the national comprehension?

LITTLE: I have no authority to discuss official thinking on matters outside this Committee's terms of reference.

ASKEW: I think the Committee and the country will draw the appropriate conclusions from your reaction.

LITTLE: My reply.

ASKEW: Your reaction taken as a reply. On whose absolute authority were directives issued to the media?

LITTLE: The PM's guide lines followed a lengthy Cabinet discussion.

ASKEW: Defied in a small number of cases.

LITTLE: Trouble-makers exist in any profession.

ASKEW: Why were not these 'trouble-makers' prosecuted?

LITTLE: They were called to Downing Street and severely reprimanded.

ASKEW: For breaching the OSA, divulging facts or for telling the truth?

LITTLE: For publicizing facts which were best left unreported!

ASKEW: No recourse to law? No prosecution? Are you saying one person took upon itself the right to—

LITTLE: No I'm not! I've said it was a collective decision.

ASKEW: Then surely you, as Home Secretary, had a duty to discipline these 'trouble-makers'?

LITTLE: In that sense I—no, I'm not in charge of national security in that sense.

ASKEW: I see ... does your reply explain the PM's refusal to allow a debate on the matter?

LITTLE: The Prime Minister made it perfectly clear a debate would not be appropriate at that time.

ASKEW: I must now put it to you that the national interest is a pretext to cover HMG's involvement in a discreditable venture and so reduces its high-minded sentiments to the level of a blatant duplicity perpetrated on the public at large.

LITTLE: Quite unmerited.

ASKEW: You mean the public was aware of your dealings with Price-Pearson?

LITTLE: I—know of it by repute.

ASKEW: The Committee will note your reply. You know Lord Betherton, also by repute?

LITTLE: . . . Yes. He's the Prime Minister's scientific adviser.

ASKEW: We're only too well aware . . . does the name Dysart have any meaning for you?

LITTLE: I have—heard of it.

ASKEW: I'm glad you have, since he purported to act on your behalf.

LITTLE: Many people do—I can't be expected to know them all.

ASKEW: But you do accept responsibility for errors committed by those acting under your authority?

LITTLE: I've said as much as I care to at this stage.

ASKEW: One last question. Bearing in mind Mr Edwards' harrowing evidence. Do you suppose, having regard to the literature sanctioned by your Department—how to take sensible precautions in the event of nuclear war, a coat of whitewash on the windows and so on—would not a public warning through the media, severely pressured into silence, have saved the lives of that unfortunate woman and her son?

LITTLE: That is an unwarrantable—!

ASKEW: You mean, it was beyond your wit, with all the sophisticated technological marvels of communication at your command—publicly to advise Mrs Jardine and other potential victims to keep their windows closed from dusk to dawn!

The night passed. Not just the staying down of the sun, but much else may augment the darkness: dream fears, death rehearsals, the universal wish for oblivion, all conspire to enrich the blackness.

She'd slept uneasily, as if aware that, in and out of her ken deformities were prowling, mannikins on four legs, snuffling, squeaking self-important syndromes of the Great Dilemma, everlastingly moving in for the kill or out for what they could get, mouse eat mouse and anything in its path . . . evil countenances graven in the image of Man. God's own mutant.

And when the last incubus retreated before the dawn it surely paused to turn its head and gaze with a changeling's malice, pointing a tiny finger at its adversary, a mirrored image seen in a distorting glass.

'We are you,' in a Disney falsetto. It vanished almost as she opened her eyes.

Real enough the perspiration cooling on her forehead, a sure sign that prodigious energy goes to repelling grotesqueries invading the never-sleeping mind.

Easing herself out of bed as not to wake him she was struck by an unfamiliar aspect, a disquieting feature—clear enough in the dawn light.

Not the low whimper and a moment's restlessness, as if her dream clones had transferred to torment him in turn, but the intense corrugation of his brow—Quentin—of all people, always so smooth and ungraven by experience. Now, hints of ruggedness, of things come home to roost. It seemed as if Life, at last, had decided to knock him about a bit.

She parodied her relentless *cri de coeur* of yesterday, palliating her bitterness to whisper softly: This geneticist is my husband.

A shower restored and refreshed. By the time Quentin appeared there were few traces of the night's incursions marring Helen's perfection.

'Such beauty,' even from the depths of obvious preoccupation he could still dredge up an habitual early morning compliment. 'Britain's ailing shipbuilding industry would welcome you.'

'Why?' as if she didn't see the point of his pleasantries a mile away.

'The thousand ships. No cornflakes. Just coffee.'

She grimaced horribly to spoil the allusion. 'Was *this* the face—? Just coffee.'

But through her smile Helen caught another glimpse of the palimpsest image that had jeered not so long ago: *We* are *you*.

After he'd gone she listened to the hourly news bulletins, puzzled and, eventually, disturbed by the simple fact that nothing was being reported, not even on the local station. The problem couldn't have gone away overnight . . . why the sudden black-out?

Nothing in the papers.

They took *The Daily Sublime* and *The Frankly Ridiculous*—Quentin's soubriquets for *The Guardian* and *A.N. Other* which he sometimes scanned after spraying it with a Jeyes aerosol. But, as he said, one had to know how one half reacted to the fact that the other half existed.

Nothing in either paper.

And how many more must be wondering how an event, monstrous and momentous, could die so tidily with not a single malediction, even allowing for the whimper of Hardcastle's yesterday morning giveaway?

Of course, the ghosts of Mrs Jardine and her only begotten were too warm, too inexperienced, to haunt public consciousness with below zero signs and portents.

But, between more thoughtful intervals, beguiled by the sheer friendliness of a late August day, she mowed the lawn, touched a favourite beech for luck, composed flowers for the house, boiled mid-morning coffee—and drank two glasses of water instead . . . walked in the maze, contemplative as a grey novice in green cloisters, but eyes raised yearningly to the benevolent blue. Took the twists and turns without hesitation, as if advancing to meet the Minotaur by appointment, today's version, six of man, half a dozen of the other—finger and thumb teasing out a thread of rebellious filaments . . .

At its very centre—a tiny roundel of green—she found in the stillness a response to no question asked or much thought on. It came in the form of a one-word prescription favoured by old metaphysicians. Acquiesce: wait on what is to come, the better to understand what has been.

It surely meant that her rare collection of irrelevancies: smashed gates, broken cars, paint flakes, numbers or formulae, would earn their keep in time because they were *there*, were tangible assets for the future.

So, patience Penelope, or Ariadne, or whoever you are. Time is the breath of life, a neglected element you breathe without which—nothing. To take in the air is to take in time: exhale the past, inhale the future, let it sustain till gates, cars and the man you love coalesce into an intelligible whole.

Thus, Helen to Helen. But if the gods heard her plea for enlightenment at about twenty past two that afternoon, it may be they condescended to fire a useful bolt from the blue only moments later.

As in a silent comedy film clip, the heroine walks safely out of the labyrinth straight into the arms of a diminutive minotaur wandering about in search of the entrance.

She stopped abruptly at sight of a not very forbidding interloper who could manage with a little ingenuity to reach her shoulder.

His beautifully stitched Chelsea grey suit—the sharp kind favoured by airline ad models—hung on him with casual grace. She looked hard for another prepossessing feature and gave up.

The stranger took her laboured regard for alarm.

'So sorry, Mrs Quarrier. I tried the front door several times—it's open you know. So I came round.'

Unconcerned to the point of slight she walked past him towards the garden seat. 'That's quite all right, Mr Dysart.'

His smile faded. 'How do you—?'

'You fit my husband's description.'

Game, set and almost the match. He tried to salvage something.

'He's never stooped to flattery in my hearing. You'll grant me an audience I hope?'

She indicated the swing seat but moved the old kitchen chair a foot further off before sitting.

'I'm prepared to listen, Mr Dysart, but nothing more. If that's acceptable you're welcome to take a sitting position.'

He did so. 'Sounds a very fair offer. I may smoke?'

She nodded, watching him narrowly as he lit a cigarette, not breaking the silence until he began to speak.

'You have some sort of identification I suppose?'

Thanks to her impeccable sense of timing he was disconcerted enough to flush, but he produced his plasticated bit of flimsy which she read carefully and, after an insulting examination of the 'mug shot' she returned it finger and thumb.

'How very elaborate,' she murmured.

He returned the ID with its grandiose signature to an inner pocket but kept a faintly puzzled eye on a woman who simply hadn't got it in her to be impressed by vain pomp and trivial circumstance, but he, poor fellow, couldn't know that.

'Your husband will have warned you he's under a cloud, no doubt?'

She nodded. Once.

'It's not much bigger than this at the moment,' extending the palm of his hand. He waited for the reaction that simply didn't materialize.

'Mice,' he continued. 'It's not a pleasant subject on such a day as this,' he flourished his cigarette at the sun-speckled garden. 'But no choice, I'm afraid. It's an escalating situation, an extremely serious one—or perhaps you're not fully aware?'

'The point, Mr Dysart.'

'How to retrieve an almost irretrievable situation—I mean the one in which your husband finds himself very nearly up to his neck.'

She glanced at the maze for no apparent reason and rough-sketched a Gioconda smile.

'I'm a bit confused: are you looking for whatever escaped from Pandora's box, or the one who opened it?'

The mouth compressed to a line, implicit and unpleasant with meaning.

'Clever and classical and deliberately missing the point, I think.'

'Which I'm still waiting to hear.'

'. . . I have a tremendous admiration for Doctor Quarrier's work—as far as I understand it—so do those I represent. It shouldn't surprise you to know we're anxious to get him off a very nasty hook. Obviously, if I approach you, I must be looking for co-operation from someone who also has his interests at heart.'

'Yes?' A moronic reply to all that, and an idiotic smile for good measure. He was bound to shift uneasily.

'Important evidence of a significant experiment is missing. The subjects of that experiment disappear only to reappear in a fluctuant and horrifying form. Your husband, against all the odds, very nearly pleads ignorance.'

'What odds?'

'The night he was hauled out of bed and summoned to the Complex by his agitated colleague. You must know about that.'

'I don't see how I could help if I do. You have to show how they disappeared. Surely a few questions to the orderlies who look after these things—'

'They *have* been questioned. They know nothing about that batch from the X700 series and what's more eloquent, they don't recall Doctor Quarrier or anyone else rushing around tearing out their hair demanding to know what happened to their mice.'

'Very likely. None of them has Latin blood I'm glad to say.'

'Mrs Quarrier—'

'Have you tried the Animal Rights people? They release all sorts of things with the greatest élan I believe.'

'. . . it's highly unlikely.'

'Then you can only be suggesting that three grown men, highly respected in their disciplines, for reasons best known to themselves, abstracted specimens from the Complex and having doctored them or something, deliberately released them at some future date?'

'It's valid.'

'Then why not have them arrested? Criminal negligence, manslaughter, sedition, misprision of mice—you could have a lovely time.'

'I need a better opportunity to admire your sense of the ridiculous. Publicity is the last thing we're looking for. And we can't decide how to handle this until we establish motives or what you call "reasons best known to themselves".'

'And so you come to me.'

'To everyone who can throw light on the mystery.'

She regarded him curiously, much as an antique dealer might study a clever reproduction.

'Go on, Mr Dysart.'

'We've established that your husband had a prior ideological commitment in his student days, that it probably extended into the postgraduate days. We need to know whether or not there was a cut-off point.'

'Why not ask him?'

'He avoids the question.'

'It really is time you made yourself clear.'

'More than I have?' He paused to choose words sober enough to withstand her power to ridicule. 'It wouldn't be the first time a man makes a brilliant discovery and decides to share it outright with the enemy.'

She thought mock-conscientiously about this, but her faint smile persisted and, she was glad to see, disconcerted.

'It's a beautifully contrived theory, Mr Dysart, only it leaves out of account one thing . . . why on earth should *two* ideological deviants free their little mutants and then allow themselves to be pursued in someone else's car?'

Noted with interest, the change in his carefully manicured expression; the more or less blue eyes grew child-like, gaping at wonders, glazed with utter dumbfoundery and the merest hint of dominance down the drain.

She leaned forward just enough to jab his defensive silence with the point that mattered.

'Don't bother to tell me you don't understand. That's obvious. But *you're* the one empowered to make enquiries—*you* have the superior intelligence raising your breed above mere mortals. When you've finished making your mistakes come back, and *then* I'll tell you where you went wrong.'

A low-key delivery of solid state vehemence had to be terrifyingly effective, had to deserve better than Dysart's patchwork response.

'It's possible to be over-protective.'

She flared at that, but regally, not raising her voice by a decibel.

'What else but your kind of over-protection generates fear, deception and sheer bloody murder in any over-organized society? You've exactly defined a symptom of our terminal civilization. Over-protection . . . do you genuinely believe you can immunize democracy from every ill and expect it to survive the first unknown onslaught of *any*thing? Or is mass euthamnesia the object of the exercise?'

'Riddles?' What kind of bankruptcy stared Dysart in the face if that was all he could pay in the pound?

'I'll give you another. A protection racket thrives on fear. Thugs practise it for gain—the rest, for reasons best known to yourself.'

It no longer mattered that she appeared to be attacking on the wrong front, but for the sake of appearance he had to explain, to preserve his identity at all costs.

'Mrs Quarrier, it's your privilege, but not my job to argue from the general to the exclusion of the particular. I came here to learn what I could about your husband, how else can I find out not only how and why he disposed of material vital to the country's well-being, but whether?'

She had no readily available answer. Had no need of one. Such a woman, like Menemoe, staring transpiciously at a stranger, is too busy drawing out the gist of a reply which, when it comes, must astonish them both.

'The Czechs have a proverb: it takes a bent pin to catch a fish. It takes a bent man to catch another.'

That was all.

Except for the long, cold vis-à-vis such as statues, met by chance in the forum, might share; a show of deaf and dumb, but not unaware . . .

After all, he reflected, I was mistaken. She fought on my ground and won, but God knows how. *Finita la commedia.*

Dysart's superb self-possession sauntered rather than fled away. He followed after without a word; a further tribute to her terrible sagacity. Relieved perhaps that it was all over, he conveyed by the manner of his departure that they both knew the game was up—never ask how.

Not just a question of defeat because the confounded woman scorned to cross swords in the conventional fashion—most of them do. But that she should have inklings enough to destroy a life's work, could stumble blindly round the truth and so, put in doubt, not Quarrier's survival, but his own.

Dared go no further; had no business there. Yet once, some yards away, he turned, lost in admiration and fear of the superstitious kind, to regard an incredible adversary.

Such a beautiful woman.

Eloquent, if dated, his slight bow, conceding, deferential; a semaphoric gesture intimating that they would never meet again. Not if he could help it.

Once more alone, Helen's mystification had to do with Helen, who no more understood her triumph than she understood her words. Most of them had come unbidden, yet she knew she hadn't spoken at random; rather, with the conviction of a Pythian oracle, *knowing* without knowing—but right about what?

And then she saw it.

Larger than a grown rabbit, it scurried askew the lawn some ten yards away stopping at intervals to snuffle the grass. Not in fear but fascinated wholly she studied the creature, its torn fur, the congealed blood about its jaws, the hideous profile until it first caught sight of her. A smile of greeting, or recognition or simply teeth bared like a celebrity's snarl of delight when cameras are by? Idiotically she smiled back, unless it was a placating grimace of pity.

It satisfied, whatever, for the creature limped on away to the left as she stood up slowly, carefully, watching its erratic progress towards . . . it stopped before the maze wall, head raised to veer and peer from side to side, questing . . .

Uncanny, the sudden movement, too human by half, as when one taps another's shoulder and the head slews round on guard; far from palatable that knowing look of a thing on the run, like the grinning glance of a prodigal returned, cocksure and knowing exactly where it was. 'I've come home,' seemed to show in that challenging expression before phenomenon vanished through the gap giving entrance to the maze.

Nemesis is circular, she heard herself musing, a hand covering her heart-beats to muffle the sound. Give no sign of troubled life, or the circle will break. Rats in mazes . . . Quentin had spoken of such things, contraptions to prove behaviourist theories . . . here was behaviour.

Fighting an insane urge to follow, to satisfy curiosity—would it find its way to the centre—she went indoors and closed up the house from top to bottom. She had to think of the children. Taking a chair to the kitchen window she sat where she could watch the maze entrance. To kill time she worked industriously to recall everything Quentin had told of his exchanges with Dysart.

As it happened Helen's controlled agitation had little to do with the second interloper. Some nervous tic of the mind was forcing her to digest a stop press item, as it seemed, from the latest edition of *The Daily Oracle*. A startling revelation, even to her dishevelled thinking, because it interwove and entirely integrated two antipathetic impressions: one of Dysart the gate-crasher, the other of a poor, sinister creature currently lurking somewhere in the bushes.

She nodded mechanically, eyes fixed on the sundrenched entrance, finger and thumb working away at the invisible tangle of a problem only partially resolved. Saw no reason to avoid verbalizing an uppermost conclusion.

'Mr Dysart,' spoken softly, 'is a mutant.'

Chapter 17

SO ARE THEY all. Mutants all. That's the penalty paid for indulging in top-tech vagrancy as against evolutionary progress harmonizing with Nature's laws.

Wonder a while who said that.

And by all means, breathe out a refusal to believe in one woman's surrealist face-to-face impression of the present, but be sure, reflexively, to inhale those moments of revelation, conceived, made flesh, and soon to be brought shrieking to bear in the not too distant future.

Even by members of a humdrum committee reluctantly convoked to enquire into a sordid break-in at Pandora's place.

Folson, the Conservative member, is questioning Lord Betherton, currently described in consenting circles as bothered, b . . . d and beleaguered. What was to be a protracted and often bitter interrogation is here reprinted in part.

FOLSON: Lord Betherton, you served on the board of the Central Advisory Council for Science and Technology and you were, till recently, its Chairman?

BETHERTON: Correct.

FOLSON: A list of your academic honours, appointments, qualifications and so forth may be taken as read, I think, particularly in the pages of *Who's Who* . . . you are, among other offices, the Principal Scientific Adviser to the Prime Minister?

BETHERTON: I am.

FOLSON: Do correct my ignorance if necessary, but I had some idea the title was Chief Scientific Adviser to HM Government.

BETHERTON: I have acted in that capacity, yes. The office was in fact abolished and my appointment as PSA to the PM was confirmed at the same time.

FOLSON: Why?

BETHERTON: I recollect it *was* explained to the Lower House. My services to the Government as such were amply covered by my chairmanship of the CACST.

FOLSON: So the separation of powers doctrine applied—I mean, a distinction was made as to what could be communicated to Parliament in general—and to the First Lord of the Treasury in particular?

BETHERTON: To an extent, yes.

FOLSON: Would you be so good as to define the extent?

BETHERTON: A matter of degree. Assuming an extremely sensitive issue, the probability of leakages among a small and volatile group of ministers would be high—but non-existent of course for a scientific adviser answerable only to the head of government.

FOLSON: Of course . . . and that's before we come to a larger volatile group of six hundred or so MPs.

BETHERTON: . . . yes.

FOLSON: I think we need to test your definition by stages.

BETHERTON: Test?

FOLSON: Why yes. Concerning the wisdom of preserving absolute confidentiality in the event of a leakage of an even larger volatile horde of mice.

Lord Betherton, will you explain to this Committee how you came to be aquainted with a Mr Jeremy Dysart?

BETHERTON: . . . in the circumstances, surely a matter for the security forces?

FOLSON: We shall decide that. At all events, and on your own admission, you exercised a quasi-security function in this affair.

BETHERTON: I advised on confidentiality—there's a subtle distinction.

FOLSON: There had better be perfect understanding on this. I'll repeat for your benefit, Lord Betherton, the terms of reference enabling this enquiry are explicit—and were fought for—a refusal to answer on the grounds of national security will be disallowed on the higher consideration of public safety.

Dysart, Lord Betherton.

BETHERTON: . . . I—attended a scientific congress in Prague in July of '73. Unless you want circumstantial details I can say I met him through the good offices of colleagues attending the conference.

FOLSON: This was well publicized I understand. Something to do with 'The Role of the Scientist in World Politics'.

BETHERTON: That is so.

FOLSON: The meeting was clandestine I believe.

BETHERTON: It was—arranged.

FOLSON: And the purpose?

BETHERTON: He wished to confide to me a fervent desire to defect to the West. Which would, of course, require my assistance.

FOLSON: Presumably it was common knowledge you had concerned yourself in another, earlier case of the kind?

BETHERTON: He knew of it, yes.

FOLSON: Yes . . . we're talking of a young man, about twenty-three, no question of status or scientific importance.

BETHERTON: He was a graduate *cum laude* of Prague University.

FOLSON: In what subjects?

BETHERTON: . . . Science and English.

FOLSON: Rather a convenient combination?

BETHERTON: Not at all. English is the lingua franca for would-be scientists—

FOLSON: His English then was very good.

BETHERTON: Impeccable.

FOLSON: A perfectionist.

BETHERTON: . . . As you please.

FOLSON: He wasn't always Jeremy Dysart of course?

BETHERTON: He was introduced to me as Vasil Manak—a Bohemian, I believe.

FOLSON: What motive did he advance for wishing to flee westward?

BETHERTON: An intense hostility towards the Communist régime of the time.

FOLSON: A sentiment with which you sympathized hook line and sinker?

BETHERTON: We are not discussing fishing!

FOLSON: Not exactly. I withdraw the question and ask simply if you sympathized with his declared aim?

BETHERTON: That goes without saying.

FOLSON: Presumably you *can* say whether your reciprocal sentiments meant that he was half-way to his goal before he started? (Laughter)

BETHERTON: I must leave conjecture to you.

FOLSON: He was given security clearance?

BETHERTON: Naturally.

FOLSON: You mean naturally in view of your strong recommendation?

BETHERTON: It—carried a certain weight yes.

FOLSON: No criminal record?

BETHERTON: None that *I* know of.

FOLSON: None that you know of . . . what, apart from changing his name did Mr Manak accomplish in the ten years or more he spent in the UK?

BETHERTON: Accomplish?

FOLSON: He was your protegé we may assume? How did he earn his keep and show his gratitude?

BETHERTON: He proved invaluable as a research assistant and in many matters requiring discretion.

FOLSON: You employed him?

BETHERTON: Substantially, yes.

FOLSON: And substantially he was your creature.

BETHERTON: . . . Your choice of words leaves much to be desired.

FOLSON: You talk of his discretion—how would this talent be employed in scientific terms?

BETHERTON: At its highest level science is bound to be a sensitive issue politically.

FOLSON: Based on the evidence we have, would it be correct to say he was frequently employed as a courier, as between you and disaffected scientists in the Eastern bloc?

BETHERTON: Greatly to our advantage, yes.

FOLSON: Facilitating a one-way flow of information—from East to West?

BETHERTON: Of course.

FOLSON: I begin to wonder whether my questions relate, if you'll forgive me, to an ideal or an ideological world.

BETHERTON: —the choice is still yours.

FOLSON: At any rate, this young Cold War crusader would have access to information incidental to his usefulness?

BETHERTON: . . . yes.

FOLSON: Classified information?

BETHERTON: ...When you say classified—

FOLSON: I mean subject to the Official Secrets Act—I mean material carelessly dropped into a waste-paper basket that could earn English charladies a committal to the Tower of London if they were caught reading it!

BETHERTON: No.

FOLSON: ... Would you care to reconsider your last response.

BETHERTON: I don't—see the need.

FOLSON: You will understand the Committee's reaction after I ask, was not Mr Dysart an important, if not a vital link in the Price-Pearson affair?

BETHERTON: He was—an element.

FOLSON: I emphasize 'important'. The experiments at issue were classified. At your insistence everyone connected with them from the Chairman to the most junior lab technician was placed under the interdict of the OSA. Is that or is that not correct?

BETHERTON: I could not insist. I could only suggest.

FOLSON: Did you so suggest?

BETHERTON: Yes!

FOLSON: Would not your suggestion as a scientific expert have the weight of persuasion if not of insistence for a head of government dependent on your expertise or why were you there at all?

BETHERTON: I can't deny it.

FOLSON: And if you similarly persuaded the PM that Dysart should be empowered by her fiat and the Home Secretary's Hocus-Pocus to act as a monitoring agent with unrestricted access to the Price-Pearson Complex *and* the London HQ, did not that confer on the ambiguous Mr Dysart a role of unparalleled importance going beyond the limits of sanity!

BETHERTON: Your reading of the situation is an exaggeration to the point of sheer naïveté!

FOLSON: ... You have just informed this Committee that, in your indiscriminate ardour to save souls from the Communist inferno, you brought a young man to this country, vouched for his political and moral health on the flimsiest grounds, allowed him access to material which not even the most distinguished scientists in the UK let alone HMG's ministers were permitted to know of, gave him powers undreamed of by our intelligence services, to oversee an allegedly crucial experimental programme—and you question *our* naïveté?

BETHERTON: I acted throughout in the best interests of my country, as the Prime Minister has publicly recognized!

FOLSON: Lord Betherton, I may claim, as a life-long Tory, to have heard that admirable justification for questionable actions many times, indeed, I will admit to having made patriotic professions of faith myself. But on the facts so far, on your evidence alone, I have to confess a sneaking suspicion that such patriotism may, after all, be the last refuge, not only of scoundrels, but of knaves and fools as well.

Her practical side knew the phone call to Jocelyn mattered more than reverie and window-gazing. It beat the indolent self, content to keep a useless vigil.

'Jocelyn. It's Helen.'

'Which one for heaven's sake! There's Helen Small who died five years ago and the other one.' He was a very old Fellow, resident in Wycliffe College. Helen smiled and left time for the wheezy chuckle to subside.

'Quentin's Helen, unless there are other Quentins, in which case—'

'Very well, yes, I take your point, my dear, don't labour it. When are you coming up or am I supposed to be coming down? My engagement book's full of notes on Creed's marvellous article on Two-spot Ladybirds as Indicators of Local Air Pollution. Have you read it?'

No time for social niceties—even to ask about his arthritis. 'Jocelyn, Q's in serious trouble.'

A pause, a change of tone, from sardonic senility to something more vigorous, more like himself.

'Is it Price-Pearson?'

'Yes. Essentially.'

Another, considered pause. 'Yes . . . there's a lot of gossipy nonsense going round the High Tables and beyond. It's about this ephemeral plague of mice?'

'That among other things—and it's not ephemeral.'

'Ah! the Hopkins thing. Too much generated rumour, based on

too few facts as televised. I was minded to ring Quentin but I wrote instead. I'll post it tomorrow.'

'They're trying to make out some sort of case against him—only it's political—nothing to do with mice or even science.'

'. . . Political.' Gravitas, and much else was in it.

'There's something odd, mysterious and phoney about the affair from beginning to end. I need your help.'

'You have it, Helen. Say on.'

'I want a piece of information. Can you find out whether a Mr Jeremy Dysart was ever enrolled in *any* of the colleges in the last fifteen—no, twenty years to be on the safe side?'

'Give me the name again. I'll jot it down . . . Jeremy . . . Dysart. Yes, that's no problem. Wonderful things computers. I'll get someone at Senate House to plug in on this Dysart and hey presto, all you need to know in one byte, eh? Stand by and I'll ring you back within the hour.'

Which he did.

'No problem, my dear. No Dysart, Jeremy or otherwise. Not a trace of him in the records. I hope it helps.'

Helps! If he could have seen the light in her eyes.

'More than you or I can know, Jocelyn. Come down soon. It's your turn.'

'No standing on ceremony. If there's anything else I can—'

'Just come down soon.'

'Blast your imperiousness! I'm packing my bags instanter.'

Well said for a seventy-six year old still living under a cloud . . . the same cloud. She smiled happily at sound of a crashed handset—he was the only telephone vandal known at Wycliffe—and returned to the kitchen in a gilt frame of mind. Surely it must all begin to fall into place at last?

Immediacy returned, euphoria vanished at sight of the maze. Had the thing found its way out and away? Should she ring Quentin, ask him to come home and deal with a biological drop-out?

Question time ended. There was his car easing along the drive. Silence, shot dead by the car door slam, a slow footfall crunching gravel. Silence, the front door squeaking open and closing softly. She turned from the window, but her homecoming smile faded under some internal and inexplicable compulsion.

Enter Man, the creator, man the eternal schoolboy taking apart and reassembling, knocking down and building up, sandwiches of triumph with a tragic filling . . . signs of defeat fighting to-hell-with-it insouciance, not to be credited till she glimpsed those tell-tale signs of shrinkage, of hang-dog hubris beneath *his* homecome smile.

'It's done.' He took a step or two towards her, found a chair on the way and sat gratefully, overcome, as it seemed, by that elegant line in fatigue we call 'world weariness'.

'It's done,' he repeated with just enough of a grin to show he knew fine about bathos and the little man between millstones weeping red tears.

They both needed to talk; both had important things to tell, the future to discuss or just tomorrow crying aloud for a solution. She was bound to listen first as he explained his ten a.m. intention to clock in at the Complex as if nothing had changed. 'But the prospect daunted me into the ground. I couldn't find a brave face big enough to fit me. The old mind did a U-turn and the car followed. I drove for hours and got nowhere until I found myself in Curzon Street. It seemed I looked for an answer and found it.'

Had 'it' been so simple?

Apparently not. To begin with, one didn't visit. One was summoned. Sir Rufus had fiddled so furiously with his scissors he'd cut a finger. Accused him of trying to get out from under. On reflection, perhaps Sir Rufus was right.

'He can't force you to stay?'

'He can demand I act out the remaining weeks of a yearly contract—at least to help clear up the mess—and he did.'

'A moral obligation.'

He sighed, as if such things were feathers, to be blown away by a little breath. 'I'm sure you're on my side but—'

'On yours *and* the side of the dead and injured.'

'For which I can't—'

She moved so quickly to stand before him he had to stop. 'Quentin, do you *know* what kind of death and injury's being visited on your fellow-men?' She supplied the answer he'd never have found. 'An insult . . . so you must want to *prove* the least degree of personal criminal responsibility. Mustn't you?'

He stared at her or at a phrase aimed to kill complacency and alert his conscience. She moved a step closer but delivered her homily a plane higher—somewhere over his head.

'It's as if there were two worlds. One under the microscope, the other through the telescope. We can see deeper, we can see further. We drown in detail, we commit our souls to suicide with big bang theories, invite anathema for all creation sucked into those gaping black holes. Why must we terrify ourselves and each other? We need a someone to invent a reconciloscope, showing us a middle way to a third, nearly ideal world.'

Over his head, as the prayer for enlightenment over an unrepentant sinner. Certainly, he misread enough to begin a defence about motives, the purity of. But something in her fixed regard discouraged Quarrier—she knew the conventional defence backwards, and it was beneath her dignity any longer to play the part of one who nods and says tut-tut, there, there, and you acted for the best, dear.

By degrees she returned to the now of things. Told in everyday tones of Jocelyn's promised visit. Quarrier was mildly surprised but pleased, even delighted.

'You should be. He's solved some of the mystery.'

'Oh?'

'You said once, Dysart claimed to have been at Cambridge some time after you.'

'Quite some time later.'

'There is no record of a Jeremy Dysart on any college register.'

'Jocelyn . . . told you?'

'I asked—he checked.'

'But . . .' perplexity verging on idiocy can be amusing or vexing. 'Helen—my dear girl, what possible difference does that make? If he's in Intelligence he's bound to have a cover.'

She closed her eyes to shut out visions of the games men play. I'm a book wearing the wrong jacket—guess who I really am.

'And why should he need a cover?'

'To show a credible familiarity with student politics surely.'

Helen would have none of it. 'He isn't what he claims to be.'

'I've *seen* the letter signed by the PM itself.'

'You saw *a* letter.'

'Helen, the man works for Betherton—'

'Who told you that?'

'Mathie, I think. But I don't see—'

She almost felt the impact of whatever had stopped him in his tracks. Plainly some odd association of ideas, or a catapulted image had struck hard. Discounted at the time but, inexplicably, and thanks to Quarrier's photographic memory, the fact resurfaced at mention of Mathieson's name. As he explained.

'After Sir Rufus had done with me I left the place without a backward glance—I felt like Lot's old woman—once put through the mangle, twice as dry—never wanted to see the place again. No sign of Mathieson—I could live without him too. The point is, his car wasn't in the company parking space when I arrived but it was there, parked in front of mine when I got back.

'I climbed in and sat awhile as I often do, winding up for an utterly boring stint of driving. Simply sat there, staring ahead . . . I can see it clearly—a London mews, a grey rainy scene, Mathie's car . . . an idiot staring at a number plate . . . Dutch liquid . . .

'And now,' he turned a wondering eye on the woman who stood listening, watchful of every nuance in his aspect.

'C284CL*T*—Rem wasn't thinking of ethylene dichloride . . .'

She was thinking: it's taken so long. The thread paid out in ignorance, paid off hopefully and in time. The maze had almost defeated them both. A price innocence is meant to pay for not knowing the ways of this brave new world skilled in microchipped skulduggery: agents, counter-agents, hidy-hole cameras, red-taped conversations and 'bugs' everywhere. Bugs! Mere musing spilled over into a verdict of angry words.

'The human race is lousy!'

'Why?'

Helen came down from somewhere up there. 'Why what?'

'Some sort of comment on humanity—its lousiness.'

Well, she knew it was just another thought off-loaded without her say-so. First signs of brain softening or simply mother manqué prattling to the non-existent?

'I suppose I was thinking of bugs—their prevalence. "He bugs me", "This room is bugged", "There's a bug going around". They don't just live behind the wallpaper anymore. So—the race is lousy.'

Bitterness. Not the most obvious of her traits. His concern beyond self showed at last and Quarrier saw how she too had trudged in his wake under an intolerable burden, hardly his fault, but much of his making.

The *per se* thing itself, to which their lives seemed committed irretrievably—almost forgotten in the spin-off any crisis generates. But Helen recovered first, spoke lightly to dispel the tell-tale signs of a badly harried man.

'By the way, one of our little friends disappeared into the maze just before you got back.'

His reaction startled them both. A pause stretched to the limit until an unsuspected glint kindled and flared in the eyes, before he leapt to his feet, trembling with fear masked by a show of angry indignation.

'You're making fun of me!'

She said nothing, let her silence do the talking. It was eloquent enough. Quarrier gestured an apology, but clearly he felt pain or anguish still; much as an animal under the knife or cankered by radiation might feel.

'How to live with it,' a hoarse explanation.

'That may take time. What's to be done meanwhile?'

'I'll—go after it.'

'It's not the answer.'

Arguably he saw her, but was elsewhere, listening to a man who played interminably with scissors as he barked to a background of trumpets blaring in pitched battle with trombones climbing, climbing to '*Your* creations, Quarrier. Rats and sinking ships, eh? Well you're staying on this ship till the decks are cleared, never mind what's left of your contract. Afterwards you can take a running jump. Now get out and get cracking!'

At the kitchen door he turned to smile bleakly. 'It's time to look for the answer. The unlikeliest places, they say.'

She gathered authority, snatching it where she could.

'You've something as important to do.'

'Tell me.'

'You must make a phone call. A belated call.'

Detective-Superintendent Whitfield, questioned by John Cherston, MP, a member of the All-Party Committee. (Abbreviated)

CHERSTON: . . . And this call from Doctor Quarrier came on the day of his attempted resignation?
WHITFIELD: That's correct.

CHERSTON: Let's go back a bit. What steps did you take following Mrs Quarrier's visit?

WHITFIELD: None immediately. It took time to find her suspicions compelling.

CHERSTON: They were ill-defined?

WHITFIELD: In a sense they appeared to defy logic. But there was nothing indefinite about that flake of paint.

CHERSTON: Navy blue, found under the gate according to her?

WHITFIELD: Doctor Remington's car was grey—as she reminded me.

CHERSTON: Very well. Earlier you told this Committee of your unease about your instructions; was that underlined by Mrs Quarrier's—what shall I call them—opinions?

WHITFIELD: Unsubstantiated statements of fact, yes I'm certain it was.

CHERSTON: . . . Yes—er, Mr Folson would welcome an explanation of the difficulties you were having prior to your first encounter with this lady.

WHITFIELD: The situation following the Wentworth disaster was highly unusual, I might say, irregular. We'd lost two officers, one of them my then superior, Superintendent Baker, and we were being deluged with enquiries. In the middle of this confusion I received a telex from the Home Office—

CHERSTON: The Home Office?

WHITFIELD: Correction, the Home Secretary, directing me to avoid publicity at all costs, and to give a Mr Dysart every facility in his investigation of the incident.

CHERSTON: Did it stress national security as a priority?

WHITFIELD: That was my reading of it.

CHERSTON: Had the Chief Constable been similarly advised?

WHITFIELD: He should have been, *pro forma*.

CHERSTON: You imply he was not so advised.

WHITFIELD: He received his information from me.

CHERSTON: At any rate you were uneasy about this directive?

WHITFIELD: I certainly wasn't happy about its unofficial—even casual nature, or the status of Mr Dysart.

CHERSTON: Why not?

WHITFIELD: Even in an emergency there are procedures to be followed. On the second point, I was being asked—ordered—to give unlimited assistance to a name only.

CHERSTON: You never saw him?

WHITFIELD: I haven't set eyes on him to this day. And I'm not likely to.

CHERSTON: Oh?

WHITFIELD: I'm convinced Mrs Quarrier scared him off.

CHERSTON: I see . . . we shall be taking her evidence on that, no doubt. With hindsight, Superintendent, how would you summarize your feelings about the total situation at the time?

WHITFIELD: I sensed an almighty cover-up at any price. Decisions taken in high places, over our heads and we were expected to react accordingly—that is, blindly.

CHERSTON: On the strength of a phrase?

WHITFIELD: Yes, national security.

CHERSTON: Many did act on it. Why not you?

WHITFIELD: Because I was handed a flake of paint, I think.

CHERSTON: And then?

WHITFIELD: I rang Twentieth Century House, spoke to an acquaintance of some standing there. I asked if his organization carried anyone name of Dysart.

CHERSTON: Go on, Superintendent.

WHITFIELD: The name meant nothing to him or anyone else in his line.

CHERSTON: I gather things moved fast from thereon.

WHITFIELD: Again it was Mrs Quarrier who'd given us a lead. I began a rethink on the smashed gate, the paint flake and that chemical formula.

CHERSTON: Which brings us back to the day Doctor Quarrier called.

WHITFIELD: Coincidence and a stroke of luck. I'd checked on Dysart and the wheels were beginning to turn. A call on the Quarriers might clear up a point or two; I couldn't expect more.

CHERSTON: Your visit was brief I understand?

WHITFIELD: It had to be. Time wasn't on our side.

CHERSTON: Were they able to assist?

WHITFIELD: That's an understatement. Frankly, Mrs Quarrier's theory was crucial and, though I normally avoid the word—sensational.

CHERSTON: What followed?

WHITFIELD: I left in a hurry, assured them I'd return when the

matter was cleared up. I owed her—them—that much.
CHERSTON: Which you did two days later I believe?
WHITFIELD: Yes.
CHERSTON: Thank you, Superintendent. Perhaps we might look at those eventful forty-eight hours in some detail.

Whitfield travelled straight from London to Alton's purlieus and found the Quarriers waiting at home. Short of his customary phlegmatic calm he rushed to the point with not a semblance of preamble. But, was he quite sure he wouldn't have coffee?

He was quite sure; hijacked a chair and doubted aloud there was time for anything else except talk.

The man's precipitancy, though it stopped short of agitation, astonished them both. Very senior police officers don't normally behave as if they've hurled themselves out of a train to fling themselves into another. Good for a chuckle in better circumstances.

Graciously he confessed some difficulty in finding the right start. 'But I'll begin with an assumption . . . Mrs Quarrier, you didn't come to me on the spur of the moment. I mean, you'd thought about this, long before the smashed gate. What was it? The "formula"?'

'. . . It—was because of someone I hadn't met. Not then.'

'Who?'

'Jeremy Dysart.'

Surprise number umpteen. Whitfield very nearly looked as if he couldn't cope with another.

'Dysart!'

'Quentin has a remarkable tape-recorder memory. He played back an account of a conversation they'd had not long since. I was struck by the singular fact that Dysart, a member of Intelligence, quoted a Czech proverb quite off-hand. I can't believe many Englishmen would be familiar with Czechoslovakian proverbs. Even in translation Ladas' and Kapek's words aren't littered with them, certainly not with the "swine's disease" one.'

'Conclusive?' sceptically.

'Of course not—any more than a coroner's verdict is necessarily the last word. But an anomaly is an anomaly. To say the least, it marked out Mr Dysart as—singular.'

197

'It ended there?'

'If it had I'm not sure I'd have mentioned the fact . . . I think he came here to test the temperature.'

'A luke-warm reception,' Whitfield supposed.

'I was ruthlessly polite—but I had my own test to think about.'

Both men watched her with more than ordinary interest.

'Yes—go on, Mrs Quarrier.'

'When I saw we were both getting nowhere, I entertained him with what I deliberately called a Czech proverb—made up of course. He left immediately—without another word.'

Whitfield didn't bother to admire. With such a woman it's reverence or nothing.

'Yes,' thoughtfully. 'That explains it.' He turned to Quarrier. 'Who told you Dysart had authority to monitor your project?'

'Lord Betherton.'

'. . . So it's true.' And quite suddenly the senior police officer who'd seen and heard much in his time seemed to fall apart at the enormity of it all. 'Dysart had the run of your mill for two years.'

'Yes—for two years.'

'And his authorization was signed by—?'

'The Home Secretary.'

'. . . I'll have a strong drink after all, Mrs Quarrier.'

While Helen pours and serves it's worth a mention that Whitfield already knew some of this and what follows, on the evidence of one man; but he, like the Intelligence officers, simply could not credit their information without cast-iron corroboration. The Quarriers could provide some and that, for the moment, was the Superintendent's brief. Hence his astonishment.

The large straight Scotch fortified.

'What seems to have happened,' he continued, 'is a massive short circuit of the regular Intelligence services. They were perfectly happy in the dark till you, Mrs Quarrier, handed them a candle.

'I'll try and give it in words of one syllable . . . Dysart suspected he was finished, but he tried a last ploy to finish you off, Doctor, anything to keep the heat off the two of them. He persuaded the Home Secretary, through Betherton, to authorize a Special Branch tap on—you. Now this must've been arranged the morning of the day he dropped in on you, Mrs Quarrier. By the time he left here the tap was on and your husband became *officially* suspect.'

Whitfield took another gulp and decided he was doing very nicely.

'Dysart was too clever by half. Just as the tapsters were chewing over your outgoing call to Cambridge re Dysart and Cambridge's incoming call saying "never heard of him", another Charley—yours truly—rings *them* from Winchester, asking "who might this Mr Dysart be?" They rang all round in a hurry and discovered no one had a clue. It was a toss-up between the incredible shrinking man and the great unknown—you're with me so far?'

They were. By the skin of their teeth apparently.

'We know Dysart didn't hang around, pack or collect his cards after leaving here. We also know he took a flight to Dublin and is probably in Prague right now, being debriefed. Considering all the years he operated it should take till Christmas.

'So we come to the crunch. Was he working alone? Who was fielding for him?'

Quarrier had no doubts. 'Surely Betherton and —'

'Ah! I said "fielding" not vouching for him. Not only do we rule *them* out of our enquiries, we don't even want 'em to know we're making any. No—there had to be A.N. Other and, very timely, I turned up with your little bomb-shell, Doctor.'

'Don't credit me. Helen got there first.'

'Well, by now we all know it was Mathieson's car the late Doctor Remington tried to speak of with his dying breath. C284CL*T* as it happens.'

'Does that prove anything by itself?'

'No indeed, but again it's your fault if the fact's in good company. We trace the car to Clarges Mews, we match your flake of cellulose to the rear *and* find a hefty dent. How can we know some idiot garage mechanic further along sees two suspicious Greeks exchanging Eurekas loitering around Mr Mathieson's vehicle and warns him accordingly to keep his car doors locked?'

'Mathieson . . .'

The Superintendent nodded. 'Very much so, Doctor. Scientific aide to your Chairman, I believe?'

'Yes—he is.'

'Was. First let's clear out of the way what made Fawkes and Fuchs die laughing. Any offers?'

'Secrecy with a capital S.'

'Right again, Mrs Quarrier,' he raised his glass to her. She refilled it. 'Much obliged. Your husband's working on a hush-hush project. I don't even pretend to know what it's all about—but I *do* know it's a computerized world we live in so, presumably, a lot of information's flowing from the Complex and flashes on London HQ's VDU at the touch of a button?'

'Yes, just about everything.'

'Passes through Mathieson's hands who interprets for Sir Rufus who probably doesn't know an isotope from an isocream. Would Mathieson see the significance of your work?'

'No question.'

'Right from the beginning? Feasibility studies and so on?'

'Certainly from the beginning.'

'Good. Enter Dysart and down comes the veil of "secrecy" . . . I take it none of you signed the pledge—for the OSA I mean?'

'We weren't asked to.'

'Of course not. That was smart. It kept the official watchdogs at arm's length and unbeknowing.'

'But you're as good as saying a conspiracy existed between the PM, the Home Secretary, Betherton, Sir Rufus, Dysart and Mathieson.'

'No, Mrs Quarrier. I'm stressing there were two dissimilar conspiracies nudging each other. Dysart and Mathieson made one, the others made a second with Mathieson linking the two.'

Pause for refreshment and to let this sink in.

'Conspiracy Number One: HMG—some of it—Betherton and Sir Rufus conspiring *with* Mathieson to keep your world-shaker under American-style wraps. Being amateurs with a dash of non-professional arrogance they leave out negligibles like Special Branch and MI5.

'Conspiracy Number Two: Dysart, in cahoots *with* Mathieson rides on the back of Conspiracy Number One.'

'Dysart yes, but I don't see what Mathie had to gain.' Quarrier's show of loyalty died under Whitfield's level gaze.

'That's where you come in, Doctor. Not wholly innocently I suppose, but not guilty of high treason either . . . Security knew about you of course—well, it's their job to know. Some sort of Marxist nonsense in your college days. Mathieson belonged too.'

And there *was* light. And great was the beholder's amazement thereat.

'That's right. But I thought he—'

'No, Doctor. He carried on after you left off.'

'But—but it was Dysart who nagged at my past.'

'Of course. He got it all from Mathieson didn't he? You couldn't challenge his credibility as a secret service gent unless you *knew* who was feeding him, and even if you did he could plead national security.'

Quarrier stared with interest at nothing in particular. 'Mathie . . . gave Dysart my pamphlet.'

'It was bright. They could use your "lapse" to create a security scare whenever they needed . . . what's better than a very red herring as things are these days . . . only—' Whitfield paused, 'you handed them something better.'

'The escape,' Helen supposed. She took the empty glass from an unresisting hand.

'Much obliged. Yes. Mathieson was on to it at once. Remember, he was watching the computer like a hacker-hawk, making notes of everything significant coming out of the Complex—'

'Why couldn't Dysart get what he needed direct?' Quarrier wondered.

Whitfield smiled. 'Because on Mathieson's personal representation to Sir Rufus, Dysart was allowed nowhere near the central computer. That made them *both* look whiter than white.'

'So when Dysart told me he'd been through the tapes three times—'

'He meant Mathieson had fed him what he needed. Mathieson was in constant touch with your activities.'

'But—'

'He notes, for example, the details, the serial number of what you call a running experiment I believe, and the date—July 7th. He refers back and discovers there's a lag, no mention of this experiment's start-up—something like that. Anyway, he's scientific enough to spot a significant gap. He's also bright enough to run through every minute of a day in the life of Price-Pearson; even searches the rest of the software concurrently coupling two and two. And he finds it—glaring at him.

'The Security log print-out gives the usual daily ins and outs and he's drawn a blank till he reads on and learns how early next morning a Doctor Remington makes an outside call to you and Alladyce. The gates open and you go through—they close—they open for Mr Alladyce. 3.07, they open, Mr Alladyce drives out. They close—at 3.25 they open. Doctors Remington and Quarrier leave in that order.

'Mathieson asks himself "what's going on?".'

'But it doesn't lead him anywhere,' Quarrier, quietly desperate.

'That's to underestimate your enemy. Mathieson reasoned correctly, if Remington led the way, you were heading for the Bowery at the end of a difficult stretch of lane. He'd also know Remington kept rabbits and things in a converted barn or something similar . . . and he knew Doctor Remington stayed away from the Complex next day.'

The Superintendent glanced at his watch. 'Shall I take it you agree with the rough outline so far?'

Quarrier saw no choice.

'I suppose it's a reverse deduction of what Mrs Quarrier half-guessed at. And it would follow that someone *with knowledge*, went to the Bowery on the fatal day, was disturbed by Doctor Remington who gave chase, smashed down the gate, smashed into the intruder's car and crashed in the end—at twenty miles per hour—and there you are.'

Little or no joy in Helen's eyes which stayed with Whitfield; becoming, perhaps, but all the same they displayed the tragedy of insight scanning and reading what's best left out between the lines. She *knew* that was not the end of it. Missing, presumed dead, one of those crucial details ensuring life will never quite be the same again.

Whitfield understood, but strangely he couldn't bring himself to tell what remained of the story. He spoke brusquely, deliberately getting in the way of a predictable question.

'Yes—you're thinking of the time factor. Everything happened quickly because Mathieson knew the game was up, probably warned from Heathrow by his control. But if he did realize the "officials" were closing in, then he'd likely know they start by playing a waiting game . . . at any rate, he never stirred out of his flat. Last night they decided to force the issue and the door . . . he never stirred out of his chair—irreversible overdoses seldom do.'

That much more known, and dissatisfied still? Or why go on

staring into existence the blank wall of a blind alley in Minos, deaf to small talk obscuring the great unanswered. Mathieson! *Who* was Mathieson!

Whitfield noted the plainsight of perplexity, that importunate, questing habit, finger and thumb kneading the air.

'Well, Mrs Quarrier?' Shrewdly, but gently, as not to distract a woman from the distaff.

'There's more to it than that; as if you've filled in the space around a vacuum—like a grave-digger preparing the ground . . . I'm sorry, Superintendent, that's fanciful. What I mean is, the picture's authentic isn't it, if it has a signature?'

He confessed long after that no woman had impressed him with the uncanny originality of her mind as had Helen Quarrier. By now he could see clearly, without rightly understanding, how she'd chanced with purpose on the leading strings of a colossal mystery, and gladly he held her in awe.

But he could regret the unwritten sadness of things as he fished a Manilla-looking envelope from his pocket, reluctant still to tell the worst.

'True enough, Mrs Quarrier, nowt's in a vacuum. They—found a longish letter on the table, a detailed confession of faith gone rotten—well, how else would I know so much? But I'll tell you why I was given several copies . . . the top people in state security took an instant decision: make sure this is published, broadcast, posted by pigeon—disseminated any way you like, but nowhere near the People who made it possible. Let's make it clear—*we're* not a party to an idiotic cover-up.'

'Despite the national interest?' strangely ironic her smile.

'Because of, Mrs Quarrier. A blow against authoritarians who insist on running *every*body's business from a corner shop in Whitehall . . . as my irate SB colleague said, "I'm surprised we haven't been privatized". Keep this copy. It'll tell the end of the story better than I could.'

'What I can't understand,' said Quarrier, 'is how Dysart got so far, for so long.'

'There'll be an enquiry—but my guess is, someone, somewhere, took advantage of Betherton's psychopathic hatred of all things red, from Marx to Spencer. If he was ready to believe Dysart was an anti-communist, he was ready to believe anything.'

Whitfield took his leave, promised to let them know of further developments, advised them to try radio and TV for news. 'Things are in the open now. They have to be.'

Indeed they had. The plague was spreading in all directions. Attacks were more frequent. Mrs Jardine and her son were no longer ill-fated exceptions. Fear flowered and ripened here and there, pervaded every walk of life, panic smouldered gently, like a slow-burning fuse.

More immediately, to bridge an awkward silence after Whitfield's departure, Helen switched on the radio, discovered it was between times for a news bulletin.

Quarrier solved the problem after a long view of the woman who'd played a star role in the wings while he agonized like a dumbstruck Hamlet on a darkened stage.

'He said nothing about the root cause—what started it all.'

'The mutants?'

'Silence implies blame—"not wholly innocent" didn't he say?'

She closed her eyes as if there was nothing thereabouts she wanted to see. 'Blame—for Dysart, Mathie and the rest? That wouldn't be sensible—or fair.'

'Fine. Then I'll plead "not wholly guilty" if that's what you want.'

'I don't want anything.' World wearily. 'I just want an end of terror—every common or garden variety of terror. That's reasonable isn't it?'

He lapsed into silence, brooding over his right of reply—knowing by heart he had no right—no answer that could satisfy.

And hadn't all been said? They were both at fault for spoiling the delicacy of perceptions with paltry words short of meaning.

Oddly and for some time, they'd forgotten—or perhaps they'd carefully ignored the envelope left by Whitfield on the sofa table. Helen came to it first, but hesitated, as if afraid to sabotage a ramshackle balance of niceties or tread a clumsy measure over his tenderer susceptibilities; Quarrier gestured impatiently, anxious to know the worst, or curious to meet a revised version of Mathieson at last.

She began, reflexively, to read the photocopy.

'For heaven's sake! Read it aloud.'

Chapter 18

THIS IS TO anyone.

I've no intention of doing a Philby. For late twentieth-century man there's nowhere to go. As for the pangs, I've endured them all—envy—pride—failure—the decline and fall of ideals—now, even drink doesn't drown the sorrow. This is literary. I'll write as I truly feel, like a thorough-going bastard. Admit first, and very likely foremost, to jealousy—well, envy of Quarrier. What a paragonic star in the firmament!

I suppose I alone could have taken him further than the sticking-point if friend Dysart hadn't come into the picture. How that happened is interesting but of no consequence. I knew him sporadically as Betherton's familiar but the hand-in-glove association really began with Quarrier's ducky little bombshell. Not just *Doctor* Quarrier, the renowned geneticist and bio-with-everything, but Quarrier the Nobel prizewinner and so, by an irresistible progression, to Sir Quentin and milord Mendel!

Give the devil his due—it *was* Nobel prize jelly and custard. Even Sir Rufus Scissors understood that without hysterical promptings from Zurich.

Enter Dysart, half-demented because Rufus had exposed his tongue in public, not about some tin-pot defence contract, but *the* project. Dysart told Betherton and Betherton warned the Godmother about another Nobel speciality—dynamite.

It didn't take long for this impressionable fellow assiduously to extend our acquaintance. I'm sorry about the Victorianisms but he *did* know my weakness well enough to ply me with drink. Of course I knew his game—we'd had dealings before—but the game was to play it as if for the first time. He tightened the strings, played like a virtuoso on my genial dislike of—not Quarrier—but of his inevitable rise to fame. Dammit—he lost nothing over the Bromouracil disaster while I—for a mere peccadillo—disgraced forever. Those damned Victorianisms again. And what did friend Quarrier throw in my face the other day? Vitriol—or Bromouracil? Dislike!

And what was Dysart up to all of two years ago? With a smile, and a nod, and a wink: 'Mathie, I suspect Quarrier ideologically. What can we make of that over a friendly bottle of Smirnoff?'

'No problem. As a matter of fact your little joke misfires,' I'd replied. Told him about the *sans souci* days in Cambridge—the hammering of nails into the Mathematical Bridge—Quarrier's prank. Told him my part in those earnest discussions in little red cells: Wither away the State?

'Well that's fine,' he said. 'But he's reformed,' I said. 'Never mind,' he said. 'All we need is evidence—just enough smoke, as from this cigarette—to suggest a red glow.'

'In support of what?' I was a bit fuddled but I remember asking him that. 'Betherton wants me to keep an eye on things,' enigma replied.

The data kept flowing from the Complex. I just passed it on to him—with the boss's permission, that's the beauty of it—even had to rein the old fool in a bit. Money for old rope—long evening sessions at which I'd explain to Comrade Jeremy some of the more arcane material coming from Quarrier's stable.

Funnily enough, all this time Dysart was programming *me*. Men are the constantly mutating mutants—not those poor bloody mice—they only reflect our change of values—of *personae*. Look what we're doing to ourselves, to our manhood, to their womanhood, to the sacred flame of regeneration. If someone spits on it shall it not go out?

Look what Quarrier is doing.

What, with luck, could an upgraded four-star office-boy do about it?

To be brief: Dysart made a new man of me. Worked on my old and tarnished ideals, burnished 'em bright—appealed to my long lost illusions—and my hatred of Quarrier. It's so easy to confuse issues when you're tanked up to the eyebrows.

It's easier still to accept propositions that can destroy . . . reputations for example. How to discredit Quarrier? Drag out the skeleton in his cupboard and make it—articulate. Yes, do the world a favour by sharing his knowledge with the rest—with the East.

'You'll be a second Klaus Fuchs—a benefactor to mankind—or a certain kind of man. And while you're about it, why not be the *first* Roger Mathieson, candidate for the Nobel Peace Prize? Certainly. Why not?'

I suppose—euphoria is born of hysteria.

I passed him the minutes of top-level meetings, strategic memoranda, progress reports, in simple boardroom language, and he passed them on . . . I remember tipsy laughter—mine—as he revelled in his part—the accredited guardian of a bloody great national secret, his sober reports to Betherton which I'd helped to prepare—read by the PM no less—or so he told me.

Yes, it was good for a belly laugh. There's farce in duplicity. And no doubt there were grim smiles in the East as his reports, *my* reports, flooded in—as they had done for years apparently. He was unassailable . . . priceless.

I stopped laughing when he'd studied the print-out for July 7th. *He* told *me*!

'I think he's got the answer.'

My head was pounding like the devil that day—all day—I was in a mood of damn it all. I explained nose in the air about random tests and nil conclusions.

'Exactly! Look at the serial number. This gives the conclusion. Where's the base-line data?'

Nowhere. He'd checked back and found the gap—good thinking! I'd have missed it. But I couldn't see the significance.

I knew Quarrier's method well enough to be categorical, convinced he *never* destroys evidence though he might scramble it. He's a continuity man—his worst failures are written in as a measure of his success.

Dysart went through everything with a toothcomb. Next morning in my office, he showed me the proof on my very own VDU. Not only the Day One deletion, but the night security log told all—well, quite a bit. So much activity in the small hours—and no follow-up after Day 42?

There had to be something in it. The smell of fish was overpowering.

What to do?

Evidently Dysart knew—maybe drunk or sober I once disclosed that Rem kept a boarding-house for small animals for his own experimental purposes. What isn't important when pride of time and circumstance is ripe? An off-hand allusion to his enormous appetite for work—especially after Linda's death—now surfaced from Dysart's insatiable memory as a fact full of meaning. He convinced me the key—the tangible proof of Quarrier's concealed success must be housed in that great stone barn behind the farmhouse.

I'm no ideologue . . . what I then did had no reference to high politics—none! From that moment it was personal—the cheap thrill of a chase if you wish—an evil genius at my elbow plus envy pure and simplistic—Quarrier was the quarry.

Nothing personal, laddie—to begin with. I just hated the *threat* of your success turning into reality.

After all, I was only Mephistopheles' fist which, as you know, is double deutsch for Faust, and I suppose I gloried in its power to punch and not a Queensberry rule in sight.

The real confession's to come.

I agreed with Dysart the need to know, to find out what was going on that our micro-chips weren't sure about. And if we needed a few rags of justification to cover our naked intent—didn't I owe it to a pair of scissors attached to my stupid employer to act in the Company's interests?

With an almighty splash I fell in with Dysart's suggestion that I go down to the Bowery—dead of night—check out the theory, make some sort of assessment.

Define my role, you hound dogs! Sleuth, spy, peeping Tom or what have you. I hardly knew myself which crown of thorns cap to wear, they all fitted my six and seven-eighths.

A dark night—a deliciously conspiratorial journey at a venture. I took minimal equipment—a few collywobbles and a torch. And a good eye, connecting the optic nerve to what remained of urbanized intuition.

Timed myself to arrive at two a.m. Managed it with three minutes to spare. Reaching the turn-off I drove on a pin-wheel along that none too negotiable lane. Interminable! I'd done the trip a few times in Linda's hey-day. Funnily enough I wasn't thinking of Rem at all—he just didn't figure in my limited field of consciousness. The quarry was some unknown, related to Quarrier —by the ties of chiasma!

Perhaps, as I clambered over the gate and crossed the grassy area round the house, stabbing at the darkness with that infernal torch to check my bearings, *perhaps* I had misgivings, some trick of conscience at large, proving I was, at least, and for the duration, stone-cold sober.

But there, before me, was the oaken barn door, closed enough to be inviting, not so shut as to be daunting. Damning my hesitancy I pushed a little, paused a little, listened for sounds from the darkened house not forty yards distant. The door gave easily and not too loudly. Mr Ever Ready helped me find a switch to the left. Should I drown the place in a hundred watts or depend on a puddle of flashlight?

An instinct for caution favoured selective darkness, so I pushed into the foetid atmosphere common to these places, went as rapidly as I dared along the rows of cages ranged about the walls at three levels. The beam picked out an assortment of caged and hutched creatures: rabbits, mice, rats, guinea-pigs and some unfamiliar exotics. The place resembled nothing so much as a broken and entered pet shop.

And they were all in ferment, twittering, squeaking . . . agitated, infecting and reinfecting each other with instinctive fear . . . *they* knew.

I—found what I was looking for by chance—tripped over a sack of feeding stuff full in my way. The light tripped with me and fell on a cage the size of a large packing crate. It stood at waist level. Fronting it an old kitchen table—covered with papers of notes, growth curves and the rest. I grabbed and stuffed them in my pocket—that was some of what I'd come for.

Too bad I lingered for too long, turning my attention to the things in the cage.

Do I need describe what I saw? But take my word for it, the reality was nothing like the electronic illusion *screened* from that reality.

Picked out in the beam were two of the most horrendous creatures it was ever a man's misfortune to see. Either I believed the evidence of my eyes or it was a dastardly trick of the uncertain light.

These—things—were reared on their hind legs, their fore-limbs wrapped about each other in what had to be a passionate embrace. I saw plainly *hands* clutching convulsively, as though to tear out the fur by handfuls . . . which they did, in their gruesome ardour. Patches of pink skin . . . obscene.

That was the background, or the foul centre-piece to a seething mass of life heaving beneath the straw; I believe now I was in shock, for I shuddered violently, yet fascinated by a self-evident evil that takes one beyond fear.

Downstage left was another matter; by a chance shift of light I found myself staring into eyes that were manifestly human, patently not human. Unearthly—or a Rabelaisian fredaine? No— none of it fits—the malignancy—the expressed threat of massive retaliation for—damnation—it *was* human—it was *human*.

Because, you see, this distortion had paused long enough to stare at an interloper, paused to let its gaze wander round the light before baring its teeth in a loathsome rictus—mocking . . . before it continued, methodically to reach through the wire mesh to a simple wooden catch holding the cage door—slowly feeling for it.

Never ask why I didn't run from that infernal sight if you know what it is to be transfixed by the inconceivable. Did I need better excuse to go from envy to abhorrence of the good Doctor when there before me—a filthy *tour de force* concocted by a depraved *maître de cuisine*?

It was attempting to escape.

Pity me. I had to do it. I was scared to. I was impelled to. In one, an eager, unwilling accomplice ignorant of what I gazed at, surrounded by darkness and a thousand sounds of fear which now infected me; sheer panic, shark-infesting the bloodstream.

Briefly, I slipped the catch to the vertical, wantonly conspired with their *intention* to escape and, hot with fear, cold with anger, I fled, stumbled to the door, not caring a tinker's cuss that I barged face to face into Remington as I supposed—I struck out blindly, too appalled by fresh experience, I think, to debate killing whatever tried to bar my way. No, it wasn't ideology at work. Yes, it was a mounting sense of outrage at the foisting of a sick joke on humanity already under the weather.

I'll not forget that moment. Even after death.

Mutants—of mice and men.

We're all sick.

Remington must have tripped and fallen at the sheer impetus of a man deserting his infernal ark. At all events, he was discomposed long enough for me to go racing back the way I'd come, maybe not fearing his pursuit so much as those obscenities I'd helped into the world . . . those little hands.

I'd made ground, reached the gate before I heard his boanerges voice, the trumpeting of an angry man. Remington was no pipsqueak weakling like Alladyce—large in every sense of the word. I knew he wouldn't give up and, in any but my present mood I doubt I could have coped.

I needed time to turn, made a decent double-quick three-pointer and had just backed up to the gate when a blaze of headlamps from behind me lit up everything. Of course his car was on the gravel drive close to the house. Well, he'd have to stop, get out, open the gate, climb in again and set off, by which time—

It didn't work out like that. I couldn't know the bloody fool would crash the gate and jam the rear stopping me dead. He was out of his car and charging at me like a demented bull. As he tugged the door open I grabbed the torch—a hefty affair—and hit out savagely—I just hit out . . . sometimes a shot in the dark goes home. And stays there. Bad luck for both of us that I hit him hard—somewhere on the temple and he just—keeled over.

I'd like to pretend so late in the day that I acted with concern. But I didn't. I searched for life competently but short of compassion. Heartbeat negligible, pulse—number unobtainable. Torchlight in the eyes—nothing doing in two redundancies. I had to face a fact and think hard on it.

To be found as he was, the gate smashed, his temple—desecrated, what price a murder enquiry leading where? To me? Justifiable homicide maybe, self-defence and so manslaughter very likely, but what were you doing there, Mr Mathieson?

What!

No time to punch out the facts on a computer and wait for a split-second answer. I was *here*, on the spot, and I had to put instant brackets round that period of my life.

The answer came of its own accord. Whence comes that Cain-like inspiration? Or do we simply follow the logic of those who say: It is written.

I hauled him up—no mean feat—drink debilitates and he was the bigger of us. Somehow I got him to his car, left him while I backed it off the gate, then dragged and pushed him in, arranging with the skill of a Californian embalmer working on some eccentric Grand Prix driver, placed his hands on the wheel, closed the still warm fingers tight round the rim. Left him to drive my car out of the way, then got in beside him, click-clunked my seat belt—but not his. I set the car in motion—the clutch—I placed his left foot carefully—realized how damned difficult it is to drive a dead man's vehicle from the passenger seat. And I had to keep him upright—that was vitally important.

You see, I had that vision of their little *jeu d'esprit* so constantly in my mind that none of this calculated mayhem seemed more than a tiresome inconvenience, to be corrected with the lightest touch of artistry.

Twenty mph in first gear seemed about right. All I had to do was keep my nerve and steer with a light touch along that serpentine lane, climb to twenty—and watch out for a tree—a suitable tree right off the ribbon of verge, take courage in both already full hands, and accelerate a little as I—Mathieson—steered straight into it. When it came, I made no bones about the business. The artist in every man urges a refinement to his least creation, good or ill. As we hit, I pushed him sharply forward to increase the force of impact.

Perfect timing! As the artist steps a flamboyant pace back from his easel to admire, I wiped the door handle clean with my handkerchief, got out and slammed the door shut, walked round towards the front and paused long enough to appreciate the perfect simulation of a car crash—the driver's head smashed against the windscreen—a bloodied mess. He had to be dead.

I wasted no more time—one could never be sure—some fool of a benighted traveller missing his way. Raced back for a mile at least, desperate to get away, breathless with a new species of panic that had to do with the irrational fear of being found loitering in the near vicinity of a crime.

Once in my car I felt safe, closeted and—the thought occurs as I write, modern crime owes a lot to that fact.

I drove slowly and carefully, passed the scene of just another traffic incident. Discovered it was only two hundred yards from the main road which appeared as I swung to the right.

And so home and to bed.

My conscience slept soundly with the help of a drink or two.

The game continued. The head-shaking and the 'oh dears' and 'ah me's' at HQ. Poor old Rem—joy-riding at his age—an inquest and the verdict exonerating me from all responsibility. I know one mourner who attended the memorial service without a pang of sorrow for the man who'd despoiled nature, desecrated its children, degraded the evolutionary theory.

I couldn't agree more. You *can* do so much with chromosomes, make lovely cats' cradles with a double helix, build *fabulous* high-rise blocks with the old-fashioned bricks used by a discredited architect. So why not a Lego man—and a Lego woman and lots of little snotty-nosed Lego brats?

Why stop at the humble mouse? Who's stopping!

Dysart rode high through it all. The notes I'd purloined were invaluable. That was his affair. I was content to watch and listen as this man and that put the screws on arch-villain Quarrier . . . I gave them a turn myself one day, as we pootered round the park.

I regret none of this. Why should I? The reports we were getting didn't touch my conscience. Why should they?

Let first causes bear the brunt or why do we condemn Adam and Eve to eternity for being accessories before and after the fact of our miserable inheritance?

Quarrier's evil creation had to be loosed on an indifferent world. After Hopkins' titillating TV laugh-in I heard that people went *looking* for these things.

I did them a favour, brought joy to their gangrenous lives. This was better than watching a Brussels tragedy. You could re-experience your favourite video nasty—sally forth and play 'Safari from Outer Space' starring Doctor Whatsisname and a cast of verminous millions.

It comes back to Quarrier. Rem might be alive now if that swine hadn't played clever games with gametes.

I plotted his decline with interest.

As for me. Undetected till Dysart's call and the incident in Clarges Mews. But *she* did the damage, he said. Giving me this last chance to bend the knee to Helen. If she helped to end this sorry business I applaud her. It means I no longer have to live with an unpalatable truth.

There are a few survivors of yesterday's men *and* women—their minds range beyond and above the narrowness, the distortions of today's version of our species. They can sound the tocsin calling what's left of 'natural' humanity to the barricades—but the meekness of green peace can never inherit this blighted earth. Tell her from me, she did well by her kind but, I doubt well enough.

Oh yes. A codicil to this will and testament bequeathing to Quentin Quarrier everything that I'm about to become.

That unpalatable truth.

Print this large, publish it wide, ponder during the TV commercial intervals: *Man* is the mutant—today's man. Forget the ETs, the video perverts, alien 'monsters' and the rest of our junk civilization's teething-rings for sub-cultural deviants and their retarded offspring.

Man is the mutant, catastrophized, drugged, polluted, diethylene-glycolized, auto-immunized to a thousand decibels, berserk, amok, turned male and not so male terrorist—in the name of what!

Let us pray *sub rosa* or under the bedclothes: Our Godperson which art rumoured to be in heaven, hallowed be thy fame. Thy kingdom has come but it's not all it should be. Your will can't be done on this stinking mudball as it is up there while Quarriers and his trespassers spew evils galore to lead us into the temptation of believing that theirs is the power and the glory for ever and ever, ament—yes truly—ament.

Now it begins to work. A toast to the fatal over-dose. I can afford to laugh a little, carefree at last. Away with it all, myself included! Death's motley will serve to shroud me from the multitudes. What better refuge from mankind?

But let there be no heaven or hell or valley of souls infested with Man's grotesque image. I'll plead *mea culpa* to murder, envy, lust for drink . . . but not to conniving unthinking in crimes against *the* Creation, not to closing eyes and folding hands against the esoteric forms of evil.

Friend Quarrier, I *do* gladly close my eyes against you and your only begotten offspring.

They're waiting . . . as if they know. Better to leave in good time before I have to look at one more—face . . .

Chapter 19

'IT ENDS THERE.' Listlessly.

Compelled to raise her eyes by silence and curiosity, she saw how age can steal a march on time, strike unawares and give Death its first glimmer of hope. No longer and by no means a man untouched by experience.

She tried and failed to find pity for this pathetic felon indicted, judged and sentenced by a foul, self-confessed killer. And it was so valid this indictment soon to be noised abroad, that she thought of the children, in his presence and silently cried out at the thought of the effect revelation must have on them.

A sudden shaft of sunlight brightened the carpet between them, but what comfort when it so nearly resembled a flashlight beam?

We're in the middle of a husband and wife act! The Comedy of Terrors. Just look at him, the malefactor! his expression furtive, eyes sidling in her general direction. 'I'm just popping round the corner to the scaffold, dear. Don't wait up.' 'Will you be long, dear?' 'Hard to say.' 'Well, don't forget your Horlicks when you get back or you won't sleep.'

But Quarrier simply repeated, without a shred of conviction, 'It ends there.' He added with more vigour: 'A Pandora's box. *He* opened it.'

'A box of any kind is meant to be opened.'

A statement of fact, but Quarrier fancied he'd heard a contemptuous note. It may be he felt the need to stand on his dignity, or avoid her unwavering regard, or to just stare out at window.

'I stand by my work whatever you ... what does he admit to? A desire to benefit humanity—a damned odd way of going about it. Alcoholic self-righteousness—pique! Mathieson murdered Remington because he couldn't beat the world left or right.

There are plenty of his kind. But I did nothing compelling me to write ten pages of confession.'

An appeal to her sympathetic understanding failed dismally. It compounded the offence that he should plead with her to judge between them. She side-stepped as best she could.

'Most of us need a volume for that. In the end a post-card will do as well.'

'I don't understand.'

She smiled bitterly. 'A volume—the vanity of authorship. A post-card—just a few lines to let you know how I stepped back and admired my handiwork . . . it's the little things that damn us.'

'And I?'

She couldn't bring herself to pinpoint Quarrier's successful candidacy for damnation, not to his face, though she knew well enough why and wherefore. Her sensibilities were a shade too fine to play that delicious game of recrimination—No, no, George, I just called your secretary a bitch, remember? It's *your* turn.

Simply, her mind closed up on the whole sorry subject. Closed up and made up. It was, after all, six o'clock. And the children had to eat whatever their parents' problems—she glanced at him, stupidly apprehensive that she'd voiced a stray thought.

'I'll get supper. Something cold?'

Il faut manger as her mother would assert in execrable French after some minor domestic disaster. Perhaps it applied, but 'one must do something' would have been nearer the mark.

He stared on at the garden scene, and his silence touched her more poignantly than any assemblage of words. She hesitated, thought better of switching on the TV, went through to the kitchen and turned up the portable radio just loud enough to catch the news before crossing to the fridge.

Something—cold.

'. . . A sense of disquiet is becoming evident in official circles as a new breed of mice continues to spread over large areas of the southern counties. New sightings have been reported as far north as Hertfordshire and the total casualty figures now exceed . . .'

True. True as the *veritas in vino*.

Through all the word-gropings of Mathieson, the heart-searching of Quarrier's and the grey-out imposed by the authorities, the deviants had spread and multiplied at a terrifying rate. Men were appalled by the gratuitous ferocity with which they attacked, not as cornered animals, but hunting with deliberation every living thing foolhardy enough to cross their paths.

Parties were formed to stalk the enemy within, but a kind of hopelessness attached to their efforts. Men with shotguns and more cartridges than courage followed up every report of concentrations or single sightings, but while they tried to deal with one incident, another group not far away might be attacking a solitary who'd ventured out of doors, and help would come too late or not at all.

The media urged those who had no essential business to stay home behind locked doors and windows. All openings should be fastened against beings adept at opening windows and shutters. Predictably this increased the sense of alarm, but it did give people an opportunity and knowledge enough to adapt to a known menace.

That, of course, is how the human race has so far survived . . .

It was late Augustan out-of-doors weather and a mother with a fretting family, gazing out at window might doubt crisis under that clear blue sky till she saw what appeared to be a pack of dogs crossing her line of vision.

Frustrated by bolts and catches the mutants showed a thoughtful ingenuity in their changed tactics; learned to rear on their hind legs and hurl stones with sufficient force to break windows . . .

Of course, animals can 'think' in their own terms. It needed time for the fact to sink deep that these hybrids could reason like humans, that their mental processes were geared to ape our unique privilege, as in a war between man and man.

They knew that glass shatters . . .

And vandalism was no longer a true blue English lout's preserve when their blood brothers learned how to use petrol and matches . . .

Professional observers were no less impressed by their ability to vary the habit of congregating after Wentworth Magna. As if the ordeal by fire had taught them to scatter and take to the surrounding countryside in troops and small colonies.

There would never be another chance to slaughter them wholesale.

It could no longer be played down: the floodgates opened by 'unauthorized' disclosure brought the crisis squarely before a nation afraid to move out of doors—and so, to the wondering world.

★

SECURITY CHIEFS DEFY GOVERNMENT *The Times*.
GOVERNMENT BAN MISHAP SPEAK-OUT IGNORED *The Guardian*.
RUNAWAY MICE STRIP MOTHER OF THREE NAKED *Daily Mirror*.

The Press made hay under a strange sun. Gave the impression of a Gulliver waking and rubbing his eyes in astonishment. The ropes and gags of Lilliput men were gossamer after all. Official Secrets Acts! Mere toilet-paper when the guardians of national security turned Bolshie and told all.

TV networks went to town. Hopkins returned with a vicious attack which, many believe, contributed to the Government's eventual downfall.

'Look who's decided at last, this country is not the plaything of pop politicians. Smiley and Co say "No" to a gigantic cover-up.

'You've heard the main facts on the news. Maybe it rings a bell. Seveso, Three Mile Island, Windscale under an alias, Bhopal, the Mexican blow-up and the rest. Fine, they were more or less chemically based. No connection. *But*—ask yourself, what's different?

'A toxic chemical escapes. Casualties. A mutant breed of mice goes missing. Casualties.

'What's different?

'Apparently, a man called Quarrier dreams up a genetic nightmare and it's classified top secret in the national interest. Silence imposed by Prime Ministerial ukase—sorry to break into pre-revolutionary Russian—but what's all this autocratic mum's the word? It's bad enough imposing silence on a couple of thousand troops—like those mug battalions in Australia ordered to keep their mouths shut when the sun burst overhead.

'It needs a minimum of words to say the situation disgusts me, and if it doesn't disgust you too, think of a mother and son torn to pieces because mandarins decreed clampdown.

'They needn't have died.

'*Hundreds* needn't have died.'

This and much more.

The reader may easily construct imaginative versions of what the pseudo-intellectuals synthesized as the trauma of therianthropic encounters.

But custom stales, however infinite the variety appears, because there *is* a limited number of basic situations: the reveller returning home from pub or club in the semi-darkness, parking his car and then savaged between the garage and the front door. The nursing staff helpless as a pack of the creatures maul patients in their beds. A class of children almost wholly massacred by a sudden irruption of predators where none had been seen before. The attack in a cemetery during an interment leaving three of the mourners mutilated and close to death. The night security men in factories and offices, lorry drivers, the bank that almost died as a dozen bestialities came looking for the softest of all currencies—flesh and blood . . . the Boeing at Heathrow that never got off the ground. They watched horrified from the control tower as a troop of forty stormed the 707 just before the doors could be closed.

The timing was uncanny. I mean, it was plain uncanny, they repeated over and over.

Enough of bizarreries under any circumstances.

Except perhaps for a last example to serve as a severing stroke of irony.

They returned to the Price-Pearson Complex.

To suggest these gargoyles went searching for their creator, returned to their roots, implies a kind of religious conviction; so it may have been, if theirs was a primitive urge to sacrifice that maker for playing sick jokes on their defenceless forebears. The fact remains, it's believed a dozen of this infima species scaled the chain fencing around the sprawling infrastructure on a moonless night. Of course they didn't find him.

Visualize them, dropping to the ground, forming into a pack with a kind of fugleman taking the lead, waiting patiently at a distance, watching the highly glazed circular building close to the main gate, a blob of light distant by a hundred yards from the huge complex.

They can see clearly three stalwarts relaxed over a game of cards. On the hour one or another would take a leisurely stroll towards the main building checking casually that it was still there. The labs and admin area were in darkness. Only the production department far behind would show signs of life as maintenance men worked on the delicate machinery used to mass-produce pharmaceutical items.

The hybrids stood motionless in unblinking contemplation of three men without a future. In their collective posture was a kind of menacing discipline hard to describe except in human terms.

Not quite suppositious this account of what happened at Price-Pearson's that night. Eye-witness accounts of similar attacks pinpoint sinister traits which are proving unbeatable, because, 'You could tell they knew exactly what they were doing, I mean, you could sort of follow their thoughts.' Thus one fortunate survivor.

At about midnight one of the security men throws down his hand, stretches and yawns, takes a mouthful of Coke, grabs his electric lantern and says something to his companions which has them laughing even after he's closed the door behind him.

The leader of the pack points with a finger, turns its head to its fellows—and nods. At once they begin to lope stealthily away into the shadows dividing into two groups as they go.

How long the other two guards waited for their colleague to return and whether they both ventured out and came on what remained of him, or whether they followed one by one can never be known.

Night workers leaving their shift at six that morning found the bodies torn to anonymity.

The police discovered a smashed window at the precinct's ground level.

Five thousand animals and clouds of Drosophila were at large from four vivariums. *Every cage had been opened*.

They had systematically destroyed or rendered useless laboratory instruments and equipment valued in millions. Adjoining offices including Quarrier's had been torn apart, filing-cabinets stank of corrosive chemicals, word processors smashed.

They destroyed the central computer.

That, of course, is the example to grasp. These—things—had fashioned a lethal calling-card out of apparently mindless destruction.

We sense, if we do not know, the source of your power. The machine and the guinea-pig are the means to your end. The crude vivisection of these men and their kind is our means to the same end . . . yours.

And then they disappeared back into the darkness to regenerate, to regroup, to work more havoc in laboratory conditions of their own choosing.

The universal realization is still slow-dawning. This *is* a crusade with implacable purposefulness and the malaise born of primeval fear still grows by what the mutants feed on.

As a co-incidental social comment, it's quietly accepted that TV companies have lost interest in screening late-night horror films.

From being a leisure activity horror has become a grisly growth industry.

Chapter 20

EARLIER PAGES HAVE shown the All-Party Committee for official heart-searching at work, wherein true democracy appeared at last to be challenging, accusing and ultimately condemning those who hate commissars but worship a Rasputin, dirty fingernails and all.

These unskilled dabblers in skulduggery might have got away with it but for one incontestable fact. So obsessed with the impossible concept of *ultra*-security they flouted the regular intelligence apparatus in the revealing belief that they alone could guard the sacred atrium of Science and so, upstage their allies and downstage their enemies.

A recent commentator on petards and how to hoist them makes this telling point.

'In conclusion, I have to say that, fantasizing a disgusting weapon of offence out of a unique experiment intended to benefit womankind, the culprits were shamed subconsciously into the kind of guilty secrecy once associated with consenting adolescents at a minor public school.'

Truly, like old soldiers, *The Magnet* never dies. Agonized cries of 'yaroo' can still be heard in Buntersland . . . I'm bound to say, you fellows, we cannot be held . . .

The talk grows wilder as the bills of mortality grow longer. Parliament demands a Price-Pearson shutdown. Many voices call for the impeachment of the PM and its familiars for constructive treason. Rumour has it that the Government may be forced to resign and call a general election.

Yes, it *does* sound improbable; a country in upheaval because of a plague of not quite nice mice. Sadly, the constant gun-fire to be heard in most counties south of the Wash wounds scepticism and kills complacency. Bands of armed police, civilian volunteers and army patrols underline the desperate state of a country occupied by a species of unparalleled malignancy unseen since before Cain gunned down Abel.

For two of those well-connected with the affair life became barely tolerable.

Quarrier degenerated with the application of a man too conscientious to do things by halves. Atonement, not curiosity, inclined him to watch all that TV could now offer on the subject, to hear every possible bulletin giving news of each outrage. He had no desire, no incentive to leave the house—the Complex scarcely functioned. Not one in a hundred experiments had survived. Friends had given up dropping by.

Morose and increasingly withdrawn, he would read and re-read Mathieson's confession as though self-laceration might do the trick while he searched for an overlooked clue in transparently clear pages. At times, Helen would find him in his study, seated in a rigid pose far removed from his once casual, almost indolent self, a lay figure, doggedly staring at the likelihood of an intervening wall. He seldom found much to say, scarcely initiated everyday dialogue that passes for the small change paid for domestic felicity.

In a worrying sense he appeared to be beating an orderly retreat, taking measured backward steps in face of vengeful furies that were to the ancients what conscience once meant to the moderns.

Furies.

Obscene letters and telephone calls, the stock-in-trade of sick mutations spawned by a degenerate society, all directed at the publicly identified architect of *homus sapiens*, and almost all deflected by Helen, so that he seldom heard their curses ringing in *her* ears.

Neither could be unaware of bricks and stones smashing through their windows.

'I hope your husband is proud of himself.'

Helen, recognizing her mother's voice with the first word, replaced the handset at the seventh. So many variants of the obscene phone-call, she'd reflected.

They scarcely moved out of doors. Reporters seemed to be permanently encamped thereabouts. Little satisfaction in viewing their house under siege on the TV screen.

Some light relief came and went with Quarrier's old tutor's brief visit. She hoped it could do more for Quentin than it could possibly do for her.

Professor Sempill spent many hours in the study with his fallen star pupil, 'bolstering his morale', as he'd explained to Helen after a longer than usual session.

But what about mine? she'd wondered. How am I supposed to come to terms with the fact that my husband is both creator and destroyer, a killer by proxy, too valuable to hale before the court of human rights? Morale! Don't I need someone to teach me how to share a Procrustean bed, to help Sisyphus roll the stone, to avoid the Damocles' sword—to protect the entrails of my lord Prometheus? Do I not!

A teenage son or daughter might have helped. She could have defended, explained, justified with the best of casuists, filling time and those long rows of asterisks between snatches of dialogue that found her nowadays in silent communion with *alter ego*. As now, while she watched Jocelyn methodically filling his venerable briar.

At dinner, a more formal affair in honour of Jocelyn, knight of the High Table, she caught herself marvelling at the brilliant repartee, so easy on the lips of those paradoxes, the cloistered men of the world. The professor played the game for all it was worth, ingenuously determined to drag Quarrier out of the slough of Despond, bullying him unmercifully into trying on new perspectives several sizes too big or fitting no worse than a pinching pair of shoes bespoke for a customer crippled by gout.

In fact, Helen hadn't been forgotten. Behind the raillery, the jarring wit intended to deliver Quarrier from louring apathy, a shrewd eye was busily assessing the effect of aftermath on their relationship. What had happened was water under the bridge, he genuinely believed. Unfortunately, he couldn't resist the opportunity to use the past for making unwanted compliments.

'I'll smoke if you don't object, Helen.'

'You'll smoke if I do,' her eyes were round with astonishment and he knew she knew he was preambling.

'Dammit, Quentin, nothing better ever happened to you than that minx. You only just deserve her.'

'I know . . . for better or worse it came up in the marriage service.' Quarrier's smile was a solitary affair, had no meaning for anyone but Quarrier. His reply seemed to throw Jocelyn who regarded them straitly for some moments. He cleared his throat, a sure sign of uncertainty and possible embarrassment. Sempill knew them too well not to realize he didn't know them that well.

'It's not easy to talk so near to—'

'We have talked about it,' defensively, 'even Mathie's discussed it—on paper.' Bitterly.

'Ah! *We've* talked of it, certainly. But, not so far, in front of the ladies. Helen, if I propose a toast to the powers of intuition would you accept that?'

'No.'

The professor lowered a glass already half-way to his lips.

'Why not?'

'Because intuition is a good servant but a bad master in the thinking process—for man or woman.'

'Very good. And then?'

'Intuition told me nothing about Dysart. It was all there—in the man. Observation, traits of character as they show themselves in words, gestures, even the shifts and crossings of legs twice in as many minutes—I'm sorry if that sounds sententious or something but I can assume, surely, if you use the microscope on a tiny organism you don't depend on sixth sense, you infer from past experience with the other five what's there, under your nose.'

Jocelyn nodded. 'I stand corrected, my dear. But I gather, forgive me if I misunderstood, you had a feeling about all this—more to it than seemed to meet the eye sort of thing?'

She glanced at Quarrier. Even with an old friend at elbow, she wanted to avoid the hurtful comment, however oblique, not appreciating the terrible truth that every word directed at him from anyone contained an implied censure, a carefully concealed accusation, a gift-wrapped brick through the front window of his defensive position.

'Yes . . .' carefully, 'a feeling's nearer the mark, because it's nearer our being—almost a tangible asset. The ancients harped on heart strings just as we still incline to talk of something striking a chord—the same idea, basically. You—can't ignore a feeling, when a thing's good or bad. It's the groundwork for speculation—and it's valid.'

'Whereas, intuition?' Sempill had forgotten his pipe.

The very question she'd sought to turn aside, Jocelyn was bound to ask. Much as she loved him she had to try hard for charity to dotards. Stared down at her share of a disordered dining table, not wanting to meet Quentin's suddenly puzzled regard. But, sentences were made to be pronounced.

'Intuition—is a terrifying insight into consequences.'

Recognized for what it was, a below-zero definition, still she couldn't apologize or disown a part of her because of its ugliness— was too clear-sighted to recognize beauty in truth. No. No apology, not to Jocelyn, not even to Quentin.

As a distracting gesture she started to clear away the dinner débris announcing over-brightly that coffee would be available in the not-too-distant future. They came to their feet with antique courtesy, confused and over-conscious that she'd spoken anoetically, beyond their understanding, certainly not aware of a momentarily lifted veil from what romantics, ignorant of anatomy, *will* insist on calling 'a broken heart'.

Later, after some desultory conversation mellowed by coffee and liqueurs Jocelyn stood and announced quite firmly that he and Helen were going to wash the dishes. Jocularly, but with serious intent, that was obvious. Quarrier seemed more relaxed, said any new experience must be a good thing but doubted the effect on their stock of crockery.

Jocelyn followed her out and to the kitchen pattering on about the perfect domestic arrangements and what hadn't he missed for all those bachelor years in Wycliffe's androecium.

'I envy you,' she retorted, ' "a dozen rufous scullions in firesome kitchens, spit-spinning beef and sucking-pigs; black Rodd the butler treads softly through ancient dust of cellary depths, nosing for port, dowsing with wand for sack in well remembered oubliettes".'

'Ah, you know that bit of doggerel, eh? It's not as true as it sounds, not any more. Times and tastes change. We actually consume convenience foods on fast days and the sherry's very common market. Where do I stand?'

She smiled, positioned him, ran hot water and noted that Quentin had switched on the TV.

'It's early for the news,' she murmured.

'Round the clock stuff, now. It's too serious to be treated as *news* any more.'

'What now, Jocelyn?' she frankly stared him in the eyes, a questing regard even her eloquent acquaintances of the past had found too—insightive.

'Quentin, I suppose, my dear. I don't want to sound alarmist but he's sagging, no question, under the weight of a world he's elected to take on pitifully inadequate shoulders.'

'Total responsibility for what's happened?'

'The only responsibility that counts rather.'

'Engineering these creatures?'

'It's an incredible feat in any language.'

She turned from the boring choring of soaping and scouring.

'I see. Do you want me to deny him the luxury?'

He too forgot what he quickly discovered he had little enthusiasm for.

'Luxury?'

'Jocelyn, I suspect enough about the masculine mentality to self-persuade there's a melancholy satisfaction in being the initiator of *any*thing.'

'You know too much—or not enough.' Sourly.

'You talk of words and shoulders. Surely Atlas sweated under the pleasant conviction he'd one day be published as a bestselling book of maps.'

'Oh come now! That's a pleasant conceit. You don't suppose he's revelling in the current brick-through-the-window animus?'

'Suffering has its reasons . . . it's important to get them right before one applies remedies.'

The old Fellow made no further pretence of dish-drying. He sat at the nearby breakfast table signifying that to discuss a man's destiny among the foamy suds of Fairy Liquid was going it a bit.

Helen sat too. 'You read Mathieson's confession?'

He nodded, cautiously.

'Then you know why and how these things are prevalent.'

'No. That's to say I don't agree as to his motive—the mainspring of this tragedy. An off-the-cuff justification doesn't wash. He released those creatures because he was, by nature, a wrecker. Which Quentin isn't. D'you follow?'

'I'm sorry, but no.'

'That's a pity. Mathieson y'know, reminds me forcefully of Loomis, Bognor Regius Professor of Greek at Clare.'

'St John's.'

'St John's it was. Well, Loomis based his whole erudition on the simple fact of knowing the Greek for "nose-picker". Disgusting Fellow, he's dead now, of course, but he took a single-minded delight in calumny—wrecking d'you see?'

'Jocelyn, we're not discussing professors of Greek.'

'Quite so,' Sempill viewed the back of his hand with a quizzical eye. Age, he reflected, positively gallops toward the fingernails.

'Let's start from the beginning and remember, I knew Mathieson at Wycliffe almost as well as I knew Quentin. They appeared to be firm friends, or at least, Mathieson chose Q as a wagon chooses a star—for advantage. Q was an idealist, Mathieson was an ideopath —I coin the word to define one of unstable character who indulges in diseased speculative theory. The colour of his ideology is unimportant. There are two kinds of Left and they parallel their beliefs with two kinds of Right. So, Mathieson passionately "believed" in change by destruction at all costs. Quentin adhered to the change-by-instruction school.'

'Isn't that a bit like saying two wrongs can make a right with a small r?'

Sempill frowned at memories of recalcitrant freshmen who'd argued the elements of genetics to his face and the point of idiocy. It didn't help that they were usually the brilliant ones. He restrained himself creditably.

'No, it isn't. I also repeat, he was by nature a wrecker. He began, you see, by self-vandalizing.'

'I don't follow.'

'My dear girl,' peevishly, 'you're not so young as to be grass-green. If a man sets out to destroy himself by a commitment to alcohol or anything else including argumentative women, it's surely an innate deficiency which may and probably does lead to higher things.'

'By which you mean lower things?'

'By which I do indeed mean "lower". But not only is Mathieson the author of his own destruction. He links with Quentin to become the co-author of *his*.'

'Fate isn't an argument.'

Counsel for the defence took another look at his brief. Wondered if it was worth continuing, and said so.

'Perhaps you know something more than I do,' she conciliated.

'Of course! Do you think I volunteered to help with nasty greasy dishes simply to compare opinions? Mathieson already had a drink problem when he begged Q to find him a place at Price-Pearson's—long before they moved from London.'

'I didn't know that.'

'Why should you? Q told you the fact. "Mathieson's got a job with us." You don't know the objectively scientific man you're married to if you think he would add "Thanks to me". But, to a man like that, such kindnesses are ammunition for a grudge . . . he lost his job in the labs, not because he distilled spirits for private consumption—but because he made mistakes in analysis. Quentin had his own department but he was subordinate to Mathieson on that scandal—'

'Bromouracil.'

'Mathieson's line was chemistry. A man called Fairburn was executive director at the time—'

'I remember him. Close to retirement—one of the old school, Quentin said.'

'Rigorous but fair. At all events, the company chairman needed a high-grade scientific adviser as the business became more complex. Quentin persuaded Fairburn to put Mathieson top of the queue for the job, which he did—and Mathieson got it. The pity is, it appeared to put Quentin in the firing line during the court proceedings which began later.'

'I remember.'

'Fairburn, *after* he retired, warned Quentin that Mathie had one of those French fixed ideas, believing Quentin had connived at his removal from practical to bureaucratic science.'

Helen smiled. 'Connived. I believe Mathie earned far more than Q.'

'Yes, well some men object to being kicked upstairs, even if it's to their advantage. He gladly used his position to further this Dysart fellow's ends and—'

'And then!' Impatiently from one who knew all that, and more, and saw no point, and then? It *was* crude, the abruptive cry of a slatternly street brawler, stopping Sempill in the full flow of his carefully assembled argument. He blinked once or twice, took another look at her seeming serenity, opened his mouth on a false start, and tried again.

'Well, then came the business of the mutants. He saw the chance to wreck Quentin's career *and* some, at least, of a social order he had no use for. QED.'

She shook her head, positively, leaving no doubt.

'You're painting grey black to make off-white seem Persil white.'

At which he frowned, as though for the first time he saw the extent of the rift. 'Believe me, Helen, I'm not playing devil's advocate for Quentin—at most, a witness for the prosecution.'

'Of whom?'

'. . . Haven't you heard a word of what I said? I've stated the situation as *I* see it, given you the facts—'

'Except one.'

Her gaze of the two was unwavering.

'Well?'

'Mathieson had to react to an act. I don't see how one cancels the other. If those things hadn't been spirited out of the Complex, he couldn't have been there to release them *and* cold-bloodedly kill Rem . . . could he?'

'. . . Cry for the moon, Miss! Quentin acted according to the laws of his vocation—unequivocal curiosity.'

'Perhaps the laws should be amended . . . before it's too late.'

Deflated a little, ego growing rusty with age, Sempill, full of years, a man of immense authority in his sphere, the disciple of Bateson, found all distinction, merit, erudition of little account in face of this woman too ignorant of the universal preference to compromise with the truth.

He recalled long after muttering something about serving mankind, not always obviously. He would remember to his death the low keening anguish of a latter-day Medea who knows what it means to lose.

'People have died—horribly . . . mankind! is an abstraction. People are real.'

There could be only one conclusion. After all, he was not a fool.

'Then you condemn him—outright?' Face her with it. Force her to retract, to think again. Give her time. But there was no reply. Only that terrible, implacable regard which answered better.

'That's—what he feels. That's why I thought a word with you would—'

He gestured at the uselessness of words, rose from the table, lead-weighted with a sense of defeat no whit improved by a faraway suspicion that it might be justified.

'We'd better finish that blasted washing-up. Must have something positive to enter in today's diary.'

Epilogue

THERE APPEARS TO be an error in the chronicle. There is no error in the chronicle.

It will be remembered that, after her encounter with Dysart Helen 'saw' clearly the vagrant mouse making its way to the maze. When Quarrier returned soon after there was much else to be talked about, but why did she mention the intruder by the way, almost as an afterthought?

To explain this anomaly is to understand something more of a complex character loosely called 'Helen'.

The vision happened nowhere but in her extraordinarily perceptive mind. Just as she could conjure a phantom family out of the air, so she had visualized and mentally rehearsed a reality out of immaterial molecules not to be found under microscopes. She played out the scene in two parts. The shadow play of the first 'sighting' and last, after an interval of despairing silence, this remarkable woman had repeated a dangerous dialogue leading to the substance—and the last fall of the curtain.

Why?

Long afterwards she favoured the author with an explanatory postscript to this narrative.

'I'm not sure you'll agree with my conviction that it was the most chilling element in the whole sorry affair. To act under an inner compulsion must always be a frightening experience—to me personally, at any rate.

'When I think about it, prevision isn't a simple act of psychic projection; more a calculated exercise in self-fulfilling prophecy. Hard to explain but, crudely speaking, much as I loved my husband, *because* I loved him, I was condemning him to prepare himself for the death he longed for, to come face to face literally, with consequences. I foresaw what I thought *should* happen—and we were not disappointed in the sequel.

'If that sounds dreadfully cruel, callous, I can't help it. I loved him too much, you see, to welcome the prospect, living through interminable years watching him slowly—disintegrate. After disgrace, the public stocks—and the private pillory. The process was beginning—accelerating . . . no—no, it wasn't possible. No comforting words from Professor Sempill or Quentin's peers could destroy that single truth: he'd preserved those ghastly creatures gratuitously, to augment a not very well concealed pride in a novelty of his creating.

'One must forgive those that trespass against one, one dare not forgive those that transgress the laws of nature in order to trespass against us—by which I mean the whole of the animal kingdom . . .

'No, I had no idea what they were doing with the X700s before all this.'

'I'm glad,' she said, 'that I never had children.'

That would have been a day or two after Jocelyn's departure.

Too dejected by half, fifty per cent bewildered, the old emeritus had readily taken his leave, before the clouds enveloped them all. He was sage enough to recognize the grey prelude to a drama not yet played out between two cherished agonistes.

They'd listened, with feelings peculiar to each, to almost continuous reports of sightings and what were inevitably described as atrocities: thus, corrosive despondency, paternal anxiety, a feminine presentiment of tragedy delayed.

Readily. Age can bear so much, but, when it can't console, when it's troubled and perplexed by a classical view of retribution, time to return to its barren set of rooms, mourn and moulder in peace along with the college fabric. Much the best.

'I'll write—yes, I'll write. And do you keep me posted.'

All three knew they were making last farewells.

And so, they'd returned home on a sullen grey morning after driving the old Fellow to the station.

Quarrier, his whole attention on the car radio, had nothing to say on the short journey back, went straight to the living-room and switched on the portable.

The timing of the gods in a foul mood contrived that an

improbable item about surrogate 'mothers' should catch her otherwise attention. Once, it had claimed first place in the public mind. Now, she at least could trace a connection between two kinds of outrage.

'I didn't hear. You're glad? About what?' he prompted.

'Not to have been a mother. These women degrading the womb to the status of a receptacle—like a chamber-pot, a vacuum-flask, pressure-cooker—saucepan!'

She seemed oblivious to any effect her outburst might have had, spoke inconsequentially enough, and yet—fancied or not—he detected accusation, forged a link between her anguish and his fault degraded to an—atrocity.

Merely the force of one destiny reacting on another. All was ordained whether or no Helen thought implacably. By every circumstance they were fated to obey a common impulse to take steps to a brink as two might run a three-legged race to an end.

He'd made no reply—the time for repartee was over—but let his gaze linger on her while hers strayed elsewhere. Had she turned and met his appeal things might have ended differently, though it's doubtful.

She went upstairs to change and tidy the children's bedrooms, came down later and tapped the hall barometer as one might touch wood for badly needed luck, and found the living-room empty. Stood undecided, listening to an alien voice that came, she realized, from a radio in the study. Like an addict he nowadays craved a background of noise, of news. News above all.

Helen assumed nothing more of those long hours of seclusion till the day she found a separate desk drawer in a corner. It was filled with slips of paper and foolscap sheets, closely written, itemizing dates, events, summaries and long, hypothetical accounts of how 'it' could have happened:

'Gratuitous curiosity! What the hell does that mean?'

'My role insignificant.'

'Mathieson no Machiavelli for the following reasons.'

'Glutathione—the berserker's friend. Did Rem say that?'

'I think the vanadium concentrate proved itself.'

'We left the notes on the lab table—I wonder if Mrs Chandrasakar —the likeliest explanation. Innocent villain! Must ask her to dinner.'

'I *had* to follow through! Scientific irresponsibility. Glib talk on just now's radio. Fastidious bastards! Science *is* indiscriminating—the discipline isn't. They simply can't see that.'

'The blare of trumpets and a peal of drums. Heard them again today. Helen's concealed bitterness—talk of wombs and receptacles—as if I could miss the point—her point! Well, silence is best. When they attack with the tar-brush, the whitewash broom is no defence. Outcome—greyness!

'And the trumpets bray louder, the trombones blare and other instruments I can't identify add their weird quota to this appalling cacophony. We're into the land of Stockhausen, God help us, or worse; the music of the spheres turns out to be inconcert howls of mankind suffering, tortured, anguished, even to the first generation —what a swelling torrential choral symphony decomposed for the outnumbering dead—it lacks the diminishing sweetness of Debussy ... murine ... mouse-like ... mice!

'It's growing in volume—intolerably. I can scarcely hear the news—or her knocking. Do I want tea?

'I must break off and go paranormally through the daily rites. For her sake.'

Tomorrow, he was thinking, I have to meet those Special Branch people who have their reasons ... he sipped his tea mechanically, almost furtively, not totally conscious of Helen, standing at the kitchen window for no apparent reason. Their attempt at conversation had petered out. Silence divided them easily as if subconscious thoughts were too charged with significance to be shared.

Yet, preoccupation wasn't so strong that he could ignore a certain tension, a rigidity of form poised rather than posed at that window.

For Helen, the prevision had come alive; there could be no stifling a gasp extorted by recognition that she had only to watch the play-back and speak on cue.

A creature, twice the size of a grown rabbit, loped towards the maze, paused and turned its head from side to side, snuffling the air before gazing fixedly at the thing behind that insubstantial stuff that shatters so easily.

It seemed to grin, the fanged rictus of a cosy conspirator—we're all in this together, eh? Then it nosed its way to the maze entrance and revulsion grew at sight of pink patches disfiguring its pelt.

'By the way, one of our little friends has just disappeared into the maze . . .' she heard the words being dragged from her—an unfamiliar voice hoarse with astonishment and horror. She tensed against a reaction she knew would be violent.

'You're making fun of me!'

Turning she started at, or rather, searched for the truth behind second-hand words, but unprepared for the light in the eye, a violent guttering such as comes before the candle's end. She thought she could see the darkness already and, true to her vision, she dared not answer.

Remembrance of the past touched her with a few pathetic words. 'I'm sorry . . . it's a dream I had you see—a presentiment. Too clear to be denied. You were there somehow,' much as a down in the gutter tramp might touch one's shoulder.

But they were not the words written into her script. She descended, almost tumbled from the pinnacle, her refuge, a vantage-point for detachment, censure on a monument, came down briefly to his level.

'Presentiment?'

He closed his eyes, like a man at prayer. 'Everything—every doubtful action—the seeds of retribution. We thought we'd fallen in love with this house—of our volition. It wasn't like that . . . fate beats free will every time. I looked at the maze and I remember saying, "That's it. I can live and die with this." Yes?'

She nodded.

'I was wrong. We're not principals, after all. Merely, agents of that universal destructive impulse we grandiose as "fate". I'd . . . better deal with it.'

'Quentin!' Very much a civilized woman, she took no more than a single step, no question of throwing herself at his feet. One step only.

They both understood the significance.

'Atonement . . . that's the name of the game.'

And he was gone, fired by some imperative too categorical to admit of delay.

Housewife stands at open kitchen door, staring tragically at a green wall beyond the Fly-mowed lawn, it's neat suburban cut dappled by shadows creeping from the nearby beech tree. Sun shines brightly after the latest rain shower, as if it's come out to see the fun.

Hubby striding in a spirit of grim derring-do, disappears into the depths of a maze composed and cultivated once upon a time by an assistant curator of Kew Gardens.

It's enough to make the gods die laughing. There's Helen just setting out on a long journey on hands and knees in quest of reasons enough to make sense of the vagaries that do so plague existence.

Nothing heard, it seems, no violent commotion, yet they found the man who'd miscreated at a venture, torn to pieces by a misconception there, at the very heart of a not terribly elaborate puzzle quite unintended by nature.

The day would come, when a woman pregnant with years would return to the house, wander into the silent study, read with a faint smile the fragment of nonsense penned by an old evolutionary and mutter Sappho's chant, the last charm left to her against the fearful spirits dwelling in the long night to come.

'Evening, thou bringst the child back to its mother.'

Turning, as if galvanized, the careworn hag becomes Helen, stepping lightly to the stairs to call:

'Martin, Harry, Esther, Jane! If you wash your eight hands quickly we'll all have tea in the garden.'

Once a week she puts flowers more or less on a desk far beneath the ground in an ancient burial ground maintained by the parish council.